Two Princes

Allison Wells

Well Versed Publications

Contents

*FOR THE BACON TRIBE, SALLIE, & MMAMMS -
THANK YOU FOR BEING A FRIEND.*

Chapter 1

Inspiration was the word of the day as Hana Willis flipped open her notebook and began jotting down her sister's words about planning her wedding. She had done the same with her best friend, who was also getting married soon. Happy couples seemed to be around every corner and Hana's career was based on the notion of love. As an author, she used the love stories of those around her to inspire her characters, the perfect date night, and unforgettable proposals.

Women loved her stories. Young single women – like herself – always wanted a sense of hope that one day their prince would come. They didn't need rescuing, of course, but they wanted someone to share their life with. And the mothers who felt anything but alluring after being up all night with children wanted to remember what those first pangs of love felt like. The older women who missed the days when they were so carefree also lived vicariously through her characters. Everyone loved love.

The problem in writing such dreamy characters, Hana realized, was that nobody ever measured up to the fictitious men she imagined in her mind. She had yet to meet a man who was dashing and sincere, attractive and smart, generous and sensitive. Those perfect men didn't exist in the real world. So while Hana wished for a prince to ride up on his noble steed, there were none to be found anywhere near Greenville, South Carolina.

Contentment found her though as she spent time with her close-knit family, her best friend, La'Anna, and her dog, Lulu. Family was everything in the Willis household. Family and church – which is why Hana found herself in her family's pew every Sunday morning. She enjoyed her Sundays with family, especially since her younger sister, Jenna, would be getting married soon and moving a few hours away.

Nudging Jenna, Hana beamed at her sister. They only had two more months left. Hana didn't know what she would do without her sister around. Even though she had not lived at home for nearly ten years, she had still spent plenty of time with Jenna and her other siblings. Their weekly coffees and frequent shopping trips would come to an end. Not to mention the gaping hole that would be left in her heart.

This day, however, was a little different. They were setting up their mother's business for a baby shower to celebrate the birth of her old friend's little girl. Merry with Min had been Min Willis's brainchild nearly ten years before when she turned an old empty commercial space into an event center. They hosted bridal showers, luncheons, business parties, and everything in between. If someone needed space for a party, Min's was the place to go.

Hana, however, wasn't putting up the pink balloons like she was supposed to be doing. She was furiously writing down details of the romantic date her sister and her fiancé

Will had gone on. It would be perfect in the book she was writing.

"Hana, stop doodling and hang up balloons." Min's stern voice echoed across the room. She was a tiny woman, but her children all had a healthy fear of their mother's wrath.

"Hang on Umma. I'm not doodling. This is work." Hana waved her pen over her head.

Min stood before her, hands on hips. "No, Hana, you are here to set up this party for your friend. Not write out steamy love scenes." Her mother's still-black hair was pulled up in a loose bun, her almond-shaped eyes glaring at Hana.

"Okay, Umma, I'm doing it. I can do it."

An hour later, her old high school friend Brittany toted around a newborn baby girl who was adorned with pink bows and white lace. Brittany's husband looked at her with so much adoration it made Hana's heart melt. This was excellent inspiration as well. Maybe her characters could have a baby.

Jenna's voice, giddy with excitement, whispered in her ear. "Brittany looks so happy. That might be me in a year or two with a precious baby to show off."

Not that Hana thought she and her siblings needed to marry and start a family in age order, but the comment stung her heart. She would never tell her sister that, of course, but it stung all the same.

"You will have the most beautiful children, Jenna." Hana sighed and turned toward her sister. "I can't wait to be an auntie."

Brittany approached and Hana noticed the dark circles under her eyes. "Hana, Jenna, how are you?"

Jenna cooed at the baby without greeting Brittany. Hana glanced from mother to child and back again. "We're good.

How are you?"

As the infant slept in her arms, Brittany blew out a long, unsteady breath. "I'm exhausted. Silver woke up every two hours last night. But that's okay. It's a growth spurt."

Without warning, Jenna's head whipped up. "What is her name? Silvia?"

"Silver. Like jewelry." Brittany nuzzled into the soft pinkness. "Isn't it unique?"

Knowing her sister all too well, Hana pinched Jenna on the arm. It was a terrible name in her opinion, but they didn't need to tell an overtired new mother that.

"It's something special." It was all Hana could think to say.

"Oh, I see my cousin, thanks for doing all this." Brittany's expression was one of exhaustion as she turned to greet someone else.

Jenna stifled a giggle. "What a crappy name. Isn't their last name Bell?"

Hana gasped. She was right. The baby's name was Silver Bell. The huge laugh that escaped Hana's mouth couldn't be helped. She hoped Brittany wouldn't think it was at her expense. After a minute, the sisters calmed and they resumed their stance at the side of the room, present but unseen.

A buzz on Hana's phone alerted her to a text. "Nari said Dad is cooking dinner." She crinkled her nose. It would be burgers again. Charred on the outside, still red in the center. Mark Willis wasn't known for his ability to cook.

"Come on, let's go out for dinner, just us two. I'm thinking Mexican. A taco salad is calling my name." Jenna checked her watch and sighed. They still had two hours until they cleaned up from this party.

As they waited, the nagging feeling that time was passing Hana by could not be shaken. She felt like it was time to stop writing about fictitious lives and start living her own. Her sister was getting married. Her friends were having children. She had been married to her career for the past five years.

Right out of college Hana won a writing contest that landed her in front of some of the industry's biggest agents. She pitched a novel she had been working on and before she knew it, she landed an agent and a publishing contract with a small press. She poured her heart into her books, but they didn't pay the bills just yet. So she worked as a writer, freelancing for magazines, producing blog articles, and ghostwriting for others. And she worked for her mother. She had scrimped and saved her entire life.

A change was on the horizon, though, and Hana felt it. Her sister was getting married and in a few short weeks, her best friend was also walking down the aisle. Things would be turning upside down for Hana whether she liked it or not. She needed to make sure she was ready for the rollercoaster ride she was about to be taken on.

<hr>

"Of course I can meet you today, not a problem. I'm free around two, how's that? Wonderful. I will make the arrangements to look at those houses. Don't worry about a thing." Chas Rossi pocketed his cell phone as he walked through the doors of the restaurant. A grand building and prime piece of real estate, he thought. His father had brokered the deal for the owners to get this land five years before. It was one of the finest establishments in South Carolina.

He plucked a menu from a gangly teenager and found his parents at their usual table behind the host stand. Visible, but not too visible. He unbuttoned his sport coat and fanned it out behind him as he sat next to his mother.

"Mother, you look exceptional today." He kissed her on her waiting cheek. Chas did not particularly care what his mother wore, but he knew she loved to be complimented, so he won brownie points whenever he saw her. His father reached around and shook his hand. "Dad, nice to see you."

He saw his parents, Chuck and Marcie Rossi, every Sunday for lunch. They attended church and he did not, but he dressed in his Sunday best and would meet them and dote on them the way they liked. As the oldest child and only son, it was his duty to care for his parents. His sister, Maddie, lived two hours away in Charlotte.

Duty was one word Chas could use to sum up his life. He did his duty and followed his father's footsteps into the real estate business. Then his father became mayor of Greenville, and now he was running for state representative. Chas would do his duty again since he was expected to run for mayor in the next few years. And he did his duty by appearing in public with his parents every Sunday.

"You should have been at church, Chas." His mother reached a manicured hand toward him.

"Let him be, Marcie." His father didn't bother to look up from his phone.

Marcie Rossi didn't know the meaning of the term. "What are you doing after lunch? Do you want to come over?"

Chas couldn't help but check his reflection in the window. He was clean-shaven, his hair perfectly styled, his suit pristine. His look told everyone who saw him that he was classy and always ready for anything. "I'm meeting a client at two, I'm afraid. Aren't you two playing a round of golf today?" They often played golf on beautiful Sunday afternoons.

"Not today. But at least we're not working. Who works on a Sunday? It's a day of rest." His mother flagged down a polo-clad server and gave them the eye. She hated it when the wait staff wasn't prompt with taking orders.

"What about the people here who are working today? They're not resting." He motioned around him as young men and women bustled around carrying plates of food and discreetly cleaning up after customers had left.

After they had finally ordered, the family was approached by Marcie's friend Regina May who pulled along a beautiful young woman. Mrs. May pushed the girl forward. "Mr. and Mrs. Rossi, this is my niece, Caitlin. She will be moving here next month to start a new job and needs to find an apartment. Mr. Rossi, might you or Chas know of somewhere she can rent and maybe find roommates who aren't, um, unseemly?"

Marcie Rossi, ever the Southern hostess, shook the girl's hand daintily and gushed over her stunning red hair. "Aren't you the vision of loveliness, Caitlin? What beautiful Irish hair to go with your Irish name!" The girl, Chas guessed her to be in her early twenties, stammered her thanks.

He stepped in and handed her his business card. "Give me a call tomorrow. I'll see what I can do for you. We don't usually handle rentals, but I might know of a few in the area that are clean and free of riff-raff." He smiled and winked at her and her cheeks flamed red.

"Thank you, Chas." Mrs. May's cheeks flushed as if he had said something flirtatious to her. The girl looked as uncomfortable as ever. "Come now, Caitlin, let's let them eat their lunch." They waved their goodbyes and hurried off.

Their food arrived and they ate in comfortable silence. Checking his phone, Chas announced his need to leave. "I have a few things to do before I meet this client. I'll see you at the office tomorrow, Dad. Mother, I will call you and we'll arrange lunch for Thursday. I'm putting it in my phone now." He kissed his mother on the cheek again and left them.

As he strode out the building, Chas noticed the Mays out of the corner of his eye. He waved, knowing they could be potential clients. Mrs. May again pushed her niece forward a little. "Say goodbye, Caitlin."

The color on Caitlin's cheeks reddened as she opened her mouth and no sound came out. She gave an awkward wave in his direction. Chas thought Mrs. May was distasteful pushing her niece the way she was.

But then, he realized perhaps the woman was more trying to play matchmaker than anything else. He rolled his eyes as he went to his car and slid into the sleek leather seat. "You can't buy taste." He shook his head as he rolled away to meet his client.

***

Sundays were pretty slow and that didn't bother Pace one bit. As the owner of Palmetto Magic, a bar in Greenville's now-trendy west end, he filled in as needed as a bartender. He had inherited the place as a run-down dump after his grandfather had passed, but as that end of the city grew, he grew the business along with it, much to his father's chagrin.

Scooping up the few dollars left behind, he wiped down the counter. They had typical bar food, but he was adamant that they not become a restaurant. They were a bar with a limited menu. He came into the office daily but rarely showed his face in the front of the house. Lisa, their bartender on schedule, had called in because her son was sick. Pace was left to fill in. They were only open from noon until nine on Sundays, and Clark was scheduled to come in at five, so Pace only had to ante up for a few hours.

A few tables were occupied with sports fans watching football on the big television. A couple sat cozied up in the corner booth, and two people sat lonesome at the bar nursing their beers of choice.

With a moment to himself, he checked his phone for emails. His main source of income may be from Palmetto Magic, but Pace much preferred working with his nonprofit dog rescue Soft Paws. People from all over the region looked to him and his crew to rescue and rehome dogs that owners claim are hard to love.

Sure enough, an email came through from someone who had found a mother dog and three puppies. He shot off a text to his sister Emmie to call them and arrange a pick up. His younger sister was a vet tech and loved helping at the rescue.

Turning to the mirrored wall filled with spirits, Pace studied himself in the mirror a

moment. He was as scruffy as one of his rescues, with a few days' growth covering his cheeks. His wild and unkempt hair was covered with a skullcap, but usually his hair was free to stick out on end at will. His appearance had never been a top priority, but he did his best to stay active and fit. His Boxer, Moses, helped with that immensely.

Out of the corner of his eye, he saw a familiar and unwelcome face enter the bar. Amanda Evans walked in and took a seat at the far end of the counter. Shaking his head, Pace wondered what on earth would have brought her back into his corner of the world.

He and Amanda had been engaged once, years ago. Her father had been a prominent member of his father's church and they had been pushed together during college. They had dated, and after two years, Amanda hinted it was time to pop the question. So he had, complete with diamond ring. With a wedding planned, Amanda
had told him it was time to stop "playing with puppies all day and do something real." When he had refused to change, she had handed him back the ring and walked out of his life forever.

Pace supposed he should have been heartbroken after that, but the heartbreak didn't come as he thought it should have. He took it in stride and realized he had not loved her anyway. He sold the ring and moved on, deciding love was not for him after all. Maybe he was like a modern day monk who didn't take time for romance.

He had only seen Amanda a handful of times in the three years since their split, and she had not been back in the bar at all. He wanted to avoid her completely but knew that would be impossible. Best to face the music and get it over with. His attempt to stay away from her did not mean she was trying to stay away from him. Her heels clicked on the floor like tiny gunshots. Pace winced at every tap.

She brushed her hair over her shoulder with pristine nails and she sighed as he approached her. "Pace McCoy, you look wonderful." Her face was all smiles and her eyes sparkled in the harsh fluorescent lighting.

Not wanting to appear overly welcoming, Pace crossed his arms at his chest. "Amanda, what a surprise. What brings you back here?"

Her made-up eyes batted at him. "Actually, Pace, I need to have a little chat with you. I was talking with my therapist and she said I needed to tell you this in person." She paused. Pace wondered if it was for effect or if she was preparing to say something

important. "You see, I'm getting married. Next week, actually. But my fiancé and my therapist both said I need to tell you first, just to get it off my chest and clear the air between us."

Pace nodded. He wondered if he was supposed to act devastated or distraught. Amanda had been the dumper after all, and he was supposed to have been the heartbroken dumpee.

Knowing he could not pretend disappointment, he nodded. "I'm happy for you, Amanda. Best of luck." He shook her hand and walked away.

Done is done, he thought. He had been over her for years.

"But wait!" *Drat.* "Pace, I am not finished. This is part of the process. You need to tell me how you feel. I feel happy, but also sad that I might be causing you strife." Her mock sad voice grated.

Turning to her, he shook his head. "Amanda, I honestly don't have any feelings about this. I am truly glad you found the man of your dreams. Like, truly glad. I feel no strife or angst, I'm sorry to say." He knew his voice was gruff and his face was rigid. But he had always needed to be more

"Oh." She blinked several times, fake eyelashes fanning her bronzed cheeks.

"Have a happy life, Amanda." He picked up a pitcher of water and went over to the few tables of patrons, ignoring his ex until she finally disappeared out the door and hopefully out of his life for good.

Pace was glad he was still single. It suited him. Sure, he dated every so often, but it wasn't worth the headache of a woman like Amanda.

Chapter 2

Hana ran through the park, peering behind trees and looking inside bushes. Where could she have gone? It occurred to her to stray from the marked path, her dog would not have had the consideration to stay on the pavement.

"Lulu!" Standing still, she turned in a complete circle, surveying everything around her. "Lulu!" She could feel her heart pounding. Lulu was her baby. Where could she be?

A familiar squeak sounded from behind a group of bushes and Hana took off after it. She prayed it had been from Lulu, the pitch was right and Lulu couldn't bark. Her new shoes were not yet broken in and were pinching her feet, but she kept going. The two minutes Lulu had been gone from her sight seemed like hours. She could be anywhere in the city with as fast as her little legs carried her.

Peering behind the bushes, Hana called again, now breathless. "Lulu!" She was greeted by warm blue eyes and the most stunning biceps she had ever laid eyes on. Beside the man was a large, mottled Boxer on a red leash, but in his arms was her little Lulu.

Breathless, Hana approached the stranger holding her pup. "Oh, you found her. Bless you. Thank you." She reached her arms out for Lulu, but the man pulled back. "Please, that's my dog!" Tears sprang to her eyes as her dog was pulled out of reach.

The blue eyes looked at her skeptically. "How do I know that? This dog has no identification."

The leash with the collar attached to it was hanging limp from her hand. "I know, because I still have it. She managed to back out of the new collar the minute we hit the park. I can show you pictures on my phone if that would prove it." She was agitated, but glad the man wasn't in the habit of handing wandering dogs over to just anyone.

Lulu was struggling to get free from the overly strong bicep holding her. The man eyed Hana again but then handed Lulu over to her. "She seems like she'll vouch for you."

His eyes were stern and his mouth was drawn into a thin line. Hana thought maybe the guy was angry at her, but it wasn't her fault the dog had slipped her collar.

Ignoring the man, Hana took hold of Lulu and held her tight. "You naughty little pup. You're not supposed to run from me." She slipped the collar back on the dog and adjusted the fit. "There. Now you can't run off again. But I'm glad you found a friend."

There was an awkward pause where they both looked at the ground, unsure of what to say. Hana bounced Lulu in her arm.

"Thank you, so much, for keeping hold of her. I was really scared." She looked again at the man straining to hold his dog's leash. She needed to get going but those arms about did her in. "I'm Hana, and this is Lulu."

Character inspiration was standing before her. Hana swallowed hard as she took the time to assess Lulu's rescuer. He stood about six feet tall and had a mop of dark brown hair on his head and two days' worth of stubble on his cheeks and chin. Hana wasn't sure if the stubble was from laziness, or if he kept his facial hair that way. Beautiful deep blue eyes stared back at her from under thick, long lashes. And not only were his biceps impressive, but all of him was. He was lean and muscular – his tank top made that obvious.

Hana quickly gauged her own appearance. Her straight, black hair was in a messy bun atop her head and she wore no make-up. She wore a bright pink V-neck tank top and worn blue jeans. Not her best look.

The man took her hand and shook it, but his expression remained gruff. "I'm Pace." He motioned to the dog. "And this is Moses."

What an interesting name, she wanted to ask the origin behind it but stopped herself. He looked anything but talkative. "Nice to meet you. And you, too, Moses. I'm sorry if we interrupted your run. I was about to—"

"We better be going." As if on cue, Moses began to jump and pull again on his lead.

Cut off, Hana moved aside so they could get past her. "Thanks again." But he had put earbuds back in his ears and jogged away without another word.

She watched him as he went, Lulu prancing at her feet. He was a gorgeous man. He could be one of those rough and tumble men on a book cover. A gruff, yet sensitive hero to be matched with a damsel in distress. What else could he be with those looks and his pup-saving nature? Hana wished she had a picture of him so she could remember his features. Her Pinterest boards were full of character inspirations.

Shaking her head, she double-checked that Lulu's collar was staying in place. "Okay, Lulu, let's get going. That was enough excitement for one day." They began the trek back to their second-story apartment.

Back at home, Hana checked the mail and made sure Lulu had food and water. She was covering an event for Suite Choices Magazine and she was running late. The messy bun would have to stay, but she quickly reapplied deodorant and put on a maxi dress. She fired off a text to her roommate La'Anna that Lulu was taken care of and she grabbed her keys.

After interviewing a few up and coming interior designers for her article, Hana meandered around the vendor tables. Suddenly, someone was waving at her. An older woman sat at a booth for Rossi Real Estate and she was wildly pumping her arms to get Hana's attention.

"I'm sorry, are you waving at me?" Hana approached the table cautiously.

The woman's cheeks flamed red and she gasped. "It is you. Hana Willis. I'm your biggest fan."

Stunned silent for a second, Hana cleared her throat to recover. "You've read my books?" Heat crept up her cheeks. Even with several books that had done well in the market, Hana wasn't used to people recognizing her out in public.

"Oh yes, all of them. I'm such a huge fan. I heard you signed with a new publisher." The woman knew more about her writing career than her own mother.

Stammering, Hana nodded. "Why, yes, I did. I'm so glad you're a fan. Thank you."

The woman handed Hana a business card. "All the ladies in our office love your books." She winked.

Another person approached the table and Hana thanked the woman and stepped away, tucking the card in her bag. What a strange experience. It was almost as if the woman was a groupie for her books. Hana snuck to a corner and did a little celebratory dance on her own. She grabbed her phone to text La'Anna about it, but saw that her friend had texted her first.

L.A.: SO, UM, WE CAN'T MOVE INTO ROB'S PLACE AFTER THE WEDDING. WE'RE GOING TO HAVE TO LIVE IN OUR APARTMENT. SORRY.

Hana scowled. What was La'Anna talking about? They had been planning on moving into Rob's place for months.

HANA: WHAT HAPPENED? SO WE'RE GOING TO SHARE OUR TINY PLACE WITH ROB?

It only took a few seconds for a reply to ding on her phone.

L.A.: HIS BUILDING HAS BEEN CONDEMNED AND IS BEING TORN DOWN. THEY HAVE SIXTY DAYS TO GET OUT. THANKFULLY WE'RE GETTING MARRIED IN JUST A FEW WEEKS. AND I HAVE NEVER TOLD YOU, BUT HE'S ALLERGIC TO DOGS. I'M SORRY.

HANA: ARE YOU SERIOUS RIGHT NOW? LULU WAS HERE FIRST!

L.A.: I KNOW. I SAID I'M SORRY.

La'Anna had been her best friend since they were six years old, and they had been roommates since they had gone to college together almost ten years before. They seemed complete opposites now, but they had always been inseparable. Hana could not love her more.

Until this moment.

Tired of texting, Hana called her friend. "You can't mean that Lulu has to leave, La'Anna. No way."

A sigh came through the phone. "We don't have time to find another place with everything going on. Look, darlin', we were hoping we could live here. With you? Maybe? If we have to."

It was clear to her that they didn't want to live with her. And Hana wasn't exactly jumping at the idea of living with a pair of newlyweds in a tiny apartment with paper-thin walls.

"Okay. Let me think. I'll see you later." She hung up and groaned out loud. "Why now?"

The thought of moving back in with her parents crossed her mind, but that was impossible. The large room she and Jenna had shared was now occupied by her grandparents. And Alex and Nari still lived at home. She did not want to share a room with her eighteen-year-old sister. While Nari would be going to college in the fall, that was still months away and she would be back frequently on weekends. Nope. That was not a viable idea.

There had to be a solution. She always found a solution. Hana walked back through the designer floor with beautifully set up fake rooms all around her. If only she could pick one of these and live in the convention center. The one with the muted yellows and pops of bright blue and orange would suit her just fine.

It was then that she saw the woman from Rossi Real Estate again. Could she possibly get her own place? Squirreling away money was one of Hana's strong suits. Maybe this was the kick in the pants she needed to buy a house of her own. Set down roots. The wedding was a month away. Could she find a place so quickly?

She did what any young American adult would do in her situation. She called her mother. Min Willis was a smart, level-headed woman who had raised four children on a tight budget. She would know what to do.

Except, she didn't know what to do. "Hana, I think you'll be fine on your own, but are you sure you want to buy a place? What happens when you get married?" Ever the Korean and southern mother, Min was sure marriage was just around the corner for her eldest daughter.

"Umma, I'm not even dating right now. I'm on an assignment right now and I just signed with the new publisher, so I'm swamped. Not to mention working for you as well." Hana had danced this number with her parents before. They had wonderful intentions but didn't understand how she felt no rush to get married.

Then her mother sighed. "Sweetheart, if you can afford a house, why not? Real estate is always good. And I suppose you can rent it out down the road if you need to, right?"

"Maybe I can find a place closer to you."

Her mother paused before answering. "You know, that wouldn't be so bad. I can teach you how to cook all the traditional dishes and maybe take you over to the Korean church every so often."

The scowl that crossed Hana's face made her glad she was on the phone and not standing in front of her mother. "I guess we'll see what's out there, Mom. I'll make some calls tomorrow."

She hung up and dug the business card from her bag. Tomorrow she would go to the bank and then start house shopping.

Chas Rossi looked in the mirror one more time. He had on his lucky suit, he cinched his tie up a little tighter, and his hair was behaving. This would be a good day, he thought. He had two new listings in downtown Greenville, three new buyers, and he was flipping his tenth house. He had a ten o'clock with a new buyer, Hana something. Meeting at the office, going over her must-haves, and then out to shop.

Chas loved selling houses just as his father loved selling houses. Together they ran the real estate powerhouse of Rossi's Real Estate. While his father had moved on from houses to cities and now looking at state government, Chas had taken over the business and had an entire team of realtors under him. But he still loved going out and showing. He had been selling for eight years, ever since graduating with a degree in business.

At precisely ten, his buzzer sounded and his receptionist's voice filled the room. "Ms. Hana Willis to see you."

He opened the door, his jubilant sales look plastered to his face. "Ms. Willis, right this way." A petite beauty came through his doorway. She was stunning with almond-shaped eyes and glossy black hair. She wore a simple peach sundress with wedge heels. "Nice to meet you, Hannah. I'm Chas Rossi. Please have a seat."

They shook hands and the woman sat before him. "It's Hana. Not Hannah." She gave him a blank stare.

"Excuse me?"

A slight smirk played on her lips. "My name. It's not Hannah, Mr. Rossi. It's Hana."

Taken aback, Chas felt sweat pop up on his brow. He messed up her name? What was the difference between Hana and Hannah? "Of course, I'm so sorry. Hana."

With a shake of her head, the woman's features relaxed a bit. "It's okay. Happens all the time." Her hands were in her lap and she blinked wide-eyed in his direction. She wasn't fussy, he could tell right away. "I had no idea I was going to see the Mr. Rossi, I feel quite special."

Chas liked her immediately, despite his own faux pas. She seemed to possess some quality he felt often lacked in the opposite gender – a sense of humility. Her expression was happy, but shy and reserved, not brazen like some other women he encountered. Many other women were too forward, shamelessly flirting with him the moment they met. It was rare indeed that he found a woman who was more modest than outgoing.

"I'm not the only Mr. Rossi, you know. My father is the one who built this business from the ground up. I'm merely maintaining his hard work." He flashed her his winning smile. "And now I plan to work hard – for you."

Yes, the line was cheesy, he knew that. But it usually worked on the people who walked through his door. He hoped Ms. Willis was no different.

"I'm hoping you won't need to work too hard, but you will need to work quickly." A pained look crossed her face momentarily before she smoothed her features. "I'm being kicked out of my apartment."

That was a red flag. Why was she being kicked out? Failure to pay rent? Not keeping the apartment up to standards? And why did she need quick? He raised an eyebrow and leaned forward on his elbows. "That doesn't sound good. Please explain the situation to me." What he was really concerned with were her credit score and pre-approval status. He did not want to waste his time.

Smoothing her long hair absentmindedly, she reassured him. "My roommate is getting married in a few weeks, and it turns out they can't live in her fiancé's apartment, so they're moving into ours. Which is forcing me out. I mean,

I am twenty-eight, and I think I can afford it, but I just thought... Well, never mind what I thought. This is where I am now. Can you help me?"

Chas relaxed as he realized the reason behind her plight. It wasn't negligent living, but a sour living situation. "Of course. Tell me what you're looking for and I'll help you find it."

The muscles in her jaw unclenched and the girl settled back into the chair. "I would prefer two or three bedrooms. One for me to sleep in, and one as a guest room and home office. It doesn't have to be large, but I want good use of space. I like the idea of large windows, they give me inspiration. I would like a small, fenced yard for my dog Lulu. I don't like the idea of Homeowner Associations, but if one was a bit more...lax...I'd consider it. A community pool is a plus. Security is a big plus."

Intrigue filled him. "What is your profession, if I may ask, Ms. Willis?" Someone who wanted security, but liked large windows seemed an oxymoron to him. Usually, privacy and security, especially in someone with a dog, meant they wanted to be isolated. Windows meant they were like an open book.

Without hesitating, Hana Willis opened her purse and pulled out a crisp novel. Sitting up taller, she passed it to him. "I'm a writer. Number one bestseller right now."

The book was titled Falling Into You and had a picture of a damsel in distress reaching out to be caught by an uncomfortably handsome man caught in a strong wind. Chas almost scoffed. Number one bestseller? With who? Bored housewives? Instead, he nodded, noting it did indeed say Hana Willis in scrolled letters on the bottom. Turning it over, he noted her picture on the back cover.

"So you write books?"

She fidgeted with a bracelet on her wrist as she opened her mouth and closed it again. Finally she spoke. "I'm also a freelance writer and ghostwriter. And I work for my family business, Merry with Min."

Ah, that was a familiar name. His mother had hosted a few parties at Min's over the years. "And what is your budget, Ms. Willis?" He passed the book back to her. She looked a little deflated that he had not been impressed by her chosen line of work.

Slipping the book back into her bag, she cleared her throat. "Under two-hundred thousand. I can put twenty-five to thirty percent down. I'm preapproved for one-fifty." She handed him the statement from her bank.

Chas took the paper and stood. "I will find you the perfect house, Ms. Willis. Can you come back here around ten o'clock Thursday morning? And be prepared to find your dream home." Within budget.

They shook hands and she left. Outside his door, he heard her speak to the receptionist, then heard Barbara squeal. His newest client offered to sign her book, and Barbara emphatically agreed, gushing over Hana Willis. Maybe he was not giving her the proper credit. She seemed to be well known and liked.

With a few minutes to spare, he checked Google for Hana Willis. Her picture popped up right away. She even had her own website and every social media known to man. He clicked onto her website. The book she had handed him wasn't her only novel. It was her third bestseller in two years. And it was, in fact, number one on the romance list. She did book signings, spoke in symposiums, and was an incredibly smart woman, it seemed. She had been raised right outside of Greenville, South Carolina.

As he jotted down notes about what Ms. Willis was looking for in a perfect home, several listings came to mind. He jotted them down as well. Then he checked the MLS. And narrowed the search to houses within ten miles of his own house. Maybe he could bump into her at the grocery from time to time. That would not bother him at all.

The door of the bar swung open, and a group of women came in, laughing and talking all at the same time. In the middle stood a tiny but colorful woman wearing a tiara that said "Bride" in glittery letters. Ah, a bachelorette party. This was why he hated it when his bartender Lisa was late. He got stuck with drunk girls.

He cleared his throat to gain their attention and was shocked to see the same girl from the dog park in the group. Except this time, she was wearing a simple sundress and her glossy black hair fell in soft waves over her shoulders. Her bridal friend, the one with ten different colors of hair, wore one of those one-piece short sets and ruby red lipstick. The other two with them were wearing party dresses that left little to the imagination. Pace tried to train his attention on the other three women, but he felt drawn to Hana, the girl with the frou-frou dog named Lulu. He decided, however, not to mention their run-in just in case she didn't recognize him.

"Ladies." He caught their attention. He kept his voice deep and gruff. "What can I do for you?" He focused his attention on the blonde at the end.

She flipped her frosted hair over her shoulder and sent him a smoldering look. "A vodka cranberry for me." She laid her hand on his forearm and licked her lips.

Pace steeled himself against her shameless flirting. He was used to it, but that didn't mean he was impervious to it. He blinked and turned his attention to a woman with dark wavy hair falling over her tawny shoulders.

With a light giggle, she batted her eyelashes. "Can I get a kiss on the lips, please?"

Pace paused and nearly sputtered. "Excuse me?"

The bride smacked the table. "Nikki!" She burst into laughter.

The one called Nikki shrugged. "That's the name of the drink. It's really good, tastes like peaches."

Ah, now Pace knew what she was talking about. A peach schnapps and mango mixture. "I think I got it, miss. And you?" he asked the tiara-clad girl.

She thought for a moment, "Um, I think a Midori sour, please, sir. And give my friend here an Alabama slammer." She motioned to Hana. He raised an eyebrow in her direction. He didn't take her to be someone who loved taking shots. Even with owning a bar, he did not find heavy drinkers attractive, no matter how pretty.

"No." She put her hand up to stop him from writing it down. "L.A., you know I don't do shots." She looked at Pace, obviously embarrassed. "I'm sorry. I'll have a glass of chardonnay, please."

He took a deep breath. For some inexplicable reason, he was relieved. Not that it should matter to him what the girl wanted to drink. "A classy choice."

As he turned to head back to the bar, the one named Nikki teased her friend, "Come on, Hana. This is our last chance to go out before La'Anna gets married. Live it up."

He paused to hear her reaction and was not disappointed. "I'm fine with a glass of wine, Nik. You know I don't drink much. Aren't I enough fun without it?"

"You know you are." This came from the blonde on the end.

As Pace worked to make their drinks, he kept looking over at the foursome. They were laughing and taking tons of pictures.

"Something interesting over there?" This came from Desi, one of his regulars who had known his grandfather.

"Oh, no, Des. Nothing." He shot a look at the group again.

"That one on the end seems to be looking at you mighty hard." Desi waggled his eyebrows and Pace glared at him before carrying their orders to the table.

This time Hana tilted her head and said something. "Have we met before?"

Flexing his jaw, Pace shrugged. "Maybe. I'm around a lot." He put the tray under his arm. "Anything else, ladies?"

"The dog park! You're the man who caught my runaway Lulu, aren't you?" Her almond-shaped eyes lit up.

Pace pretended to think a moment. "Oh, yes, the little terrier. I remember. I hope you got her collar to fit her better." When she nodded, he asked again if they needed anything else. With no additional orders, he went back behind the bar.

Moments later, Quent came in with Pace's sister Emmie on his arm. Pace greeted them and pointed them to a corner booth in the back of the place. He'd join them as soon as Lisa showed up for her shift. They often gathered to talk about what was happening at their rescue.

"What can I get you two?" He made a show of pulling out his pen and his paper to write their order.

Quent Rogers had been a go-getter since they were kids and had become a veterinarian two years before. When Pace's little sister Emmie started working as a vet tech at the same office as Quent, sparks had flown. Emmie had always had a crush on her brother's best friend and Quent, being the go-getter he was, didn't waste time making Emmie his girlfriend.

Now the pair sat cozied up together, taking up very little space in the large booth. Emmie beamed at her brother. "Coke and nachos, please."

"Dr. Pepper and a burger. You know how I like it." Quent kissed Emmie on the cheek.

"Gross you two." Pace made a gagging noise before tapping the table and walking off to put in their orders.

A loud noise caught his attention and one of the girls in the bachelorette group was banging on the table. "Hear ye, hear ye!"

Hana looked mortified as she grabbed her friend's arm and pulled her back down in an attempt to shush her. Their eyes met and Hana's grew wider before she quickly looked away.

"I'm here, Pace, I'm here. I'm so sorry." Lisa scurried through the kitchen door, tying an apron to her middle. She immediately set to work. If she wasn't such a great bartender, Pace would have fired her months ago. But she knew her stuff and Pace didn't want to go through the effort of finding someone to replace her.

With Lisa in place, he could finally sit down with Quent and Emmie to talk shop. He slid in beside his sister, passing out their drinks as he did. "How's that new rescue, Q?"

"The hound? She'll be okay. Just needs to put on some weight and get used to people being nice for a change." Quent leaned his head back against the seat and sighed. More noise from across the bar caught his attention. "What is going on over there?"

"Bachelorette party." Pace rolled his eyes.

Emmie looked from the ladies to Pace. "That one seems to be eyeing you pretty hard."

Sure enough, Hana was practically staring him down. "She's embarrassed. And we kind of met yesterday at the dog park."

The drink in Emmie's hand almost slipped, but she caught it just in time. "Whoa. Pace met a girl?"

He stopped her. "No. I just barely met her yesterday when I rescued her pet rat."

Emmie's blue eyes grew wide. "A rat?" She loved small animals like rats, guinea pigs, and the like.

"Well, it looked like a rat compared to Moses. This little terrier slipped its collar and was tearing through the park free as a bird. Somehow Moses got her to stop and play. I scooped her up as the owner came running around the corner." The thought of the gorgeous girl with silky hair made his lips twitch up into a grin. "The girl chasing the dog down had looked panicked. I knew they belonged together, but I made her prove it just in case."

"And?" Quent winked at him.

"And nothing. I gave the dog back and she put the collar back on it. I hope she keeps better track of that thing in the future." Caught having feelings, Pace tried to stiffen up again. "And now she's over there with her friends."

"Did you invite her to come here?" Emmie sounded way too excited and Pace groaned.

Now he was annoyed. He had sat down to discuss business, not who he had met at the dog park. "No, of course not. And the dog's name was Lulu, anyway. Lulu!"

Quent raised his eyebrow. "What was the girl's name?"

"Hana." Her name had hung in his mind since the encounter. It wasn't Hannah, it was Hana, and it was a name that matched its owner perfectly. Then he muttered under his breath and put his head in his hands. He had played right into that one. He knew his friend and his sister could see him turn red, but they were silent for a minute.

When Emmie got up to use the restroom, Quent leaned in closer to Pace. "If you're interested in her, go talk to her."

"She's with friends. And I'm not interested. She's attractive, yes, but I'm not looking." Pace knit his brows together and gave a stern look to Quent.

Shaking his head, Quent clapped Pace on the back. "Just because you ain't looking, doesn't mean someone won't show up. You of all people know that your plan isn't always how things work."

Of course he knew that. But as a stubborn man, Pace needed to see the writing on the wall. And right now, the writing was erasable. Pretty girl or no, right now he wasn't interested, even if he was interested.

Chapter 3

"No, no, no. This is all wrong." The client, a perky blonde woman, screeched as she approached Hana at Merry with Min.

Hana had to stop herself from rolling her eyes as a bride nitpicked over every little thing for her bridal luncheon that afternoon. Hana hated dealing with bridezillas, yet here she was bright and early, hours before the event, and the bride wanted everything changed. Again.

"Miss Palmer, this is exactly how you drew it for my mother last week and we used the specific links you sent over to purchase the balloons and centerpieces." Hana tried to stay calm. She needed the money from this job to keep her dreams of a house afloat.

"Where is Min? Why isn't she here?" An expensively heeled foot stomped the way a child would.

Hana felt bad for whoever this woman was marrying. Maybe Amanda Palmer would be a good antagonist for her next book. "She is picking up the flowers for your luncheon and will be here shortly. You can tell me what's not right and I can see what can be done."

"The centerpieces should be yellow. These are orange. I can't have orange."

Deep breaths. "These are the exact ones you chose, Miss Palmer. And they did say they were buttercup yellow, but you're right, there are orange undertones. I'm afraid there is nothing that can be done at this point."

Turning, the woman searched for something else to complain about. "And the chair covers are supposed to be black, not white."

Looking at the form this very woman had filled out for the event, she clearly noted white chair covers, but they had black in the storage room. "We can switch those out. Perhaps that will help the centerpieces look more yellow in color." Hana composed her best smile and looked to the nervous bride.

"Oh, I bet so. Get that done. And make sure there's more room between tables. My father hates my mother's parents. And Mrs. Cooper Brian's mom can't stand Mrs. Cooper Brian's stepmom. We just need more breathing room." She put her hands to her temples and pinched her lips together.

That explained why she was so worked up. Family strife. It wasn't about the set up at all. Hana tried to look sympathetic and told the bride she would get the chair covers changed before disappearing in the back as her mother came in.

"Your luncheon client is out front and in a panic. I'm changing the chair covers." Hana hefted the box with the covers inside. This day couldn't go fast enough.

As she worked, her mind wandered to a new storyline featuring a bartender with rugged good looks and maybe a power couple who wouldn't accept anything remotely subpar. Maybe the girlfriend in the couple would be dumped by her flashy rich boyfriend and she would fall for the bartender. That might work. Hana pulled her phone from her pocket and made herself a note.

"Let me help you." Her brother Alex's voice startled her and made her jump.

"No, no, I got it. I need to do something mindless. It helps the creative process."

He shrugged. "Whatever. I told Mom I would do something."

"Run the vacuum, then."

More chair covers. More daydreaming about this new storyline. That's what Hana did best.

With the room complete and their own lunches hastily eaten, Hana, Alex, and Min worked the luncheon for the families of the Palmer-Cooper wedding. Alex kept the food trays full, Hana refilled beverages, and Min did whatever it was she did to make things run smoothly. Hana never knew quite what her mother did aside from hold the client's hand before and during their events.

"Miss, where's the coffee?" This came from an older gentleman with kind eyes.

"I'll bring you some in just a moment, sir. Do you want regular or decaf?" Hana had a weakness for sweet old men. There was something about them that made her feel all warm and fuzzy.

"No coffee, Dad. You know what your doctor said." The bride's mother shook her head at the older man.

The man on the other side of her spoke up. "Oh, let him have his coffee, Kim. He's old." Then, so the older man couldn't hear, he spoke under his breath. "Maybe he'll keel over."

This must be the bride's father who can't stand his own in-laws. Hana gave the trio a fake grin. "Coffee will be out in a few minutes and you can decide then." She hurried away, imagining them as characters in a book. At least they weren't her family.

She absently filled empty cups of water or tea, then brought around coffee for any upturned mugs she saw. As she wove through the tables - now spaced wider apart - she incorporated the sweet old man into the story as the grandfather of the dumped girl. She's his caretaker and had planned on marrying the rich guy in order to afford better care for him. But the bartender has a heart of gold and he helps her because he missed his own grandfather.

This was coming together nicely.

An overturned chair clattering to the ground broke her reverie.

"Brian is not your son!" A well-dressed woman with graying hair stood over a woman a good ten years her junior.

"Sheila, really. This is not the place. Heather has been in Brian's life for fifteen years."

Stepping back to observe the debacle before her, Hana figured this was the groom's parents and stepmother. She bit her lip, knowing whatever unfolded before her would make a terrific scene in a book. Though she did feel bad for the now mortified bride and groom.

Brian stepped in and touched his mother's arm. "Mom, it's okay. I can do a dance with just you and do one with her later on."

"You will not dance with her, Brian. She's a predator, she's always had an eye on you."

Whoa, this was getting a little too heated. When Hana saw her mother step towards the group, she and Alex followed behind.

"Mrs. Cooper, let's chat, shall we?" Min had a way with people. Her small frame, her easy smile, and her soothing voice always put people at ease instantly.

Alex managed to pull Mr. Cooper and Heather aside and out of harm's way. Hana went to Amanda and her fiancé to talk them down as Amanda looked like she was about to burst – into tears or flames.

Clapping her hands together, Hana tried to look professional. She felt anything but. "It's okay, y'all. It's okay. No harm done."

"She's going to ruin my wedding, Brian."

For his part, Brian looked defeated. "Let me talk to my mom." He strode past Hana and stopped at his stepmother's side. "I'm sorry, Heather." He grabbed his mother by the arm and pulled her back towards the bathrooms.

Amanda looked at Hana and began to cry fat tears as she wailed. "I knew this would happen! Why aren't the centerpieces yellow?"

I'm so glad I deal with fictional relationships.

Chas sent a few home options to his new client Hana Willis. Hopefully she could look over them before coming into the office. As Chas picked out his suit for the day, he wondered why he had woken up with the raven-haired beauty on his mind.

He had even dreamed of her during the night. Of course, in the dream she had picked out a million-dollar home, making Chas giddy over his commission. He was choosing to ignore the part of the dream where he had taken her in his arms, bent her over, and kissed her inside that million-dollar home. Dreams about clients happened, but never where he was kissing them.

A chirp from his phone sounded and Chas grabbed his favorite tie from the pristinely displayed options. He looped it around his neck before grabbing his phone and checking his messages. It was from Hana Willis. She couldn't wait to see the houses he chose for her. A few cute emojis were peppered into the message and Chas's chest grew warm.

It must be because he had mentioned her to his parents and his mother had practically had a mild heart attack over it. She claimed to be Hana's biggest fan, having read all her books. And in true Marcie Rossi fashion, she had told Chas in no uncertain terms that he needed to ask this woman out because she was a rising star. His mother was convinced that Hana's family must be old money and that tying their families together would be akin to creating royalty in South Carolina. Chas had only laughed.

In the office, he returned calls and set up viewings for a few clients. His days followed a schedule, yet it was always a little different and exciting. Just enough to keep him on his toes and interested in what was going on with the housing market. He also met all manner of people, from local celebrities to politicians to salt-of-the-earth types.

Barbara buzzed his intercom. "Your father just walked in."

His father didn't frequent the office often, enjoying his semi-retirement and campaigning for office. Chuck and his iron fist usually ruled from his home office. A slight sweat popped up on Chas's brow.

The door swung open causing Chas to jump. "What happened with the Linder building?"

"What?" What Linder building? Chas shook his head. "I don't know what that is, Dad."

Chuck smacked the desk between them. "The Linder building. Historic building with ten retail spaces downtown that went up for sale. Why did we not jump on that? I told you to make sure you got it and you didn't even put in an offer."

"You mean Queen Street?"

"It was owned by Joe Linder back in the sixties. It still says Linder across the side. Everyone knows it as the Linder Building." Now Chuck was agitated. "The point, son, is that you were supposed to buy it."

This was absolute news to Chas. At no time in the past month had his father once mentioned the big property on Queen Street with Linder across the side. He had seen it go up for sale, looked at it online, and then promptly forgotten about it. They weren't business landlords, they bought and sold only.

"When did you say anything to me about it? Not once did you tell me to go look at it, to put an offer on it, anything." Chas wracked his brain. No, nothing. Sweat now beaded on his neck.

Veins popped out on his father's brow. "I went and looked at it. I talked to Linder's son-in-law about putting in an offer. Then I told you to file the official paperwork."

"When, Dad?"

"I don't know. Weeks ago!" Again he smacked the desk. "We lost it to Martin and Shale."

With nothing else to do or say on the matter, Chas looked blankly at his father and kept his voice void of emotion.

"I'm sorry, Dad. I didn't realize you wanted to start acquiring property to rent out. We can look into other places."

"I don't want other places. I wanted that one. Never mind. I should have done it myself and not trusted you do get it done."

On that note, the senior Rossi exited the room just as furiously as he had entered it. Chas was left in his father's wake, wondering what had just happened.

Of course, it didn't matter what had just happened. The point to be taken away was that in his father's eyes, Chas had mucked things up. Again. It didn't matter that Chas ran the office, brokered deals, showed houses, scheduled everything, and still found time to entertain his parents. It was never good enough, never fast enough, for his father.

Barbara appeared a moment later, her coiffed hair and round eyes peeking from behind the door. "Chas?"

"Come in, Barbara." He sat back down in his office chair and put his head in his hands and took several deep breaths.

"Coffee?"

"Sure." He heard her scuttle away and he kept his focus on his breathing. In for four counts, out for four counts. Repeat. Think of something positive and beautiful. "The beach, the streets of Paris, Hana..."

He stopped, his breath hitched. Where had that thought come from? Sure the girl was cute, but why was she invading his thoughts like this? Again, he tried to chalk it up to his mother's meddling and the dream he had the night before. Certainly it wasn't her glossy hair, her full lips, and her easy laugh. He hadn't even noticed those features.

The smell of coffee wafted to him as Barbara entered with a huge mug prepared just the way Chas liked. He didn't often ask her to fix him coffee, but he was grateful she knew how he took it.

"Can I get you anything?"

He looked up at her. "Did you know anything about that building? Did anyone? Did he send an email? Call?" He threw his hands up. "I don't get it."

She shook her head. "Nothing. I never saw anything or heard anything about him wanting it. You would have mentioned it."

"So I'm not going crazy?" He took a long drink of the coffee and wished it would bolt through him.

"Not today, hon." Then she backed out of the room quietly and closed his door behind her.

It was almost time for his next appointment and Chas couldn't decide if he was looking forward to it or not. Way too much of the previous twenty-four hours had been spent thinking about Hana Willis. Maybe if he sold her a house he could get her out of his mind. He had about thirty minutes before she came in and he needed a quick break to calm down from the encounter with his father.

He slipped out of the office, waving to Barbara as he went. There was a park just down from his office that many people used to walk, have lunch, or just hang out. He made a beeline for it, breathing in the cooling breeze. Chas wasn't much of one for exercise and he was naturally slim. Between his job and a few of his active hobbies, he felt like he did just fine. When his shoes began to pinch, his plans for a quick walk disappeared and he just stood a moment.

If he could have, he would have taken his shoes and socks off and walked in the grass. Then he would have screamed wild obscenities into the void. But there were people, families with children. He couldn't do that. So he did it in his head. Then he went back to the office.

Soft Paws was his happy place and Pace needed a little happiness. Lately he had been in a terrible funk. His parents were pressuring him to sell or completely change the bar. Employees were making things a nightmare with scheduling. Even with the rescue he had to coordinate things and talk to too many people.

The dogs were better. They were always happy to see him. They never talked back. Even the more stand-offish ones were better than ninety-nine percent of people. Sadly, most of Pace's time was relegated to the office, but he would run with the dogs every day and pet the few cats that always ended up there.

"We have a chinchilla, Pace!" Emmie greeted him when he came into the kennel area. She was cuddling a small ball of fur. "Oh, he's so soft."

"How did we get a chinchilla?" Pace reached out and stroked the soft fur. The animal twitched under his touch.

"Ken picked up a little terrier this morning and it was in the home. The house was abandoned." Emmie's bright eyes stayed fixed on the chinchilla. "I might have to keep this one."

"Em—"

"I know. But since Jasper died a few months ago, that corner is lonely." Her pet hamster, another rescue failure, had been Emmie's companion for two years. "As long as Q gives him a clean bill of health, I'm adopting him."

Emmie always got her way. Pace blamed the big blue eyes and youthful, round face. She looked like a movie princess.

"There was a terrier?"

"In the back." Emmie went back first and put the chinchilla back in the quarantine carrier. "She's in number two."

Pace went over to the kennel and saw a tiny little terrier trembling in the corner. Wiry hair was matted down and her nails were grossly overgrown. Sitting down at the door of the kennel, he pulled a few small treats from his pocket and put them just inside where the dog could get them. Then he waited.

While he sat and Emmie checked on their other quarantined guests, they chatted about their day. Emmie reminded him of their family dinner the next night.

"Yeah, I have to work, Em."

"All you do is work."

"Someone has to." He shrugged. The terrier moved a few inches closer to him.

"Nobody should make work their entire life. Go have fun. Find that raucous bachelorette party and kiss one of them." She giggled.

He knew she was talking about the one he had met before. Hana with the dog Lulu. At least he knew she was an animal person. Not like Amanda, who had never liked Moses and liked him smelling like dogs even less. Hana had definitely been sexy without being over the top. Pace appreciated an understated woman.

"I'll stay here with the terrier, thanks. Does she have a name?" Pace hoped it wasn't Lulu.

A scowl came across Emmie's face. "Ursula."

The laughter that erupted from Pace couldn't be helped. "Oh, that's terrible. We can change it. Ariel?" With approval from his sister, he softly called to the dog. "Who would name you Ursula? We'll call you Ariel and treat you like a princess. Come on."

Again his mind went to the little dog he had met the other day. She had been fluffy, a good weight, and was obviously cared for. Hana had to love her dog. Pace was convinced that only terrible people disliked dogs.

He worked on his phone while the terrier inched closer and closer. Pace wanted to give her a bath and trim her nails, but it was all about trust. He would have to build that up. And she had survived this long with matted fur, a few more hours wouldn't hurt.

A text from his brother Trey popped up. Trey had just finished seminary and would become a minister just like their father.

TREY: I PROPOSED TO CAROLINE. SHE SAID YES.

Apparently it was a group text because congratulatory replies started rolling in and Pace was glad his phone was on silent. Privately he texted his brother back that he was happy for him.

TREY: THANK YOU. THAT MEANS A LOT.

PACE: YOU DESERVE IT! COMING TO SOFT PAWS TONIGHT?

TREY: PROBABLY NOT. KINDA CELEBRATING MY ENGAGEMENT AT THE MOMENT.

PACE: OH, RIGHT. I SHOULD HAVE FIGURED THAT.

Trey had been shirking his duties with the rescue for a few months. But animals weren't his passion like they were for him and Emmie. Thankfully, they had enough volunteers rotate through to make up for Trey's slack. Emmie had said soon Trey would abandon the rescue completely, but Pace had refused to believe her. This was what they did together. They had stared the rescue together. One couldn't just leave.

Ariel the terrier was now at the door of the kennel, gingerly picking up a small, round treat. With as much speed as a sloth, Pace lowered his hand to the floor right in front of the dog. He didn't look at her, didn't move anything else. The dog sniffed the air, then got ever so slightly closer to him.

After almost an hour, the dog touched her nose to his hand. Pace's heart swelled. Who needed people when dogs were so much more trustworthy? He felt confident that within a few weeks she would be ready for a new home. Perhaps Hana would consider adding another little terrier to her home.

Whoa, where had that thought come from? Why was she on his mind? He had run into her twice for a few minutes at a time. There had hardly been any interaction between them, so why did he find his mind wandering to the way she looked when she found him holding her dog? She had looked like an angel with the light behind her, her skin glowing and her face radiating pure joy.

"Psst, earth to Pacey!"

Blinking several times, Pace looked up to see his sister furrowing her brows at him. He raised his own eyebrows in return. She then pointed to the terrier beside him.

Ariel had curled up against his hand and fallen asleep. He hadn't even noticed. How long had he been daydreaming? He attempted to shake Hana Willis from his head. That was the danger of women. They were a distraction he didn't need.

When he stood, Emmie looked him up and down. "Are you feeling okay?"

"Of course."

"I only ask because you were completely spaced out. You didn't see me, you weren't paying attention to the dog. You were in la-la land." Emmie nudged him with her shoulder. "Whatcha thinking about?"

No good answer came to mind and there was no way he was admitting the truth. "Nothing. Nothing at all."

Definitely not Hana.

Chapter 4

Hana followed Mr. Rossi into the third house of the day. The first one had been too cramped, even for one person and one dog, and way overpriced. The second had strict rules from the Homeowner's Association she did not want to deal with, and now they were at a quaint little cottage not far from downtown Greenville.

"You do have this nice little driveway all to yourself. As you can see, the neighbors are nearby, but not so close they can peek in your windows at night." Chas Rossi fiddled with the lockbox for a minute before it finally popped open. "This home has three bedrooms, a wonderful kitchen, and even an additional half-bath off the living space. There is a community pool as you requested, and they have a neighborhood watch program. There is an HOA here, but I can show you their outline, it's nothing extreme."

When the door opened, he allowed Hana in first. The walls were a creamy yellow and cheerful. The living room was large and let in a ton of natural light. Hana threw open the blinds to see the view. Across the street was another identical home, but it was offset, so the houses were not staring at each other. At the back was a dining area perfect for a round table for four. The back door revealed a little fenced-in yard with a few shade trees and a concrete slab for patio furniture.

"What do you think?" Chas peered around and flipped on a light switch.

Hana ran her hands over a door jamb and looked at the kitchen. "I like it. Nice size, it's fenced, and doesn't seem to need paint out here. What's the price?"

He checked his phone. "This home is a steal at one seventy-two nine. Let's keep looking, shall we?"

The kitchen was laid out well and had plenty of space should she ever entertain. And down the short hallway were three bedrooms. They appeared to be identical in size, though one was squarer in shape, the other two more rectangular. At the end of the hall was a full bathroom with a large wall mirror.

"Didn't you say there was a half bath?"

"Yes, this way." A door off the living room revealed a small mudroom with the washer and dryer hookups and a small half bath attached to it. Through the mudroom was a door to the driveway.

"How long has this been on the market?" Hana had done her research. She knew the longer something was on the market, the less money the owners would take for it.

Chas again checked his phone. "It seems it's been on the market for about three months."

That was what Hana wanted to hear. She liked the house and pending an inspection, she thought it was the perfect bachelorette pad for her and Lulu. "Perfect. I love it. I'd like to put in an offer of one fifty-eight."

But Chas did not smile back. "That's more than ten thousand less than the asking price, Ms. Willis."

"I'm well aware of that, Mr. Rossi. I may be a writer, but I can do the math. After three months on the market, that's what I am prepared to offer. This is a negotiation, is it not?" She blinked her eyes at him, offended that he thought her offer too low. It wasn't even his house. Was he only concerned about his commission?

Now the look of amusement came back. "Of course, of course. Let's head back to my office and we'll write it up and get it sent in to the listing agent." He showed her to the door and began the process of locking everything back up while she inspected the outside of the brick house.

With her offer submitted, Hana felt almost giddy. And despite Chas Rossi's hot and cold demeanor, she was happy to have the head man on her side. As she stood to leave his office, she thanked him again for his help.

"It's no problem at all, Ms. Willis. May I take you out for a congratulatory drink?" He flashed his mega-watt smile to her and rolled his shoulders back as if in a mating dance.

Hana eyed him suspiciously. "Do you take all clients out for drinks after they make offers?"

This time he winked at her and Hana felt a blush creep over her cheeks. Chas Rossi was a handsome man. "Not all of them."

She looked down at her hands and played with a ring she wore on her right hand. "I'm not much of a drinker. I'm afraid it's not my scene. But thank you anyway."

His voice came from her side of the desk now. "Well, then I must insist on taking you for a full meal, then. Please."

Was he asking her for a date? It has been months since her last date. Quickly she scanned down to his left hand. She had not checked him for a wedding band. But the hand was now in his pocket. "Won't your wife mind?"

"I'm not married." He pulled his hand from his pocket and wiggled his finger as if reading her mind.

"Girlfriend?" Hana tilted her head and pursed her lips.

He chuckled. "I don't have one of those either. You can ask Barbara if you don't believe me." He gave her a look that she would have described in one of her books as a smolder. He looked like Flynn Rider from Tangled and she almost laughed.

The real estate agent was an attractive man, but Hana didn't have time for this. She was too busy, on too many deadlines. She really needed to go home and start thinking about packing. Home, where La'Anna and Rob would be cozied up and she'd be the third wheel for dinner. Again.

"You know what? Why not? If you're willing to buy, I'm willing to eat." She did like to eat, and who knew? He could turn into a good character inspiration. "But it's not a date and I'm driving my own car. Where shall we go?"

He nodded his understanding. "Are you familiar with The Q?"

"Of course, who in South Carolina isn't?" The Q was famous across the Southeast for its barbeque, and Hana considered herself an amateur barbecue connoisseur. "I'll see you there in about fifteen minutes, then?"

With a nod, Chas walked her out of his office and bade Barbara goodbye. The older woman winked to the two of them as they left side by side. Hana wondered how many clients – single female clients – Chas actually took to dinner. The thought soured, but she told herself to enjoy the evening. Regardless, it was a meal she didn't have to cook or watch La'Anna and Rob make gross faces over. She could survive this one meal.

In her car, Hana quickly applied lipstick and ran a brush through her hair. Her blue maxi dress was casual, so she was glad he didn't suggest somewhere more upscale. After pulling into a parking space, she texted La'Anna her dinner plans – just in case – and got out of the car. Chas approached her and his dark eyes sparkled in the sun. She couldn't help but return the smile.

His confidence was attractive on top of his well-put-together look. He had taken the blazer off and now sported only his khakis and a green pinstripe button-down shirt with the sleeves rolled to his elbows. Hana thought he looked like he belonged in a catalog ad. He'd make a great character. The problem with these types of characters, though, was that they were always hiding something. The façade wasn't their true self. It made her wonder what Chas Rossi was hiding.

Chas opened every door for her like a true gentleman and Hana couldn't help but think her mother would be thrilled. He even held out her seat for her, even though the atmosphere was rustic and the table coverings were butcher paper.

After ordering, Chas was quick with the questions. "I know you're a successful writer, Hana, but what else? Tell me your story." He took a drink from his mason jar filled with tea and bore his dark eyes into hers.

"Oh, well, I'm the oldest of four children. My dad is an engineer and my mom runs an event space. My sister Jenna is getting married soon. So I guess I'm officially the Old Maid big sister." Her laugh was sad, she knew. "But at college, I majored in Journalism where my sister majored in boys." This time she laughed for real. It was always a good joke.

"I didn't know one could major in boys." Chas's eyes shone as he chuckled.

"She did graduate with a degree in marketing, but she's much more interested in getting married than anything else. She chose her classes based on who was in them."

Chas shrugged. "So she's young and in love? Who wouldn't want that? How old is she?"

"Jenna is twenty-five." Hana sighed, tired of talk always revolving around her sister. Though she guessed she had been the one to bring Jenna up in the conversation. "Tell me about you, Mr. Rossi."

He thought for a moment, "Oldest child as well. My sister is a news reporter in Charlotte. My father is Charles, or Chuck, Rossi, you should know his name. My mother Marcie is the perfect wife of a businessman. I've been married to my career for the past several years, but when my grandfather passed away last year I realized I needed to prioritize."

Their food was placed in front of them, and the tangy scent of mustard-based barbecued chicken wafted up to Hana. Chas didn't finish his thought or explain what he had been making a priority.

"My mother said I'll never meet the right person if I don't meet anyone." His smile faltered and his eyebrows shot up. Was this his new priority? "Not that I'm saying you're the right person. Or the wrong person. Just someone I'd like to get to know better. Because of your books, I mean. That kind of came out wrong. I apologize."

Feeling a little awkward, Hana laughed a little. "No problem. I know what you mean. My mother thinks I spend my life holed up at my computer. She wonders how I can write about romance if I don't experience it. I guess I'm also married to my career."

"Married to the career, single to the rest of the world."

The comment made Hana nod in agreement. "And I plan on staying that way for a while. There's just too much I need to do before I settle down. I mean, I want to, but I'm not looking for forever." Maybe that would relay to him that while she was happy to have dinner, she wasn't looking for anything serious.

Only a nod came in reply as Chas proceeded to eat everything on his plate. "This is delicious." His eyes rolled back and he groaned.

Hana wasn't sure he had even chewed the food first. At least it was a free meal.

Chas's phone went off and he gave it a quick check. "Wait, this is about your offer." After a nod from Hana, he took the call and spoke in hushed tones.

Her knee bounced as he spoke and nodded a few times. Impatient, Hana waited for him to hang up. But when he did she thought the call was way too quick for good news. "Well?" She closed her eyes and wrung her napkin in anticipation.

"I'm sorry. I don't usually take calls at dinner, but since it was about your offer, I thought you wouldn't mind."

Opening her eyes again, Hana saw him taking a bite of potato salad. She was ready to jump across the table. "What did they say?"

With a sneaky smirk, he winked at her. "Oh, you want to know, don't you? They actually accepted your offer. But with the house as-is. If an inspection reveals anything is needed, you're on your own with that price."

"Deal!" She shouted, drawing the attention of several people around them. She blushed and lowered her voice, wiggling in her seat as she spoke. "Deal. I'm so excited. Thank you, Chas!"

She could have hugged him then, but seeing as this was mainly a professional relationship and she did not want to give him ideas, she was glad that wasn't an option with a table full of barbecue between them.

"I hear you went on a date last night, Charles." His mother's southern drawl came through the phone. "Was she a nice girl? How did you meet? Who are her people?"

Chas was trying to get dressed and out the door so he could officially accept the deal on Hana Willis's new home. He put his Bluetooth earbuds in and tied his tie as he spoke. "Did Barbara call you again, Mom?"

"No, it wasn't Barbara. It was Kitty McInnes, she said she saw you with 'a very attractive girl at the barbeque place downtown' and had to call and tell me all about it." His mother, ever the drama queen, practically sobbed. "I didn't know you had a girlfriend, Charles. Why are mothers always the last to know?"

"She's not my girlfriend, mother. She's a client, albeit an attractive one." He grabbed his jacket and slung it over his shoulder and moved toward the front door. "She made an offer on a house, I took her out to dinner. Nothing more."

"She must make good money to purchase a house all on her own." Nosy woman. She was fishing for information without even realizing it.

"She's actually an author. A romance novelist, apparently. Hana Willis." Chas maneuvered his car down the street toward his office.

The screech that came through his phone could have raised the dead. "The Hana Willis? Author of Falling into You? Chas, you must bring her to the house!"

He shook his head as he turned into his office parking lot. "No, Mom, I must not. She's nothing more than a client. End of story. Now, I'm at work. I will talk with you later, Mother." With the push of a button, his mother's voice disappeared.

And just in time for Barbara's to fill his ears. "Mr. Rossi, the Adamses called again. Several times. You are interviewing two potential realtors today to take over Desiree's place, a Graham Black at eleven, and a Nicole Hood at three. And Ms. Willis' offer was accepted. But I think you know that part already." She eyed him and raised her eyebrows.

After hearing enough from his mother, he chose to skip over his secretary's look of amusement. She was often like a second mother or concerned aunt. He took his stack of messages from her hand and went into his office, closing the door behind him. Sitting down, he read through his messages. They were unexciting, he decided. He opened the email concerning Hana's offer and replied that he would send the contract over immediately.

He sat back a moment and thought about Hana Willis. It was a shame she was buying a house so soon. He would love an excuse to show her around more, spend more time with her. He could not deny the strong attraction he felt for her. What if she was the one? The One. And she was buying a house solely for her and her dog. There would be no room for him in a small house. Chas shook his head. What was he thinking? He had gone on one quasi-date with this girl and suddenly he was moving into her house? He needed to busy himself with other things.

Looking at the stack of messages, he sucked it up and picked up his phone. He dialed his least favorite client, Joe Adams, and shoved Hana Willis from his mind.

✻

He spotted her at last. Not that he'd been looking, Pace tried to tell himself. Oh, who was he kidding? He had taken Moses to the dog park every day for a week hoping to catch sight of Hana and her little dog Lulu. Something about the girl pulled Pace in, making him want to find out more about her.

Then he spotted her. She was sitting on a picnic blanket, wearing cutoff jean shorts, a tank top, and Chucks.

"My kind of girl." Then he caught himself. Women were not worth the effort. He argued with himself. "Cute or not, Pace, the answer is no. Don't go over there."

She sat hunched over, reading a book, a half-eaten apple in her left hand. Lulu the dog was leashed and the leash was staked to the ground. She dozed, content in the sunshine.

Pace jogged Moses by a few times, hoping to catch her attention. Relief would fill him when she didn't look up, but then he'd jog by again watching her. Her black hair covered her face and she was absorbed in her book. Finally giving up, he unhooked Moses from his leash and threw a tennis ball for him to fetch.

The ball landed on the edge of her blanket.

Hana looked up to see Moses bound over to her. Lulu jumped from her nap with a start, but otherwise seemed happy to see her friend again. Pace watched as Hana petted Moses and looked around. He ran up, waving as he approached.

"I'm sorry. I wasn't watching where I threw that. I hope it didn't hit you. Or that Moses is bothering you." He quickly reattached Moses's leash and knelt down beside him.

With her hand over her eyes, Hana's face broke into a huge grin. "No bother at all. Moses? Oh! You're Lulu's rescuer. The bartender, right? Want to sit a minute?" She motioned for him to sit in front of her.

Settling in a little more beside Moses, Pace let Lulu come sniff his hand. She looked a lot like Ariel. "That's right. Pace McCoy is my name." She shook his hand.

"Pace. I'm Hana Willis. It's nice to see you again." She looked in her backpack a moment and produced a bottle of water. Holding it out, she made a simple observation. "You look hot."

Unable to resist smiling, Pace accepted with thanks and twisted the cap off. He had remembered her name, but didn't tell her that. Several cool gulps slide down his throat. They had been at the park for almost an hour. He poured some out and Moses lapped it up as it fell through the air.

Unsure what to say, he looked to the book in her hand. "What are you reading?"

She put the book aside. "Oh, I'm just proofing something for work, that's all. You must come here a lot."

"We try to come often. It's good exercise for Moses, and me. And it helps me get my vitamin D since I spend so much time inside." Most of it was spent in the stuffy office with no windows and iffy air conditioning.

"How did you become a bartender?" She tossed her long, glossy hair over her shoulder. She appeared to be genuinely interested in the answer. Most people who asked were more interested in how to judge him rather than actually wanting to know.

"I guess I fell into it. I'm not actually a bartender – I have my license but I inherited the business from my grandfather. I fill in up front as needed." It was a vague response, he knew, but for most people, it satisfied the curiosity. The response was either utter horror or absolute delight, followed by asking if he could work their next party.

She sat up a little straighter and clapped her hands. "That's awesome. I'm an author, and I would love to have a character who's a bartender. Would you mind if I picked your brain sometime?"

She was an author? To Pace, it sounded both flighty and mysterious. He had never met a true author before. Without much thought, he agreed.

She looked at her phone. "I'm sorry, I do need to get going. Can I come to your bar tonight? Will it be busy?" He shook his head unsure what he was signing up for. "Say around seven?"

He hadn't been planning on working that night, but he had nothing else going on. "Sure, that would be fine."

They both stood and he helped her gather her blanket. She shoved everything in her backpack and grabbed Lulu's leash.

"I'll see you tonight. Thank you." Hana wiped her hands on the backside of her shorts and Pace couldn't help but follow their movement. Then she jogged away, her raven hair flying out behind her and her little terrier happily running along.

Pace was left scratching his head looking after her as she went. He should have asked what kind of writing she did. Regardless, the butterflies he felt at the idea of her coming back into Palmetto Magic left him wondering what was going on in his mind and body.

Romance was a bad idea. A horrible idea.

<h1 style="text-align:center">Chapter 5</h1>

Palmetto Magic was in a brick building shared with a florist. A blue neon palmetto tree cast a bluish shadow over the sidewalk. Hana snapped a photo with her phone. It was perfect for the story forming in her mind. She envisioned lots of neon, low lights, dark wood.

As she pushed through the door, the first thing she did was inhale. It wasn't filled with a smoky scent as she expected, even though she knew businesses were mostly smoke free these days. The scent of some fried food mixed with a general alcohol smell and lemon met her olfactory senses. It wasn't a bad scent at all. She nodded her approval.

It wasn't worn, dark wood as she had thought it would be. Instead it was all chrome and silver with pops of blue everywhere. The bar seats and booths were covered with an electric blue vinyl to match the neon sign out front. There was a matching one on the far wall. Two booths and three tables were occupied with customers, five men sat at the bar either talking or watching a television on the wall.

Pace was behind the counter cleaning glasses. His expression was grim, like he was unhappy or deep in thought. When he looked up and saw Hana, he waved her over, coming to the side of the long counter. He wore a fitted t-shirt that showed off a full sleeve tattoo and impressive biceps.

Hana blinked. She was not impressed by guys covered in muscles, but his were just the right amount to show strength without showing off. But the tattoos would make a great feature for her character. She made a mental note. Sliding into a cushy stool, she put her bag on the counter.

"Thank you for letting me invade like this." Her notebook and pen, along with her camera, were pulled from the bag. When she noticed his eyebrows raise she tried to assure him. "I hope you don't mind. I won't take pictures of customers, or you if you don't want me to. But I would like pictures of the bar, how it's set up, so on, so I can reference it later."

He shrugged. "Um, Ms. Willis, what kind of writer are you?" He wiped down the surface of the bar between them and Hana watched the damp pattern he made.

She opened her notebook and clicked her pen. This was going to be fun. So many nuances she had not considered before. "Call me Hana, please. I'm a novelist. Romance, if you must know." She leaned in and wrinkled her nose. "I know it sounds a little corny, but my last three books are on the bestseller list. I promise I'm legit."

The look on his face told her he doubted her legitimacy, but he didn't say anything. She jotted a note about the set up and about how he laid his palms flat on the lower part of the counter in front of him. She licked her lips as she often did when thinking. Her pen flew over the paper, her writing legible only to herself.

"So what—"

Her head shot up. She had started working without telling him anything more. "I'm sorry, forgive me. When the ideas start, I can't stop them. Act like I'm not here for a few minutes, I want to see you in action and take notes on the bar atmosphere." She bent down over her notebook again.

"Can I get you a drink?" He held up a bottle of vodka that was sitting in front of him.

Hana shook her head at the alcohol. She needed a clear head and she had never been much of a drinker. "Do you have Sprite?"

Pace nodded and filled a glass for her, placing it behind her notebook. She thanked him and continued to take notes. After a few minutes, she took a satisfying sip and looked up to see him watching her. He averted his eyes, but not quick enough. The music changed to something with a moving bass line and Hana closed her eyes to absorb her surroundings.

When she opened her eyes again, a group of men came in wearing the telltale blue shirts of a local mechanics shop. Their stained fingers would have given them away if the shirts had not. This was a perfect set up for watching Pace interact with customers.

The characters came to life in her mind. A plucky bartender who had big dreams, his regulars who gave him sage life advice, and a woman who would blow in on the breeze one day and turn his life upside down. Hana needed to nail down her female protagonist. Her pen flew furiously across the page as ideas poured from her mind.

Once the ideas staunched a little, she put the pen down and stretched her hands. She lifted her camera and caught Pace's attention. "Mind if I take a few?"

What she really wanted was to take a few pictures of him. He really was the perfect look for the character she was thinking. Maybe she could name him Patch. No. Payne. No. Pax. That was it. She wrote it down before she forgot.

Pace agreed to the photos and Hana snapped pictures of the bottles on the wall, of the tap, even under the counter. She got a detailed shot of what the taps looked like. Sure, she could look it up online, but there was something about seeing them physically in front of her, being able to touch them and feel if they were cool and smooth or warm and rough.

"Can I take a few of you?" The question came out before she thought about it. The look of sheer panic on his face, however, made her second guess the idea. "It's okay. I don't have to. I just wanted to note the way you wore your apron and towel there. But I can write it down."

He fidgeted with the apron for a moment. "Oh, that's okay. I'm not used to being in front of the camera these days. You can take a picture if you need to." He smoothed his apron down and ran his fingers through his hair.

A smile spread across her lips and she nodded emphatically. She stepped back from him and looked through her lens. Pace stood rigid, as if he was facing a firing squad instead of a girl with a camera. Hana giggled, he was way too serious. But when he interacted with his customers, he was relaxed and almost pleasant. Almost.

"Um, can you, like, lean against the bar? Act casual."

Leaning his hip and arms on the counter behind the bar, Hana watched Pace attempt casual. It seemed he didn't understand the word. Cheeks pinked, Pace's eyes shot to the side when the men in the blue mechanic's shop shirts began snickering. Not wanting him to be embarrassed, she raised the camera again and snapped several pictures of him as quickly as she could.

Knowing he would be the perfect inspiration for this character, she stepped toward him. "One more." She turned the camera to his face and held her breath as his hazel eyes reflected the camera back to her. He did not change his expression, having neither a smile nor a grimace. Yet she could read his thoughts. She knew she could.

I dare you to come closer, they seemed to say. See what happens when you run your fingers over my tattooed skin. But don't get too close, I don't let anyone in.

Goosebumps erupted on her arms and her breath hitched. She looked at the picture on her camera and back up at him. She swallowed hard and furrowed her brow slightly. She was pleased with the photo, but it wasn't the picture that had her so shaken. "Thank you. I think that will do."

She put the camera away and made a few more notes before the unsettling feeling was too much for her. Pace was one of the most ruggedly handsome men she had seen in a long time and her body was apparently having some sort of metaphysical reaction to that. It was also getting late and she had to be at Min's bright and early. Her bag packed up, she asked Pace what she owed.

Adam's apple bobbing, he cleared his throat. "It's on the house. I think I can spare a Sprite." The faintest hint of a smile played across his lips, but it disappeared before it ever arrived.

"That is so kind of you. Thank you."

Before she could stand to leave, he put his hand on the upper part of the counter. "It, um, looks like my regular bartender just walked in. I can sit down with you and tell you more about running the business. If you think that would be useful."

Stunned, Hana agreed. A buxom blonde in a tight shirt came into the bar area tying an apron around her waist. Hana immediately wanted to take notes on the woman's clothing and how she wore her apron differently. Pace did not introduce them, though. Hana wondered if this was his girlfriend, but then thought the air between the coworkers didn't change, so likely not.

A few minutes later she and Pace were sitting in a back booth, a plate of nachos and an order of buffalo wings between them.

"I am famished. Thank you for getting these." Hana pulled a chip covered with cheese and jalapenos from the pile and popped it into her mouth. She didn't worry about how she looked to him as her stomach truly was growling.

"Don't worry about it. I'm hungry, too. So we may have to fight over the last chip or wing." His eyes grew wide as he watched her devour the food she had in hand.

"I will fight you over the wings." And she meant it. Buffalo wings were among her favorite foods. She eyed him and winked. "You inherited this place from your grandfather? That's so cool. Tell me more."

"He opened Palmetto Magic in seventy-three and ran it until a few years ago. He still owned it but couldn't be here. I majored in business at Clemson, so he had me managing the place. My father was livid. He hated that Mom's father ran a bar. And my running it almost gave him a heart attack. It's been tough with me owning it now."

Hana furrowed her brow. "Why is that?" She thought any parents would be thrilled that their child was financially independent and running a successful business. Hers certainly would be.

Pace sighed and wiped his hands. "My father is the pastor over at Haven Rest and he says drinking leads to debauchery. He's disappointed I didn't go into ministry with him, but he's pleased with the dog rescue."

"Dog rescue?" This piqued her interest. The hot bar owner also worked at a dog rescue?

Now a genuine smile appeared and Pace's shoulders relaxed. "Soft Paws. My sister named it. We started it several years ago, my sister, brother, and I. We have room for twenty dogs and several cats. Currently we also have a chinchilla my sister thinks she's going to keep."

He runs the dog rescue? Hana had heard of Soft Paws and their splendid work in the community to run spay and neuter programs, to rehabilitate animals, and find homes for all their charges.

"You own Soft Paws?" Her mind was spinning with possibilities.

A sheepish look came across his face. "We don't say that we own it. We run it. More my sister and I now, along with my best friend Quent. Trey, my brother, is still on the board, but he's not as active as he used to be."

"I would love to learn more. Tell me everything."

A closing was always a reason to celebrate in Chas's mind. Hana Willis had closed on her new home the day before and Chas had surprised himself by asking her on a proper date. She was so humble but had the makings for being a real celebrity author like a few others. Having her on his arm would be perfection and maybe – finally – impress his parents.

But Hana had turned him down. She claimed she was under tight deadlines and now needed to move her things into her new house. Chas had thought momentarily about offering to help, but he didn't want to haul boxes or deal with meeting her family, so he kept quiet.

Still, he wanted a way to see her again. He figured bringing her a housewarming gift to her new home would be a brilliant idea. Maybe a hanging plant. Not knowing what she might like, he loaded his car with two potted ferns, a spider plant in a macramé hanger, and a bouquet of flowers. After pulling in behind her little sedan, he placed the potted plants at the front door and held the others while he knocked. He practiced his smile while he waited.

The door swung open to reveal a stunned Hana with a messy bun on her head and wearing workout gear. "Chas, what are you doing here?"

The sight of her made him exhale deeply. She was gorgeous no matter what she wore. He had to shake his head to think clearly. "I brought a housewarming gift. Well, a few of them." He motioned to the potted plants.

Shock registered on her face. "Oh my word. That was so thoughtful of you. Please, come in while I get a vase." She took the bouquet, then stopped and turned. "I think there's a hook right there if you want to hang the spider plant. I love the macramé!"

There was a hook on the eave, so Chas hung the spider plant before following Hana inside. He stepped into the small home and looked around. He was shocked at the progress already made. A small brown dog came over to him with its tail wagging. It sniffed his shoes and Chas tried not to shoo it away.

"Cute dog."

Hana beamed. "That's my Lulu. She's always happy to make a new friend."

Chas made a show of bending down and giving the dog a pat. "Hello, Lulu." Then he stood back up and ignored the little thing. "How did all this get set up so fast?"

He noted the complete living room, even down to the table lamps already in place. Through a doorway he could see a bedroom also furnished, the bed made. Aside from boxes stacked in corners and empty walls, it looked like she had lived there for more than a few hours.

Laughing, Hana looked around her place. "I have a large family and lots of friends willing to help."

The laughter drew Chas's gaze over to Hana where he finally looked at her. She stood to the side, beaming, the bright colors of the flowers accentuating her olive skin. Chas thought she looked radiant.

"You look stunning." His voice was low and he wasn't sure she heard him, but then she looked up to him and blushed.

She put the flowers in a vase and arranged them. "This really is so nice of you. No wonder you're such an in-demand realtor." Satisfied with her handiwork, she moved the vase to her small dining room table. "Can I get you coffee? Water?"

"No, thank you. I just wanted to congratulate you again." What he really wanted to do was ask her out, but he was terrified she would say no again. "Do you need help getting around the area? I should have brought you a map."

"I have a map on my phone."

"Oh, right." Foot in mouth again. Of course she had a map on her phone.

She leaned on the counter and crossed her arms. "And I know the area well. My favorite coffee shop is just a few blocks away. I think we can even walk there. I was going to take Lulu, actually, when you knocked. So good timing."

"Oh, I guess I should let you go, then."

Hana licked her lips and raised an eyebrow. "Do you want to come with us?"

Dressed in chinos and wingtips, he was not dressed for a walk. "I appreciate the offer, but I do have work to do. I just wanted to stop by. I hope to see you around more."

She went to the door and grabbed a pink leash with a harness attached to it. The little dog now jumped with excitement while Hana hooked her up. Chas opened the door for her and waited for Hana to lock up.

"Thanks again, Chas. I'll see you around." She started to turn from him.

But Chas's mind screamed at him to do something. Ask her out again. An idea came to Chas at that moment. His friend was getting married and he still needed a date. Hana would be the perfect person to take. She was demure, gorgeous, easy to talk to. She seemed to embody everything Chas had been looking for in a date – and perhaps more.

"Wait." He stood with his hands shaking, the keys rattling. He shoved them into his pocket.

"Yes?" The sun was casting a glow on her cheek and a stray hair had found its way down her neck and Chas wanted to reach out and touch it with every fiber of his being.

"This may seem out of line, Hana, forgive me, but might you be interested in joining me for a wedding I have coming up in a few weeks?" He checked his phone. "It's on June twenty-seventh, right here in Greenville."

She looked down a moment as her cheeks grew pink. When she looked at him again, her eyes meeting his, Chas felt his heart thud into his chest. Hana shifted her weight as she pulled out her own phone. "Oh. What was the date again?"

"June twenty-seventh." It came out as a croak as his mouth had suddenly gone dry. He needed her to accept his offer. Needed, as if his life depended on it.

When her face fell, Chas felt his whole body fall with it. "My sister's wedding is on the same day, I'm afraid. I'm in the wedding. I'm sorry. I hope you find someone else, though."

Attempting to save face, Chas shrugged and smiled. "That's too bad. I hope you can find a date as well. Not that you couldn't find a date, I know you could." He rolled his eyes and grimaced. "I put my foot in my mouth there."

With a giggle, Hana laid her hand on his arm. "I know what you meant."

An awkward pause hung between them as neither knew what to do next. Finally, Chas spoke. "I guess I better go."

Hana tucked the stray hair back up into the bun. "Actually, my best friend La'Anna's wedding is next Friday if you're free around four. I know it's short notice, but..."

The phone came out of his pocket at once. He had a closing at two, but he could see about bumping it up an hour. "You're in luck." He looked at Hana and winked. "Or maybe I'm the lucky one. I would love to join you."

"I'll text you the details." When Chas nodded, Hana gave into Lulu's pulling and jogged after the little dog.

Chas watched them a moment before getting into his car and backing out of her driveway. He was curious about the coffee shop she liked, so while he went the other direction, he circled back around and found her as she turned into another neighborhood.

A few minutes later, Hana and the dog stopped in front of a little hipster coffee shop on the corner of a trendy strip of stores. He made a mental note to try to bump into her there if he could. Until then, he had a wedding date to prepare for.

Saturdays were never a day off for Pace. He spent the morning at Palmetto Magic when it was empty and he could clean and sort. And his afternoons were spent at Soft Paws, again when it was mostly void of people, where he would do the same. Between them he would take Moses to the dog park or go to the gym.

He was mildly surprised when the chime on the door at Palmetto Magic sounded right as the door was unlocked. Most people weren't thinking about drinks at noon. He had his bartender Jake out front so Pace continued to sort the stockroom. A moment later, Jake's voice beckoned to him.

There was probably a salesperson or a Girl Scout at the bar trying to sell something. Pace pushed through the swinging door, ready to turn away whoever it was.

"Hana. What a pleasant surprise." He was even more surprised that he meant it. He had enjoyed their conversation a few days before once she was done taking horrible photos of him behind the bar. She had been genuine and engaging.

She tucked her hair behind her ear and bounced a little when she saw him. When Pace's heart hammered in his chest, he reminded himself to maintain distance. She had said she was on deadlines and incredibly busy, just as he was. Any thoughts of liking this girl needed to fly out the window.

"I'm sorry to bother you, but I'm glad you're here. I loved everything you said about your animal rescue and how we need to keep dogs and cats off the streets. So I, I mean, it's not much, but I wanted to bring you this." She thrust a piece of paper out to him.

It was a check for two hundred dollars. He knew she had just bought a house and was struggling a little, so this was a huge sacrifice for her to make.

Pace swallowed the lump in his throat and fought the urge to hug her. "This is so generous of you. But you didn't have to do this."

Her cheeks pinked. "I know that. I wanted to. I keep money set aside in case Lulu needs emergency surgery or something and there's plenty in there. I wanted to make sure other animals are afforded that same care."

It was Pace's turn to blush and he felt the heat rise. Not many women were as passionate about animals as he was. Amanda certainly hadn't been. His talk with Hana earlier in the week had turned into comparing stories of rescuing rabbits, stray cats, and watching bird nests. And now she was giving her hard-earned money to his cause?

If Pace wasn't careful, he could fall into serious like with the woman before him. And he couldn't have that. He set his jaw and tucked the check in his back pocket. "Thank you. What we really need are volunteers, though."

The hopeful smile on her face faltered, but then came back even stronger. "I would love to volunteer. I have a crazy schedule right now, but give me about two weeks and I can do it. Just tell me the time and place."

Sensing the two week timeline was an excuse, Pace felt his hopes fall. No woman would ever understand his dedication to Soft Paws. "Right. I sure will. I better get back to work."

He didn't wait for her to reply before he turned and walked back through the swinging kitchen door and into the stockroom filled with bottles of liquor and wine. Now he had lost count and would have to start again. He cursed under his breath.

At Soft Paws later on, he slapped Hana's check on his desk to add into their other donations for the month. Emmie jumped at the noise.

She was pinning puppy profiles to their corkboard. "What did that paper do to you?"

He sat with a huff. "Nothing. It's a donation."

"Since when are we upset with donations?" Five new profiles were hanging on the board, making a total of twelve. They needed to get some dogs adopted.

He rubbed his eyes. "I'm not. It's from someone I met the other day. An author. But when I asked if she'd volunteer she just made excuses."

Emmie sat across from him and looked at the check. "Hana Willis. I know that name, I've read her books. Wait – was she the one at Palmetto Magic with the group? The lady staring you down?"

He had forgotten about that. A groan escaped his lips. "Yes. But don't make a thing of it, Em."

"What was her excuse?"

"That she was really busy for the next two weeks but maybe after that."

Emmie stood, walked behind him, and slapped him on the back of his head. She ignored his cry of pain. "So this girl, an author you happened to meet, that came into the bar with friends, wrote a two-hundred-dollar check and wants to volunteer after her schedule clears up. Where's the excuse? And how did she know about this place? You must have talked to her again."

When Pace didn't answer, Emmie lifted her hand again as if she would slap him. Not wanting to experience that again, Pace relented. "I saw her again at the park and we got to talking. She said she wants to make a character that's a bartender and asked if she could come and ask questions."

She would read too much into it. His sister always did.

"And she came to Palmetto Magic to ask questions about the bar. But you told her about Soft Paws?" Her expression turned smug. She was reading too much into it.

"Right."

"And then she just magically showed up with money? Gee, she sounds awful."

"Em."

When Emmie put her hands on the desk and leaned in close to him, Pace knew she was getting serious. "Not everyone is Amanda. This girl has a dog. She listened to you prattle on about this place, brought a donation, and wants to volunteer. She sounds amazing."

"I'm not interested, Emmie."

She stood to her full height and flipped her blonde hair over her shoulder. "Of course not. But it doesn't sound like an excuse. It sounds like she has a busy few weeks and wants to volunteer after that. Her number is on the check, write it down."

He wasn't going to tell her, but Hana's number was already in his phone. He had put it there earlier in the day. Purely for volunteering purposes, of course.

Chapter 6

Meeting at the wedding location, Merry with Min of course, made the most sense in Hana's mind. There was no pressure of Chas coming to pick her up, or possibly standing her up, and he was free to escape if he felt the need. But it didn't stop her from having sweaty palms at the thought of bringing a date to La'Anna's wedding.

Why had she asked him in the first place? She'd been told to bring a date, and she had felt bad when he asked her to a different wedding the same day at Jenna's. She was relieved at not being able to go with him because while he was handsome, she didn't have time for dating. Then she had opened her big mouth and invited him to La'Anna's. She shook her head as she tried to make sense of it.

"Can you stop daydreaming and focus on me for a minute?" La'Anna snapped her fingers at Hana and she jumped to attention.

"I'm with you. Just wondering if he's here yet. And if Jenna has spotted him. Thank God Mom and Dad will be too busy to notice I have a date." Hana was thankful the wedding was small. While her parents would be there, they would be working and hopefully not paying attention to her.

But La'Anna's mother would more than make up for the parental part of meeting Chas.

"Is my necklace straight?" Long, thin fingers groped for the large aquamarine. La'Anna's grandmother had left the necklace to her when she passed away the year before. It was her old and blue.

Hana pulled the clasp to the back of La'Anna's neck. "Perfect. You'll knock Rob out."

One final glance in the mirror before exiting the room for the aisle. Hana was simple in a blue chiffon tea length dress with her hair curled over her shoulders. But La'Anna was stunning in a mermaid gown with crystals covering the entire top. A birdcage veil perched on her hair and covered the top of her face. Sparkles reflected everywhere and Hana thought her friend had never been so lovely.

Once the music started, Hana proceeded down the aisle alone. With only a maid of honor and a best man, her counterpart was standing up front with Rob and the minister. She glanced to the left and spotted Chas who looked stunned. She raised her eyebrows to him in greeting and he gave a small wave. As usual, he looked impeccable in a navy blazer with a shirt that perfectly matched her dress.

At the front of the room, Hana turned her attention to the door where La'Anna would enter. Rob bounced from one foot to the other as he waited and his best man, Justin, clapped him on the shoulder. Tears filled her eyes as the door opened and La'Anna stood there. The music started and La'Anna walked down the aisle on her mother's arm.

The ceremony was a blur to Hana, she spent the entire time looking at her best friend and marveling at the fact that she was becoming a married woman. Before she knew it, music was playing again and the happy couple was retreating. Rob held his arm out for La'Anna and she beamed. A quick glance at Chas showed him grinning ear to ear.

Chas was attentive during the reception, getting Hana a drink, telling her she looked beautiful, and staying by her side. When Rhonda, La'Anna's mother, approached, he congratulated her and told her she looked wonderful.

"This one is smooth, Hana. How did you manage to get Greenville's most eligible bachelor as a date?" Rhonda preened a little in front of them. Despite her fifty years, she was still good-looking and she knew it.

Hana scoffed. "Most eligible bachelor?" When Rhonda nodded, she looked to Chas. "Really?"

A cough and a hand through his hair told Hana that Rhonda was right. Chas looked at her sheepishly, his head still a little bowed. "Well, it was two years ago. My mother nominated me in hopes I would find a suitable up and comer for a wife." He mimicked a female voice as he spoke.

Hana's hand went in front of her face as she giggled. "Oh, I understand meddling mothers all too well, don't I Rhonda?" She looked to the woman who had been like a surrogate mother to her for years. "Min Willis is nothing if not meddling. She means well, though."

Hana had thus far managed to avoid her mother as to avoid both the question roulette and being put to work. She kept hers and Chas's backs to her mom so she didn't make eye contact.

"My mother is much the same. I think they would get along, then." Chas raised an eyebrow and ran his hand down Hana's arm, giving her goosebumps.

Rhonda leaned in to kiss Hana's cheek. "He's adorable, Hannie."

"Oh, no. It—we—" But Rhonda walked away to chat with someone else.

Once the bridal couple had left and Hana dried her tears yet again, Chas offered her his arm and she readily took it. He cleared his throat, something Hana noticed he did when he was going to speak. "Care to go for dessert?"

Did she care to? Sure. Should she, though? Perhaps not. She caught Rhonda and Jenna watching them out of the corner of her eye. She pressed her lips together, they were dry. "I would love to, but I can't I have to help Rhonda clean up and I promised Jenna we'd have a sleepover tonight."

Chas's curiosity was piqued. "A sleepover?"

A roll of laughter escaped her. "Yes, a sleepover. Complete with ice cream and cheesy chick flicks." Hana looked at her sister and made her eyes really big. "Jenna, what movie did you want to watch tonight for the sleepover?"

She prayed Jenna would take the hint. They didn't have a sleepover planned, but one could be set up within minutes. They could call Nari to join them.

There was zero hesitation in Jenna's reply. "The Princess Bride, of course."

Turning back to Chas, Hana shrugged. "Maybe another time? I really appreciate you coming and being my date tonight. You are a gentleman."

A dimple showed on his perfectly smooth cheek. "As you wish." He lifted her hand and kissed it gently. "Another time then?"

"I would like that. Don't get captured by the Dread Pirate Roberts in the meantime."

"Of course not, Princess Buttercup." He winked and Hana nearly swooned.

The dog park was packed, but that didn't stop Pace from picking out Hana and her little scruff ball within seconds of arriving. This time she was sitting on a bench with the dog's leash in her hand, a little girl on the ground giving the dog belly rubs.

The girl called over her shoulder. "Momma, I want a puppy like this one." Pace watched as a woman approached Hana and they chatted a moment.

Not wanting to interrupt, Pace walked Moses around the back of the bench before approaching. Recognizing his little friend, Moses went straight for Lulu. The woman with Hana lit up while the girl quickly got out of the larger dog's way.

"I'm sorry. He's very friendly, just big." Pace knelt down and held Moses's collar. The little girl approached with a timid look on her face.

"That's the kind of dog my husband wants. But Violet clearly thinks otherwise." The woman put her hand out for Moses to sniff.

It was then Pace noticed Hana's dimpled cheeks. She was happy to see him and it made his heart beat wildly. He didn't know what to do with how he was reacting to seeing her. He should tamp it down and tell it no. Firmly. But then it was such a light, pleasant feeling, one wholly foreign to him, and he didn't want it to end.

"This is my friend Pace McCoy. Pace, this is Violet and her mom Wendy. They're scouting out dogs to see what might be a good fit for their family."

This was right up Pace's alley. "I run a dog rescue right here in town. Soft Paws. All our animals are screened before being adopted out to make sure they're good with kids, other dogs, cats, what have you. Give us a call." He fished a card from his wallet and handed it to the mother.

She studied the card a moment. "I've heard of Soft Paws. Thank you." She patted Moses again and looked to her daughter. "Time to go, Violet. Thank her for letting you pet her dog."

"Thanks."

Hana nodded as the pair left and Pace took the mother's seat on the bench. "It was nice of you to let people pet Lulu."

"She's used to it. She loves attention. And because her bark is broken, she's not scary." Lulu curled up in the sun while Moses leaned hard into Hana's bare leg. "Just like this one I'm guessing." She scratched behind both ears, making Moses wag his backside.

"He sure does." Then Pace wasn't sure what to say. He hadn't been out with a woman in a long time, at least not to where he truly liked being around the person in question. Instead, he sat in awkward silence. Or maybe it was comfortable? He wasn't sure.

"Are you working tonight?" Hana ran her slender fingers over her tanned and toned knee.

At that moment, he didn't care if she noticed him noticing. Pace licked his lips as his eye went over her flawless skin. "No, actually. I took the entire day off. But I do have to go over to the rescue later."

"Tell me more about the set up. Once I meet this deadline with my publisher I should have time to come see it."

That was all the prompting Pace needed. He described the kennel, his favorite dogs, how he felt when one left. It was a mixture of sadness but extreme pride that his canine friend was going home. He told her about the office and his sister's puppy profile wall. He described the veterinary room that was used by Quent and another vet who helped out.

When he finally looked back at Hana, her face was lit up. "You really love this place."

Pace rubbed the back of his neck, a little embarrassed at his overzealousness. "I run the bar and it is my primary source of income, but Soft Paws is my passion. Working with the animals." He loved to talk about the rescue's mission but talking about himself and his involvement wasn't always easy.

A soft hand came over his own and gave a light squeeze. "Oh, I think it's wonderful. You have to have a huge heart to be so selfless."

Unable to hold back, Pace reached up and tucked a stray piece of hair behind Hana's ear. He swallowed hard and wondered what it would be like to kiss Hana's soft, full lips.

Breaking the silence, Hana hummed a little tune. "Pace, do you work every Saturday night?" She peered at him from under her lashes, her hand still resting on top of his.

"Most every Saturday. If I'm not at the rescue, I'm at the bar." He pulled a water bottle out of his back pocket and took a swig. "Why do you ask? I have a feeling that one wasn't for research."

She smiled and tucked a stray hair behind her ear. "Busted. My sister is getting married at the end of June and I need a date. I thought maybe you would be willing to go with me." She took a big gulp of her own water. "But if you can't – or don't want to – I understand."

A date to her sister's wedding? That seemed serious. It wasn't just a date, but meeting the family as well. But he did like Hana. Maybe more than a little. Perhaps they could go out a few times before that.

Out of the corner of his eye, he spotted his ex-fiancée waving wildly and dragging a man behind her as she hurried toward them. Pace whispered closely into Hana's ear. "Play along for me and you have yourself a date."

He picked her hand and kissed it gingerly. Hana's gasp was audible. She spotted the wild-eyed blonde coming towards them and must have understood what was needed. She immediately leaned into him, tucking her shoulder under his. She felt so good in that spot, but Pace didn't have time to enjoy it before Amanda called out.

"Pace? Pace look at this! We run into each other again. You have to meet my new husband, Brian. Brian Cooper, this is Pace McCoy." She tapped the man's chest as she spoke and pulled his arm around her waist.

Pace nodded. "Amanda. Nice to meet you, Brian. This is Hana." He motioned to the dogs. "You know Moses, and this is Lulu."

Amanda stopped short as if she had just noticed he wasn't alone. With her head cocked to the side, she squeaked. Literally squeaked. "You're from Merry with Min. You're Min's daughter. Hannah?"

Did they know each other? Pace stifled a groan.

"That's right. It's Hana, but yes. Hana Willis." Hana shielded her eyes from the sun. "It's nice to see you again. Pace, love, we really should be going if we're going to get to Emmie's on time." She ran a hand over his thigh and squeezed it.

Pace's brain forgot how to function with her fingers on his leg. It had been a long time since anyone had run their fingers over his skin. The sound of Amanda's voice brought him back to the unpleasant reality in front of him.

"Oh, you know Emmie?" Amanda looked mildly panicked as her eyes flitted from Pace to Hana and back.

Flicking Lulu's leash, the dog stretched and stood. Hana followed suit. "Of course I do. When you're as in love as we are, you also fall in love with the family, don't you?" She turned to Pace and ran a finger along his jawline.

Pace would have married her on the spot for that comment. Amanda had never much cared for his family or Moses. He stood beside her, pulling Moses closer to him. Amanda stared, slack-jawed.

"Always a pleasure, Amanda. Enjoy the day." He took Hana's hand in his own and they walked off together, dogs leading the way.

On the outskirts of the park, they finally stopped. Hana burst into a fit of giggles. "That was too much fun. She was a witch to me at her bridal luncheon. Old girlfriend, I'm guessing?"

Rolling his eyes, Pace nodded. "Yep. We were set up and I never did love her. She hated Moses and hated the rescue. I broke it off with her like five years ago and she still can't seem to leave me alone. You met her at her wedding?"

Hana looked horrified. "Good grief, no. We hosted her bridal luncheon before the wedding at my mom's event space. And who could hate Moses? He's amazing." She knelt down and hugged on the slobbery dog. Lulu jumped around them.

"I can't thank you enough, really. I owe you big time for that."

Hana looked him in the eye, crinkled her nose, and took his hand. "You will at my sister's wedding. And you'll have to take me to meet Emmie for real. I want to see this rescue."

It was Chas's day to do some schmoozing and elbow-rubbing around the city and today he was hitting up the west end. The bar he approached had gone from eyesore to trendy over the past few years. He had heard of Palmetto Magic from friends and colleagues. Perhaps the owner was interested in expanding.

Edison lights were hung from industrial looking overhead lamps, everything was steely gray or silver with the exception of the stool covers and booth cushions, which were electric blue. Sapphire-colored lights also lined the rows of spirits on the back wall. Even though it was late afternoon, tables were occupied and the latest song by Beyonce was playing.

As he approached the bar, a perky blonde bartender made her way over to him. "What can I get you today?"

Chas scanned the wall. "Gin and tonic. And I would like to speak with your manager, please." He slid onto a barstool.

The girl smiled at him and leaned closer. "Already? I haven't even messed your drink up yet." Blue eyes sparkled, but Chas was indifferent.

Not that the girl wasn't cute. She was dew-faced with long, blonde hair pulled into a high ponytail, and she had curves in all the right places. But Chas's mind went straight to Hana and this girl didn't compare.

When he didn't respond, the girl backed up and scrunched her nose. "Gin and tonic and I'll get the boss for you. Just a minute."

She disappeared in the back, then returned and set to making his drink. Chas pinched the bridge of his nose, preparing his winning expression and charming banter.

"Chas Rossi, what do you know." The familiar voice pricked his ears and gave him goosebumps. It had been a long time since he's been around Pace McCoy.

Chas turned on the charm anyway. "McCoy. It's been a while." They did not shake hands.

It wasn't that there was bad blood between them, just sour blood. They had both been on the same wrestling team in high school and in the same fraternity in college. They had never meshed well. Then throw in a cute girl their junior year and they had come to blows. Chas didn't even remember her name. But he remembered Pace's.

A little older but still fit, Pace put both hands on the counter of the bar he stood behind. The girl beside him busied herself but stayed within earshot. The tension was heavy in the air.

"What can I do for you, brother?"

Signature smirk on display, Chas passed Pace his business card. "I'm sure you've seen my picture and heard my name around town. I'm the top real estate broker in the Upstate."

The card went into Pace's jeans pocket without a glance. "And you've worked up a thirst?"

"I go around every so often to see if businesses are interested in selling, expanding, or the like. I like to personally offer my services, especially to locally owned businesses. I also still work in the housing market, if you're ever in need." Chas leaned on the bar and took a sip of his drink. It was incredibly strong.

"Palmetto Magic has been in his location for going on fifty years. We're pretty well established. But thank you." Pace started to turn.

"How long have you had this place? As I recall, your father was a preacher." Chas straightened his tie as he looked around the place again.

"He still is. I took over from my grandfather right after graduating. It became mine a few years ago. And I have a great loft within walking distance, so no needs there, either." Pace began mixing a drink, tossing bottles around like they did in movies.

Chas raised an eyebrow. "A loft? So no family then? What happened to what's-her-name?"

A pair of rolled eyes told him what happened to the girl they had fought over. "Amanda hasn't been my business in years. I should have let you have her." A soft chuckle broke Pace's hard exterior.

"Oh, ho, ho. No thanks. She was too much for me. I'm seeing a real gem of a girl from right here in the west end, though." Chas thought of Hana. They weren't exactly dating, but he figured it was close enough and he wanted to get one up on Pace McCoy. "Maybe I'll bring her here one day."

Pace crossed his arms and looked straight into Chas's eyes. "Anything else? I'm in the middle of payroll."

Standing, Chas laid a twenty on the counter. "For the drink and your bartender. I'll let you get back to it. I'd say it was a pleasure, but..."

Pace's eyebrow went up and his mouth cocked to the side. "Right. Goodbye, Charles." He turned his back to Chas and disappeared again behind a closed door that read 'management only.'

Looking to the bartender, Chas winked. "He's a kitten. Just like in college. Thanks." He threw back the rest of the drink and left the dimly lit bar for the still sunny outside.

As he walked to the next business, Chas thought he would bring Hana back to Palmetto Magic and show her off. Pace would be instantly jealous when he got an eyeful of her gorgeous skin and silky hair. Pace McCoy had nothing on him, slinging drinks as if he was still a kid. Chas pitied him, really.

Chapter 7

Family dinners were always hard for Pace. He knew he was loved, but he was the black sheep middle child. The square peg that didn't fit into the round hole. Trey, older than him by a year, had followed their father's footsteps and become a pastor. He was always ready to quote scripture as an argument for anything, and their father was beyond proud. Emmie, the baby and lone girl, was the golden child their parents doted on. She worked as a vet tech, helped run the rescue, and still lived with their parents.

On this occasion, the family was gathering because Trey had asked his girlfriend Caroline to marry him, and they were having a celebratory dinner. Pace was thrilled for his brother, and he thought Caroline was a nice enough girl. A little stuffy, but she matched Trey in about every way.

Except when he arrived, he was met not only by his parents and Trey with his fiancée, but also Emmie and Quent. He was the proverbial extra wheel. He rolled his eyes when his parents' backs were turned, but his sister caught him.

"What now, sourpuss?" She poked him in the arm.

"I didn't know this was a bring a date type of situation." He folded his arms.

Emmie kissed his cheek. "It's Quent. If I hadn't brought him, you would have. It's not like you have a girlfriend. Unless you talked more with that author who loves dogs?"

"No, of course not. I mean, I have talked to her, but she's not—" His mind immediately went to Hana Willis and her little dog. She would fit right into this scenario with his family. She would be warm, gracious, smart. Everything he could want. "She's not my girlfriend."

But did he want that? Pace had figured he would spend his life alone. Not that he was looking to be single forever, he hadn't factored in spending time on dating apps or hitting on random women. He had never accounted for the fact that the perfect woman might simply fall into his life.

A finger snap in front of his face startled him. "Earth to Pace. She's not your what? Come on. I've never seen you make that face before."

Redness crept up his neck and colored his cheeks. "It's not like that. She's just a nice girl I've run into a few times. We're barely friends. Acquaintances."

"Right." Emmie jumped up and down, a silly grin on her face. "You really like her don't you?"

Trey and Caroline came into the room as Emmie hugged Pace, her arms around his so he was held captive. "What are you talking about?"

Emmie played up her role as the youngest, and therefore most immature child. "Pace has a crush on a girl. Hana Willis.

Caroline's eyes grew huge and her jaw hung open. "Wait. Hana Willis? The author? Author of Falling into You? She's my favorite." This was the most excited Pace had ever heard Caroline. He didn't even know she was a reader.

Pace didn't realize Hana was so well known. He had looked up her books online and saw that she was fairly popular, but he never would have guessed that so many people were fans. "I helped her with some research. She has a character who's a bartender. And Moses adores her. I mean, adores her little terrier."

Blue eyes crinkled as his sister squealed in delight. "And you adore her. Oh my..."

"Emmie." There was a warning in his voice.

"I want to meet her."

"Emmie."

Caroline smiled shyly. "She's such a great writer. And it's all so sweet. She must be an amazing person."

Their parents called to them, ending their inquisition over Hana. Dinner was served. At the table, Gerry McCoy sat at the head of the table, his wife Rosalyn at the other end. The newly betrothed couple sat on one side, while Pace, Emmie, and Quent occupied the other.

It wasn't awkward at all, everyone being part of a couple except Pace. Besides, where would a date fit at the table? Across from him? But the idea of staring into Hana's enchanting inky eyes all night was appealing. She could be swapping recipes with his mother and making jokes Trey would laugh at but not understand.

Glasses filled with sparkling juice were raised. Alcohol was not allowed in the McCoy household, so all events were toasted with overly sweet juice. Even though Pace wasn't much of a drinker himself, special occasions warranted a proper toast and this was not a proper toast.

"To my eldest son, Gerrald Paul McCoy, the third, and his beautiful fiancée, Caroline Grace Banks. May you live a life pleasing to the Lord. Be fruitful and multiply. Serve one another and the church. Cheers."

Everybody's glasses clinked together and they took a sip.

Without planning to make a toast, Pace found himself standing, then panicking. "Apparently I feel led to make a toast as well." His mind blanked but his tongue kept moving. "Trey, you are a wonderful brother, and I'm sure Caroline will be a wonderful sister. I hope you have a long life together full of love. Enjoy each other in all that you do." He raised his glass and took a sip. Everyone followed suit.

His mother laid a hand on his arm as he sat back down. "That was lovely, son. What a touching thing to say."

Pace could only nod. His father waited a few seconds before bowing his head and saying a prayer over the food. The dinner conversation centered around wedding plans and Pace wondered if he went to Hana's sister's wedding if she would come to Trey's for him. It would be mutually beneficial. The thought made his chest grow warm.

After dinner, the three siblings sat on the couch and discussed Soft Paws, something they always seemed to naturally gravitate to when together. For the past few years, they had hosted a charity gala and auction to raise money and it was always a big success. Several corporate sponsors donated goods and a few threw money at them in order to get their names attached to a charity.

Pace went over the list with his siblings, everything from restaurants to florists to boutiques. Even a few large corporations were attached this year, bringing a larger crowd. Pace was hoping they could exceed the previous year's donations.

"Enough of that fancy talk. We need to muck out the whole place this weekend. You all have to help." Emmie, who hardly ever dressed up, was more comfortable in duck shoes and jeans than heels and sparkles.

"Oh, I don't think that will work. We're going to see my dad." Caroline's gentle voice was never loud. She looked to Trey for confirmation.

For his part, Trey furrowed his brow. "Oh, that's right. Sorry, Em."

Again, Pace's mouth seemed to take control ahead of his mind. "I can ask Hana to come. She actually asked about volunteering."

"Finally!" Emmie's eyes lit up.

Pace pulled out his phone and began typing a text message. "No promises, but I can ask." It didn't even take thirty seconds for a reply to come through. "Looks like she's in. On the condition that she gets to play with puppies at some point."

Emmie beamed. "Oh, we can make that happen."

Pace wondered what he was getting into by arranging for his sister to meet Hana Willis.

"With Rossi Real Estate, you never have to worry. Home is waiting for you." Chas waited for the director to call cut before he dropped the fake smile from his face. Commercials were the bane of his existence.

Starting when he was a little boy, he had been pushed into the family commercials for television ads. Now the ads went mostly online. And they had moved from his father in the starring role with the family in the background, to him being the face of the company and his parents in the background. The cheesy smiles and the overly dramatic movements were too much for Chas. And every time they shot one, his mother reminded him that he should have a wife and child already to attract young families.

Because, apparently, the only reason to have a family was to bring in business.

They shot the closing line two more times and Chas's jaw ached from the way he was holding his mouth. A natural, happy expression was one thing, this was excruciating.

"What's left?" Chas checked his watch. Studies had shown that a watch made people look smarter, so he wore one at all times.

The director looked over a paper on a clipboard. "I think all we need is you walking up to your parents with the glass of tea in hand."

"That's my favorite bit." Marcie fluffed her hair and went to the patio where they would shoot that part.

Three times Chas had to walk up to his parents and hand his mother a glass of tea. Some assistant wiped the condensation off of it each time. There were so many better things he could be doing with his time, Chas thought. He had two showing that afternoon and a closing in the morning. Being a pretty boy for the camera was not high on his priority list.

Once the director said they were done and Chuck gave his okay, the crew began breaking down their equipment. It was seconds before Chuck singled Chas out and began giving him a list of things to do.

"Dad, I know what I'm doing. I have two showings scheduled, one being in about an hour and I need to go by the office first. The Grants are closing tomorrow on the house in Hardy Estates." He went over the checklist in his head. "And I'm interviewing a new agent tomorrow as well."

"How about that girl you're dating, son?" His mother was never accused of being indirect.

Were they dating? Nothing official had been said, but then, he wasn't sure how that worked anymore. He hadn't had time for anything beyond a single date for an event in a long time. He had seen Hana several times and had been her date for a wedding, but he didn't know if that qualified them as 'dating.'

"Honestly, Mom, I don't know if..."

"Chuck, I told you she's a bestselling author, right? She's famous across the country." Being able to name-drop, especially if the name was connected to her family, was huge for Marcie Rossi.

"Mom." Chas raised an eyebrow at his mother.

"Invite her over, Chas. I would love to meet her. I have all of her books." Marcie squeezed his arm, her talon-like nails digging in ever so slightly.

"We're not there yet, Mom. Okay, I need to get going. I'll see you all later. Dad, I'll call you after I interview that agent tomorrow." Chas lifted his hands as if in surrender and began to walk towards the cars lined up out back.

Sitting in his car, Chas went over the emails that had piled up. One caught his eye – a charity gala his father had agreed to sponsor. Chas needed to make an appearance. He loved an occasion to dress his best, but wasn't fond of having to suck up to anyone and pretend. He did it every day for work, he didn't want to do it on his own time.

But it was a good way to show support for local non-profits, gain some new clients, and remind people that Rossi was a name that meant values, quality, family. He wondered if it was too late to invite Hana as a date. But then he had a better idea.

He emailed the coordinator and requested that an invite be extended to local author and celebrity Hana Willis. That way he didn't look desperate for a date, it gave Hana publicity, and they could potentially leave together. Yes, that plan was the best as it benefitted everyone.

Hana was always glad her literary agent lived nearby. It had been a godsend that the Issaqueena Agency had taken her on and was based less than an hour from where she lived. It made meeting with her agent much easier, and they had become fast friends. Kendra Lamont had bent over backward to get Hana's books in with Puffin Essentials Publishing and it paid off big time for them both.

Today they were meeting for coffee at a little place Hana adored and was within walking distance of her house. She put Lulu on the leash, put her laptop in her backpack, and off they went. The weather was phenomenal with blue skies and the perfect amount of breeze. The walk took less than fifteen minutes.

A silver sedan pulled up in a parking spot right as Hana approached the cafe, aptly named That Coffee Place. Kendra jumped out of the car and leaped at Hana. "Hana! Lulu! Perfect timing."

The dog jumped and trotted in a circle and Kendra bent down to pet her quickly. Popping back up, Kendra held up a well-manicured finger and ran to the passenger side of the car. Hana laughed and went over to the outdoor seating area and chose a table with an umbrella. She tied Lulu to the chair and pulled out her little dish and a refilled bottle of water for her. A pup muffin would definitely be ordered.

Kendra sat at the table with a happy huff. "How are you? What's new? How's the house?" The woman never stopped for a minute. Her red-lined lips moved constantly.

Hana was exhausted from watching her. "Good. Working hard. And it's fantastic."

They caught up on pleasantries while they waited for the server to take their order. An iced coffee with an everything bagel for Kendra and a green tea, blueberry muffin, and a pup muffin for Hana and Lulu.

"Down to business. Not Prince Charming comes out in July. I hope your edits are coming along." Kendra peered over her glasses at Hana, but kept going. "You're doing a meet and greet that week for the launch. And then we have you booked on a signing tour throughout the southeast in early Fall."

Checking her phone, Hana confirmed that she had all the events on her calendar. "I got it. Four stops in South Carolina, three in Georgia and two in North Carolina. Unless you were able to book the one at Duke?"

Kendra pulled out her laptop as their order was brought to them. Hana got Lulu set up with her muffin while Kendra pulled up Hana's file.

"It looks like we did get that. It's all on the agenda I'll send you. Will La'Anna be joining you again?" Kendra pulled her bagel apart and savored a bite.

It hadn't occurred to Hana until then that neither La'Anna nor Jenna would be able to join her for her tour. "No, I guess not. She and Jenna will both be enjoying the married life." A pout momentarily crossed her face. Even Nari would be off to college by then. She would have to tour alone.

Distracting her, Kendra kept going. "How are you with edits? Doesn't Franca need them next week?"

Nodding as she sipped her green tea, Hana grabbed her own laptop. "Yes, next Friday. And I have them. I really want to read through one last time and I'll send them back over. And I should be getting the cover any time now." A notification popped up as she logged into her computer. "Oh, this is from the design department. Let's see if that's it."

Sure enough, a mock-up for No Prince Charming was attached. She pushed the screen to where they both could see. A confused-looking princess and a scruffy guy with a crown dangling from his finger popped up. It never got old to see her work come to life. Covers were one of her favorite parts. The girl looked exactly like how she envisioned her heroine, Callie.

"I love it. The guy is sizzling hot." Kendra mooned over the cover, leaning in to study it closer.

It was almost perfect, but something wasn't quite right. The words didn't match the photo in Hana's mind. "I think the font might need to be different, but otherwise I think it's great." She looked again, squinting her eyes. "I'll email them back when we're done. But there you go. Cover."

They chatted more over the next forty-five minutes, making plans, going over Hana's current work in progress, and talking about life in general. When Kendra finally checked the time and announced that she needed to go, Hana was almost relieved. Kendra did everything fast paced and it exhausted her.

On the walk home, Hana mulled over her career as an author. She always dealt with something called imposter syndrome - a feeling that she wasn't good enough, that her books were terrible and that her best work was behind her. She wasn't alone in these thoughts, it seemed every author had them. Even in her article writing she battled the same fears.

At some book signings, Hana would sign hundreds of books and take so many photos with fans her mouth would hurt. Occasionally there would only be a dozen or so people and nobody would ask for a photo. Those were the times she wondered what on earth she was doing wrong. Not that she was only out for acclaim and taking selfies, but it did wonders for her confidence when people were happy to see her and tell her their favorite characters or scenes.

Her mind went to the secretary at the realty office. The woman had been so excited to see her and meet her. Hana had realized early on that fans of her books always thought they were friends of hers, and she was happy to count them as such. Signing the copy of Falling into You and giving it to the woman had filled Hana with so much joy.

Her phone rang, pulling her out of her thoughts. "Hello?"

"I totally forgot to mention that you've been invited to a gala." Kendra's voice practically screamed through the phone. "It's a charity auction and gala."

Never one to turn down a chance to dress up, Hana was all too happy to listen. "Tell me more. When?"

"It's in two weeks. Black tie. You were actually requested to come twice, believe it or not. The charity organizer and one of the financial backers both contacted me to see if you could come."

A gala sounded like a fun time and dressing up would be an added bonus. "Send me the details. As long as the date and time works, I would love to do it."

"I gotcha, Hana. Okay, have a good one." With that, the phone went silent.

A gala in two weeks? She needed to go shopping – after she finished her edits and emailed the artist department about the cover. But that didn't stop her from looking up designs online as she and Lulu finished the walk home.

She texted La'Anna that a shopping trip was in order and her best friend did not disappoint. They made plans to shop the next day.

As she rounded the corner into the neighborhood before her own, Hana heard a voice call out from across the street. "Lulu! Lulu!"

Stopping and turning, Hana saw a young girl drop her bike and dash across the road. Hana's heart stopped a moment in fear that cars might be coming, but thankfully the girl made it across unscathed.

Searching for the girl's parents and seeing none, Hana scowled and crossed her arms. "That wasn't very safe, running across the road like that." The girl was vaguely familiar, but she met a lot of people.

The girl finished petting Lulu and stood. She was close to Hana's height, which wasn't saying much, but was quite young. "I'm sorry. I didn't want to miss seeing Lulu. Remember me?"

The girl at the dog park, that's who she was. "Oh, yes. You were with your mother before. Looking at different types of dogs. Did you get one?"

The girl frowned, her brown hair falling into her squinted eyes. "Yes, a Labrador Retriever my dumb brother named

Rocket."

"I take it you don't care for Rocket?"

With a heavy sigh, the girl sat cross-legged with Lulu on the sidewalk. "No, Rocket is fine. He's just really big, and I wanted a little dog I could play with, like Lulu."

Her heart went out to the girl, but Hana realized she really needed to find the girl's parents or someone in charge. Though she was tall, she couldn't be older than ten. "What was your name again?"

"Violet."

"Violet, honey, where are your parents? It's not safe to be running across the road on your own." Hana looked across the way to the girl's bike. Thankfully it was a neighborhood without too much traffic, but she knew she would have to play crossing guard to get the girl back to her bike.

Standing back up, Violet pointed across the street and down two houses. "I live right there. My mom is inside."

Relief came over Hana. She wasn't far from home. "Okay, I'm glad you stopped to say hello, but next time don't run across the road. I live in the next neighborhood over, actually. Let me stop traffic so you can get back to your bicycle."

Checking both ways, Hana went to the middle of the road with Lulu and watched as the girl made her way back to her bike. "Be careful, Violet."

Ignoring her, the girl made kissy noises at Lulu. "Bye, sweet puppy. Bye, Lulu!"

The rest of her walk home was uneventful, thankfully, and Hana collapsed on her bed, glad the girl hadn't been hurt. She looked to Lulu and shook her head. Maybe she better stick to dogs on leashes. Kids could get loose.

With her work finished the next morning, Hana prepared to meet La'Anna at their favorite boutique, Inspired Inclusion. It featured clothing from minority designers and their prices were reasonable. Donning a pair of black gauchos and a purple rouched top - both from Inspired Inclusion - she kissed Lulu on the head and went to the boutique.

La'Anna was already inside perusing the goods when she got there. Hana spied an armload of items already weighing her friend down. "What have you found?"

Dark eyes cast her way and La'Anna's hip jutted out. "Nothing for you, girl." Then she held up a black sequin dress. "But maybe try this one."

Hana grabbed the hanger and her eyes lit up at the way the lights hit the dress. "We need to get a dressing room started." Like magic, an attendant appeared and whisked their selections off to wait for them.

"Will you be taking a date? Hot business man or sexy bartender?" La'Anna wagged her eyebrows at Hana.

"I hadn't thought of a date yet, but I guess if it's in two weeks I should think about it. I need to ask Kendra if my invite included a plus one." She pulled her phone from her purse and fired off a text. "Besides, I think you should be my date. I miss you."

La'Anna sent an air kiss her way and rounded the corner of a sales rack. They pulled a few items to try on and the attendant again swooped in and took them to the dressing room. Thinking she had pulled everything in her size and preferred color palette, Hana said she was ready to try everything on.

The black dress La'Anna had chosen was too slinky for Hana's taste. It showed too much cleavage and the slit was almost indecent. Next came a velvety sheath dress, but the material did not appreciate her ample hips. A plum-colored cocktail dress with a high, lacy neckline and back cut-out piqued Hana's interest.

She came out of the room at the same time as La'Anna. "What do you think?"

Her friend had her spin around. "Oh, Hannie, that's it. The perfect amount of shimmer, a sexy back and demure front, it practically screams Hana Willis." She made the chef's kiss gesture. "Now, how about me?"

La'Anna was an office manager, so while she had to look professional, she often sassed it up. And the outfit she had one certainly did that. Fuchsia pants, topped with a fuchsia and green shell blouse, were paired with green boots. On anyone else it would have looked ridiculous, but on La'Anna, it was enviable.

"It's fantastic. The colors are excellent on your skin." Hana released a wolf-whistle and pulled out her phone. They snapped a selfie Hana would put on her Instagram page later. La'Anna had quite the fan base from Hana's fans. They all loved the duo together.

With an outfit chosen, Hana still needed to find out if a date would be in order for the gala. And then to figure out who to ask if she could invite one.

Chapter 8

The bar had become a familiar place for Hana to work. A round booth nestled in the back, away from the football games and soccer matches on the gigantic television, was perfect for her to cocoon in. She could spread her research around her, pop in her earbuds, drink Sprite to her heart's content, and work almost completely uninterrupted. It helped that Pace had invited her to make herself at home after her third trip there to hide away in the corner. Her dishes and unmade bed weren't staring her down, and Lulu wasn't giving her the stink eye for not playing fetch.

After a text message from her sister with a wedding emergency - that was probably completely in Jenna's head – Hana told her sister to come to Palmetto Magic and sit with her and decompress.

Jenna stood before her and cleared her throat. Hana had been so engrossed in her work, she hadn't seen her sister approach.

"You invite me here then ignore me, huh?" Jenna flopped next to Hana on the bright blue cushion. She bounced a second on the soft seat. "This is really comfy."

"Isn't it? These booths are like magic. Pace had them put in a few years ago." Hana ran her hands over the cool plastic. It shouldn't be soft and supple like leather, but it was, and it felt like sitting on a cloud.

"Pace, huh? Is that why you're hanging out here?" Jenna winked at her sister and nudged her with her shoulder.

Glad for the darkened booth that would hide the color in her cheeks, Hana shook her head. "No, no. Pace is a nice guy who tolerates me and appreciates that I keep his rotation of Sprite and nachos fresh." For effect, Hana lifted her glass, the carbonation bubbles still jumping from her last refill. "What's this emergency?"

The ability to create drama was one of Jenna's specialties. She laid her hands on Hana's arm and looked her in the eyes. "It's the paebaek. Will's family doesn't get it. His father refuses to participate and his mother has giggled at every Korean word I've said to her. It will be a disaster."

This wasn't fabricated drama. The paebaek was a tradition with Korean weddings. Done mostly in private, it was a way for the groom to show his commitment to his bride and to their now-joined families. They had seen their cousins' paebaeks and had dreamed about their own for years, creating elaborate hanboks on paper in every shade of red imaginable.

Hana bit her lip. "Can't Mom speak to them? And explain the importance of the paebaek? And surely there are videos you can show them. It's not embarrassing or overly hard. It's a fun wedding ritual." She thought back to her cousin Suki's paebaek where they caught the dates and chestnuts, supposedly symbolizing how many children they would have. Suki and her husband had managed to catch nine and she was then horrified at the thought of being pregnant nine times.

Together the two sisters brainstormed ways to get Will's parents on board with non-western customs. After about a half hour, they had what they thought would be a good compromise to present to the groom's family and Jenna was more relaxed.

It was then that Pace approached their table. "Hana, I'm going to have to start charging you rent. Or put you to work." He laughed at his own joke. Upon seeing Jenna, he extended his hand and Jenna shook it. "Pace McCoy. I'm the owner and resident sucker here at Palmetto Magic."

Hana looked to her sister. "This is Jenna. You'll be attending her wedding in a few weeks."

"Ah, congratulations. Hana has told me, well, almost nothing about your wedding." Pace winked at the sisters.

Jenna's face lit up. "You're Hana's date? Well, well, Hannie. I had no idea." Jenna motioned for Pace to sit with them. "She hasn't told you about how you have to perform in the paebaek and wear a jeogori?" The smirk on her face was hard to hide.

"What now?" Wide-eyed, Pace looked from Hana to Jenna and back again as he slid into the booth.

Instinctively, Hana's hand went to cover her giggle. "She's teasing. They're parts of a traditional Korean wedding. The groom's family is hesitant."

"Is the groom on board?"

Jenna nodded. "Oh, yes. Will is very much on board. He loves Korean customs and ceremonies. And they're part of the whole day." She batted her eyelashes and looked off in the distance like a love-sick heroine in a Hallmark movie.

Pace shrugged. He picked up a paper straw wrapper and folded it like an accordion. "Then they should do it for him. Has he told them this is important to him? My parents would be hesitant about something unknown as well. More because they'd be afraid of messing it up. But if he tells them it's important to him, they should be able to get on board quickly. But the key is that it comes from him."

Jaw dropped, Jenna stared at Pace. "That's brilliant. Up to this point, it's been all me telling them and they're not getting it, nor are they wanting to. But because Will is still learning himself, he told me to do all the talking. But I think you're onto something there."

Hana sat back while her sister and Pace talked. He was at ease with her and appeared quite open about different cultural aspects of her life. It endeared him to her all the more, though she knew he only thought of her as a friend. And she had been out a few times with Chas.

Jenna announced that she was going to go explain things to Will right away and made Hana get up so she could scoot out of the booth. "Thank you so much, Pace. Hannie, I'll call you later." She kissed Hana on the cheek then leaned into her ear. "He's hot and sensible. I like this one."

Instead of watching her sister walk off, Hana looked to Pace, who was still sitting in the booth. Hana sat back down and smiled shyly. Her palms began to sweat a little as Pace looked at her. "You give good advice."

He ran a hand through his already mussed hair. "Oh, it's just common sense. And as a son with conservative parents, I know how to work the system."

"You'll enjoy the paebaek. It's a lovely ceremony. Very brightly colored. I'm glad you're going." Hana began collecting her papers and sorting them. She needed to get home and it was clear she was done for the day. "I guess I'll get out of your hair. I appreciate you letting me set up camp here."

A strong, calloused hand laid over hers, stilling it. Hana swallowed hard and looked up. Pace had scooted closer to her. "You know I don't mind. At all. I enjoy having you here." His eyes spoke far more than his words and he licked his lips.

"Pace, I..." But the thought was cut short as he kissed her.

It was like something straight out of one of her novels. It was sweet and sincere. While it wasn't more than a peck, it was testing the waters, Hana knew. And test them it did, as warmth bloomed across her chest. Calloused fingertips grazed over her knuckles sending shivers up her spine. Her mind went from comparing the kiss to one in a book to saving it and tucking it away for herself. This one wasn't for sharing with an audience.

"I am not looking for anything, and I don't think you are either. But as someone once told me – just because you're not looking doesn't mean something doesn't find you. Is this, maybe, do you feel something growing here?" His green eyes searched her own.

The nod was barely perceivable, but Hana managed the slightest movement. Her voice was soft and low while her heart hammered inside her chest. "I think so."

Showing up somewhere unannounced wasn't Chas's style, and he would hate it if someone did it to him, but he found himself standing on the other side of Hana's door knocking. A tall caramel macchiato burned in his hand as an offering.

Small yips sounded on the other side of the door and he could hear footsteps.

Chas checked himself in the window reflection. He was casual in a polo shirt and pressed chinos. His most comfortable loafers were on his feet instead of the stuffy oxfords he usually wore. He had gone to lunch with an old friend and happened to be on the west end so he thought he would surprise Hana. In a short time, the girl had easily made her way into his mind more often than not.

It really shocked him how much he looked forward to seeing her. Perhaps her hair would be up in a messy bun. Would she be wearing a tank top and jean shorts? For some reason, he longed to see her dressed so relaxed.

The door cracked open and a dark eye peered out at him. "Chas?" The door opened further. "What are you doing over this way?" She stood back and gestured for him to come in.

"I met with an old friend and realized I was close by, so I thought I would bring you a coffee." He held up the disposable cup and offered it to her.

She beamed at him, and Chas thought he would love to put that look of contentment on her face for a long time to come. He could spoil her rotten and love every minute of it. After sniffing the top, she giggled.

"Caramel macchiato? How did you know?" She took a sip and closed her eyes while she moaned a little. "Come sit down."

Chas was rendered dumb by the pleasured expression and little moan that came from her. She had to call his name again for him to realize she was inviting him to sit, which he readily did. The little dog jumped up next to him and he was instantly glad he wasn't wearing a suit.

Animals were great as long as they were behind a fence or in a cage. He was happy to give his sister's little dog a pat before shooing her away, so he gave this one the same little pat then ignored her, focusing his attention on Hana.

"Lulu likes you." Hana sat on a high back chair, curling her legs up underneath her. She wore an oversized t-shirt and baggy cotton shorts. As predicted, she had her raven hair piled atop her head in a wild mass.

Chas wanted to run his fingers through that hair and see what Hana Willis tasted like, but he refrained. Hana's comment registered finally and he tilted his head. "Who's Lulu?"

Laughing, she pointed to the dog. "Lulu. Remember you saw her when you brought me the flowers?" The little wiry dog lifted a paw toward him. "She wants to shake."

Shake? The dog wanted to shake hands with him? How? Never had Chas seen a dog want to shake hands before. Slowly he took the paw and shook it a few times, looking from dog to owner, his eyebrow raised. "Nice to meet you?"

Satisfied, Lulu jumped down and disappeared behind the couch, where Chas could only assume she was taking up residence on her own dog-sized furniture.

"Not a dog person?"

Sensing that this would be a major faux pas in Hana's book, Chas chuckled and brushed the awkwardness away. "Oh, I am, I adore dogs. I guess I'm just used to bigger ones. She's so...petite. And smart." He described her the way he would a client's ill-behaved child. They always loved it when he called them smart.

Hana was no exception. The pride on her face was evident and she puffed her chest a little. "Isn't she? She was at the top of her obedience class. I know she's a dog, but she's my family. Especially now that we live alone."

Unsure what to say, Chas looked around the modest home. It was well decorated, a bit minimalist, but felt comfortable and warm. "I love what you did with the place. Who's your decorator?"

"Decorator? Ha. I will tell my sister you said that." Hana looked around her own living room. "Nari actually talks about becoming a designer. Maybe she could stage homes for you one day."

Nodding, Chas agreed. "She has the touch if she did this. And home stagers make good money. Is she local?"

"Yes, but she's only eighteen. She just graduated from high school. My parents don't think design is a good career choice, but maybe coming from you will change their minds. You're a respected businessperson in our family." Hana blushed and looked down at her coffee.

"I'd love to talk to them." Silence filled the air and Chas wasn't sure what else to say. "I guess I should get going. I just wanted to pop in to say hello. So, hello." He hated how tongue-tied Hana made him. He didn't usually put his foot in his mouth.

Hana put the coffee down and made an excited noise. "Oh. Can you help me with something?"

"I can try."

She stood slowly and went to the dining room table, grabbing a computer bag. "This computer company is making a new computer and tablet for writers and creatives. They want me to be a spokesperson and appear in social media ads. I can use basic software, but I am not a tech person. I can't even set this up. Do you think you might be able to?"

Standing, Chas took the bag from Hana. He opened it and pulled the computer out. It was lightweight and opened easily. The login screen popped up and he looked to Hana questioningly.

"User is Hana, of course. The password they sent me is..." She fished a scrap of paper from the computer bag and sat down on the couch. Chas sat right next to her, their knees touching. She passed him the paper. "The password is this."

He typed it in and watched the screen come to life. "Welcome, Hannah." It spoke to them with a voice similar to Siri's. "Set up computer?"

"It talks." Hana looked stunned, her eyes wide open and her mouth puckered. "It's talking to me."

"It sure is." Chas couldn't help but burst into laughter. He had never seen such a thing before. It reminded him of that old movie where Meg Ryan's email would say, "You've got mail," every time she opened the app.

"First thing, you have to teach it my name. I'm not Hannah. As you well know." The look she shot him was trying to for pure evil, but her eyes sparkled and her mouth would not stay downturned at all.

He remembered when they first met and he had mistakenly called her Hannah. A mistake he would not repeat. "Let's set it up and then we'll see how to adjust your name." He clicked where a little word bubble had popped up asking if they wanted to set the computer up.

Within about twenty minutes he had set up most everything on the new laptop. It was fairly intuitive, and Chas wondered if Hana really had no clue or she was looking for a reason to have him stick around. Either way, he was happy to help her, and he was grateful it was something he actually knew how to do. Had she needed plumbing done, he would have had no clue.

"Now, to fix your name." He went into the computer's settings and found the user's name. "Oh, it looks like you can adjust pronunciation. Should be simple." With a few more clicks, the laptop was properly saying Hana and not Hannah.

A squeal came from Hana and she hugged Chas around the shoulders. "You are my hero. I've tried twice to do this and couldn't get past the login screen. Thank you so much. I owe you the next round of coffee."

Flustered and blushing, Chas shook his head. "Oh, no, it's fine. I'm happy you couldn't do it. I mean, not that I'm glad. I'm glad I could help you out." He stood and wiped his hands down the front of his chinos.

Hana stood with him and placed the laptop on the coffee table. "Really, I appreciate it. I'm so glad you stopped by."

"Me, too." Chas started for the door and the little dog came out of her hiding spot. "It was nice to meet you, Lulu." Chas could have sworn the dog nodded at him.

At the door, Chas hesitated. He turned back to Hana and kissed her on the cheek. "Bye, then." Electricity ran through his body and he walked off without looking back. The scent and taste of her skin, something like oranges and honey, filled his senses and stayed with him the entire ride home.

Maybe it was more than her occupying his mind. Maybe she was beginning to take up residence in his heart as well.

❧ ⚶ ☙

"Emmie, how's Hank doing today?" Pace went over to the kennel that held Hank, an old beagle who was blind and recently had a few rotted teeth pulled.

Glancing over her shoulder, Emmie cooed at the old dog. "Oh, my sweet Hank is doing well. I think we can put him in the little run today, maybe with Buster."

A majority of the dogs spent time in the big dog run a few times a day. Emmie, Quent and Pace rotated them through depending on their personalities. Each one got out three times a day, keeping their kennel time to a minimum. Pace needed to go over the books, but he wanted to spend time with the animals first.

He opened Hank's kennel and kneeled in front of him, offering his hand for the dog to sniff. "Hey, Hank. Are you feeling better without those bad teeth in your mouth?" The dog licked his hand in response. "I wish we could get you adopted out for the time you have left. Not many people want an old hound."

"Actually, I got an application for him this morning." Emmie hefted a bag of dog food over her shoulder. "An older couple going empty nest. They asked for the dog nobody else wanted. I'm hoping they'll come this afternoon to meet him."

Tears welled in Pace's eyes. Nothing got him like an unlikely adoptee getting a home. "Hear that, boy? You might have a family to go home to." More licks came, and Hank nudged his head under Pace's hand.

Grabbing a leash, Pace hooked Hank up and urged him from his kennel. Hank obliged willingly, tail wagging. Pace walked the old beagle in the sunshine and got him to run a little in the open. When Hank began to slow down and had done his business, Pace brought him into the office where he unhooked Hank and showed him to a cozy dog bed

Moses usually used when he was there. Hank happily laid down for a snooze.

Sitting at his desk, Pace pulled up the financial reports for Soft Paws. Money was always tight, but with prices of everything going up, they needed their support to go up as well. Thankfully, their gala was coming up in a little over a week. It had been a great fundraiser for them over the past few years and corporate sponsors were always eager to write a check to have their name and logo on the side of the Soft Paws building.

Once the checkbook was balanced and supplies ordered, Pace checked the guestlist for the gala. He had made sure Hana was invited, but he didn't ask her to be his date because he wasn't going to be able to spend much time with her. He had to do the one thing he hates – play up to other people and kiss their butts.

"Nothing is worse than pretending you like someone just for some money." He looked at Hank who snored softly. "But you're worth it, Hank. Help the helpless." He repeated that mantra as he looked over the names on the list.

Hana was on there. His entire family. He noticed the name La'Anna, and he could only assume it was Hana's friend. Nobody else could have that name. The next name made him scrunch his nose. Chas Rossi. Rossi Real Estate would be a great corporate sponsor, but he wished Rossi would write a check without showing up for the event.

"Help the helpless."

The door opened and Emmie peered inside. "There you are. This is the couple I was telling you about to see Hank. Mark and Min Willis." A couple followed his sister into the office, another woman trailing behind. "And their daughter. I'm sorry, I didn't get your name."

A voice Pace knew all too well filled his ears. "I'm Hana."

"Wait. Hana Willis?" Emmie stood with her mouth agape. She looked from Hana to Pace and back again. "This is your Hana?"

Pace stood and ran his hands through his hair, making it stand on end even more than usual. "She's not my Hana. She's my friend who happens to be named Hana." He looked at Hana and raised his eyebrows while she became wide-eyed and turned a lovely shade of pink.

"You know this man, Hana?" The older woman turned to Hana. She was attractive for a woman of almost fifty and Pace could imagine Hana looking much like her at that age.

Hana almost rolled her eyes but nodded instead. "Yes, Mom. I told you that. He's helped me with my book and his dog likes to play with Lulu. We've become friends." An exasperated look crossed Hana's face, but she quickly masked it.

Mark looked to the floor where Hank was now awake and staring at them from under heavy eyelids. "Why are you getting rid of your dog?"

"Oh, this one isn't my dog. He's a rescue. My dog, Moses, is at home. Probably itching to go to the dog park this afternoon." Looking to Hana, Pace noticed her shy smile and the slight nod of her head.

Emmie called to Hank and he stood up and wagged his tail. "Now he is blind, but he does a great job once he knows the layout of a place. We've worked hard with him. He recently had some teeth pulled, so I would suggest soft foods." Bending down, Emmie scratched Hank, making his back leg go up and down rapidly. "We have all his records and he was well-loved. His owner passed away and he was brought here. Hank is twelve years old and while he doesn't have more than two to five years left, we think he will brighten the lives of those who want to bring him home."

While Emmie and the Willises talked, Pace sat back down and eyed Hana. She listened to Emmie but stole glances at him every so often. She wore cutoff jeans and a simple V-neck t-shirt. Her hair was pulled in a low ponytail that ran down the length of her back. Pace had never seen her look so beautiful.

"Pace, do you want to pull out the adoption paperwork for Mr. And Mrs. Willis?" Emmie looked at him and cocked her head to the side.

Standing, Pace moved from behind the desk. "Actually, Em, I'll let you handle all of this. Hana, didn't you want to see the rescue? I can show you around while your parents fill out the paperwork."

"Yes!" The toothy grin on her face was unmistakable. She brought her hand up to her face to cover it, but she did a poor job.

Pace shook hands with Mr. Willis and nodded to Mrs. Willis before opening the office door and allowing Hana to go out before him.

They walked into open sunshine and Hana turned to him. "I'm your Hana, huh?"

He had forgotten about his sister saying that. "Oh, totally Emmie's words. I mentioned that I knew you and apparently every female I know has read your books."

"That's sweet." Hana continued walking toward the building in front of them. Several of the big dogs were in the run, happily barking and jumping, especially upon seeing people coming toward them. "How many dogs do you have now?"

"These are the big ones." Pace went to the chain-link fence and petted a mixed breed that stopped to see if they had any goodies. "We have eighteen in total, well, seventeen if Hank is going home with your parents. We have room for twenty. And off the side of the office is our cat room. We have six in there right now. And I think we have a rabbit as well. Not with the cats."

Hana squatted down and scratched the ear of a brindled mix breed. "Did your sister keep the chinchilla?"

"Of course she did. Because Emmie is Emmie." Pace went to the door and opened it for Hana.

She looked around and made a little gasping noise. "It's much larger than I thought."

"Our biggest thing is cost. It's not cheap to house, feed, and get medical services for these guys. So adoptions aren't cheap. Plus, we want to know the families are caring for our animals properly, so the money is a good way to know they're serious about the animal being part of their family."

Hana entered the door but then stood still. She looked deep in thought for a moment before turning her face back to Pace and showing off those dimples again. "Show me around. I want to pet everyone!"

Of course she did. And she was true to her word. Hana didn't bat an eye at having to clean her shoes and she got on the floor and petted every dog that was in a kennel, no matter how they looked or acted. The ones who were a little scarier to Pace came up to her and submitted to her gentle hand willingly. She had a magic touch and Pace was awed.

The animals loved him, but they adored her. And she was sitting on a dirty floor without a care in the world. If he wasn't careful, Pace knew he would end up adoring her as well.

Chapter 9

It was too dark to see, but Daphne knew Jackson was there. She could sense him. She could smell him. If only she could see him.

"Jackson? Please tell me where you are." Searching with her hands, Daphne felt her way around the room. A couch, a table, the brocade fabric of a lampshade. Until...

The next object was warm, alive. Ah-ha! Jackson stood before her, unmoving despite her hands on his plaid-covered chest.

A ringing snapped Hana out of her groove. Finding that sweet spot of concentration wasn't always easy and a ringing phone could certainly ruin the moment. She glanced at the name on her phone and rolled her eyes.

"What's up, L.A.?" Sensing the break, Lulu jumped into Hana's lap and rested her head on the desk.

"Did you know you're on the Insta for a shelter?"

"A shelter?" Hana sat up straighter.

La'Anna scoffed. "Well, it's you, petting some scruffy dog behind a fence."

Realization hit Hana. It was the rescue. "L.A. that's Soft Paws Animal Rescue. Not a shelter. They're no-kill. It's run by the bartender, Pace McCoy, and his sister."

Putting the phone on speaker, Hana pulled up Soft Paw's Instagram page. Sure enough, there she was, petting an adorable retriever and laughing big. Pace stood behind her, though he was cut off. The caption read, "Author Hana Willis enjoyed playing with Barney yesterday at Soft Paws. All our animals got the royal treatment from the Queen of romance novels." It was followed by several hashtags, and she was tagged, as well as Pace.

"Okay, so it's legit?" Right. La'Anna was still on the line.

"It's fine. I wish they would have asked before using my photo, but I don't mind at all." She could only guess that Pace's sister, Emmie, had snapped the photo after finishing with her parents and Hank.

A laugh sounded through the phone. "You don't mind an incredibly hot and rugged guy with a soft spot for animals." Before Hana could reply, La'Anna snorted. "And a thing for clean-cut, handsome go-getters like Mr. Rossi. You have a dilemma on your hands, my dear."

Hana thought a moment. She hadn't considered that both men liked her, but Pace had kissed her, albeit quickly, and Chas had given her a lingering kiss on the cheek. Much like Pace had said, even though she was not looking, it seemed two guys had found her. And she found herself liking them both.

"Oh, La'Anna." Sucking in a breath, Hana felt sweat bead on her neck and her heart pound inside her chest. "Oh, do I have a problem?"

A cackle of laughter rang through the room. "Oh, sweetie, it's the best problem to have. Two guys to choose from. And I'll bet you didn't even try."

Hana stood, Lulu jumping from her lap. "Oh, geez. Of course, I didn't try to be attracted to them both. But I am.

They're both so different, but they have many of the same qualities. They love their family, they support my writing, they're friendly and generous to a fault. They're both sexy. I love Chas's suits and take-charge demeanor. But then I love that Pace is relaxed and down to earth. They're like two sides of the perfect man." She paced back and forth in her office, Lulu sitting a few feet away, watching.

"It's like you're living in one of your own books."

Blinking, Hana looked into a mirror mounted on the wall. "It is like I'm living in one of my own books. But unlike my characters, I don't know what to do." A mild panic rose in her throat. Did she really suddenly have two men interested in her?

Ever the voice of fun and reason, La'Anna shushed her. "Hey, hey, it's okay. You don't have to pick one right now. First, you have to figure out if they're both actually interested in a relationship – assuming that you are." She paused, but then went on. "I can sense that you're ready even if you don't know it. But you need to figure that out, then make sure they both know there's competition. Otherwise, you'll lose them both. Remember Georgia in Home Town Decision?"

In her Home Town series, Georgia found herself in a love triangle and tried to juggle both guys only to lose them both for a time. But unlike her novels, the odds of one coming back and being her true love was slim. In real life, if you burned someone they were likely to stay out of your campsite forever. And Hana didn't want that to happen with either guy.

"So I have to tell them there's someone else, even though I'm not actually dating either one?" She sat back down in her office chair and Lulu rested her head on Hana's foot. A comforting gesture if ever there was one.

"Afraid so, Hannie. But first, you have to figure out if they're serious. If one of them isn't, then cut him and move on. I got to run, Rob is home. But I'll be thinking about you, girl. Keep me updated."

"Bye." The phone went silent before Hana finished the word. She stared at her phone for a minute, then up to her laptop. Knowing she wasn't going to get anything else in Daphne's story written at the moment, she closed the computer and went to her kitchen. She pulled out a can of Sprite and popped the top.

Chas and Pace were like her two favorite drinks, Sprite and caramel macchiato. One was a little zingy, fun, and gave you unexpected bursts. But the other was smooth, rich, and warm. Both hit the spot depending on what she was looking for, and both were the same no matter where she had them. Pace was her Sprite, and Chas her caramel macchiato. How would she choose one over the other?

<hr>

"Chas, darling, do you think you can get your girlfriend to come to my book club? We're reading her book this month." His mother had not greeted him, just came out with the question. Though Chas did like the idea of Hana as his girlfriend.

"I can ask, but I am pretty sure there's a way to contact her through her website. She has an agent." Chas kissed his mother on the cheek and sat next to her at the table. La Cucina was a family go-to, after all. The servers treated them like royalty, and Marcie wouldn't stand for anything less. "And she's not my girlfriend, Mom. Not yet, at least."

"Sweetness, you're thirty. You're not getting any younger. I want to see you settled and happy, and I want to be able to play with my grandchildren." She clasped her manicured hands and sighed.

It wasn't that Chas didn't want to get married. Why did his mother always assume he was the problem? The right woman had yet to present herself, though, with the thoughts he had been having of Hana lately, a change might be on the horizon.

He didn't know if there was marriage potential there, but a dating relationship sure seemed like the next logical step. He had been pretty clear about how he felt the last time he saw her. Though he hadn't said anything outright, he had looked into her eyes and kissed her on the cheek. Women understood those things, right? It's not like they were kids and he had to throw rocks at her.

"If you will go to her website and put in a request for an appearance, I will make sure to tell her you did so and try to nudge her to accept." It was going along with his mother's request without actually going along with it. He could certainly tell Hana that his mother had sent something in.

With a roll of her eyes, Marcie waved the server over to them. "Well, if that's all you can do, Chas." She turned to the young man that appeared before them. "Water and hot tea, please. Chas, do you want an Earl Grey?"

"A sweet tea, please. *Grazie*." Chas looked sympathetically to the young server. He was in for a world of training with Marcie Rossi at the table.

"*Figlio*, what does your social calendar look like for the coming summer?" There was always a need to see and be seen. As a wanna-be socialite, Marcie was the queen of being seen.

"Mother..."

The server returned with drinks and took their orders, scurrying away as quickly as he appeared.

Marcie swatted Chas on the arm. "Now, Chas, I'm simply looking out for you and for our company. The more you're seen, the more women will be interested. And the more people will come to Rossi for their buying and selling needs. I'm not trying to be a meddling mother, I only have your best interest in mind."

The only winner if he were to argue would be his mother, so Chas huffed and pulled out his phone. "I have that gala fundraiser this weekend. Will's wedding at the end of June, and I'm the grand marshal for the Independence Day parade."

"And is Hana Willis your date for all three?" A wink came his way.

He only wished she was his date for any of them. "I'm afraid not. She is going to the gala, but not as my date. But I do hope to dance with her. As a corporate sponsor, I thought talking up the people was more important. And she already had something planned for the day of Will's wedding. And I don't know if I can bring a date to a parade, Mom."

Plates piled high with pasta were laid before them. Scallops seared to perfection made Chas's mouth water. His mother only had a small plate of pasta with a salad. Marcie quickly bowed her head and blessed the food, her voice almost inaudible. Chas barely had time to register that she was praying before she said amen and shot him a disapproving look.

Not caring to open his mouth and invite more scrutiny, Chas relished the flavor of the scallops. His uncle was a fantastic chef and trained his staff well. They ate in relative silence, something Chas was grateful for.

As soon as her napkin hit her plate, Marcie started again. "Who are you taking to the wedding if not the lovely Hana?"

"Nobody you know, Mom." Of course, he didn't have a date yet. He added it to his mental to-do list.

Marcie leaned in and studied Chas. "Nice girl, but you would prefer Hana. As would I. Who are her people again?"

Lifting his hands in exasperation, Chas sat back in his chair. "Yes. Yes, I would prefer to go with Hana. I really like her, okay? But she can't make it and I don't want to go alone. Can you stop now?"

A satisfied smile crossed Marcie's lips. "Yes, *figlio*, I will stop. But I'm glad to know how you really feel." She folded her arms and leaned back, looking as though she had unlocked all of Chas's secrets.

After lunch, Chas got into his car and felt like he had done ten rounds in a boxing ring, except his opponent was a petite brunette with three-inch heels. He knew his mother meant well, but her inquisitions often felt him feeling slightly beat up. His entire life there had been nothing but pressure to be and do the best. While it was something Chas and his sister excelled at, it didn't stop them from feeling anxious every time their parents looked at a report card or a date or their career progress.

"I'll never do that to my children." It was a vow he had made years before. To not push his kids, but encourage them to pursue everything and anything their hearts desired. Maybe it was time to take his own advice.

"Two whiskey sours and an old-fashioned, coming up." Pace had better things to do than tend bar on a Thursday evening, but yet again Palmetto Magic was slammed with an after-work crowd and Jake needed a hand. He was going to have to hire someone else for all these people coming in for a post-work drink.

He made quick work of the order, presenting the three drinks to the trio on the corner of the bar. They all wore polo shirts with a company logo embroidered on them. They thanked him and he went on to the next pair that had come in and sat down at the bar.

Even though he was rushing around, he did so with a smile on his face. He told himself it wasn't because Hana had stopped by earlier to do some work, but it was. She had spent a few hours holed up in the booth in the back, papers spread around her, her laptop open. She stuck her tongue out when she was concentrating, not that he noticed. Nor had he noticed how expressive her eyebrows were when she was looking at her screen and mouthing words silently.

He had told Jake not to bother her and Pace had taken her a fresh Sprite every so often. No words were exchanged, just a nod if she even noticed him. It was like they were spending time together but not. Pace wondered if she noticed him as much as he noticed her.

Before the after-work crowd appeared, Hana packed up and left. She would wave on her way out and Pace would go clean up. She would always leave money on the table, not that he would have charged her. The money went into the donation jar for Soft Paws that sat on the counter by the register.

The influx of customers finally died down about nine and Pace went back to the office to work on the books. His mind was wandering to the thoughts of expansion and doing more market research when a knock sounded.

A head poked through the office door. "Visitor for you."

Looking up, Pace saw his father come through the office door. He sat up straighter and cleared his throat. "Dad?"

An older version of himself, Gerry McCoy had graying hair and glasses, but still looked younger than his years. "Patrick."

Nobody ever called him by his given name. He had been Pace from the day he was born. Blood began to rush through his veins and he swallowed hard. He steeled himself for whatever his father would say next.

The stern expression on Gerry's face softened a little. "I'm sorry, I'm not trying to panic you, son. Mom is fine. Everyone is fine. But Caroline called off the wedding with Trey and he's beside himself. Actually, he's drunk as a skunk and was picked up by the Sherriff's department a bit ago. He's lucky he didn't kill someone."

To say he was shocked would be an understatement. Caroline had been with Trey for five years. She had patiently waited for him to complete seminary and become a pastor before getting married. And for Trey to then be drunk? He never touched alcohol.

Pace scratched the scruff on his chin. "Do you need me to go get Trey?"

Gerry sat in a chair, then stood again. He looked completely baffled, much the way Pace felt. "Come with me? I figure you will know how to handle him better than I would."

"Because I run a bar?"

His father sat again and reached a hand out to the desk as if to steady himself. "No. No, because you're his brother and you two have a bond. Maybe he can stay with you tonight?"

"Yeah, Dad. Let me tell my crew to lock up on their own." Pace began to sort a few papers. "How much is bail?"

"Five thousand. We have it covered."

Trey would regret more than the break-up and the booze in the morning once he realized his parents had bailed him out of jail. The clean-up from his debacle would take a long time, considering Trey's new church wouldn't likely want a preacher with drunk and disorderly on his record.

In the car, Pace considered his father. The look of disappointment when Pace took ownership of Palmetto Magic and turned it into an up-and-coming place had been heartbreaking. But going into a church ministry wasn't Pace's calling. The rescue was. And, apparently, running the bar. He employed good people, he provided a safe and clean environment, and he called car services for any customer who had imbibed a little too much. He even kept their cars and keys safe until they could retrieve them.

Gerry McCoy didn't see it that way. He saw a son who was a sell-out, giving in to sin at every corner. At least, that's what Pace assumed his father thought of him.

"Dad, am I a disappointment to you?" The question surprised even himself.

His father glanced his way. "What? No. I don't love that you own and operate a bar, causing people to stumble, but I love you."

"I'm not questioning your love, Dad. I'm asking if I'm a disappointment. Trey has always been golden. Emmie is the perfect daughter. But we're all imperfect humans doing our best in the world." Pace sighed as they slowed at a red light.

"Yes, I own a bar and yes, I serve drinks. But I do so responsibly, I know every taxi and Uber driver in town. I take the safety and well-being of my customers seriously. And you know Soft Paws is my passion."

The Sherriff's department loomed ahead of them, barbed wire around the back. Gerry adjusted his glasses and looked pained. "You are an excellent businessman. You turned your grandfather's hole in the wall into something new and upbeat. But it's still a bar and I can't condone that. But your work with the animals is beyond compare. I am very proud of all you have accomplished, Pace."

The war over his business would likely never be won, Pace realized. But at least he knew his father was proud of him. "Thanks, Dad. Let's go get Trey."

Chapter 10

Being overdressed was never a bad idea in Chas's mind. When most of the gala attendants were dressed in suits with seersucker bowties, he donned a double-breasted tuxedo with satin lapels. Standing out was what he did best, and he saw people look at him and whisper to their companions. The Rossi name on everyone's lips was why he was at this blasted charity event.

That and seeing Hana Willis. He was going to finally make a move and let her know he wasn't casually flirting with her. He saw the potential for a future with her and needed to act on that. She was the perfect balance of focused and fun. She understood business and the drive to succeed. And together they would make a perfect power couple. They could be South Carolina royalty.

The evening included a cocktail hour, dinner, silent auction, and a litany of boring speeches about whatever this charity was. Oh, right. Animals. Animal rights? Animal rescue? Save the birds? Whatever it was, Chas was there to schmooze and be seen. Preferably with Hana on his arm for part of it.

He grabbed a glass of wine and an hors d'oeuvre. Not caring what was on the toothpick, he popped it into his mouth and chewed. Not bad. Prosciutto.

"Chas, it's so nice to see you here. Representing the company?"

The voice caused him to turn and swallow quickly. The groan that threatened to erupt from his mouth was thankfully swallowed with the food as he saw the mayor, Jaclynne White, standing before him. While she was a nice enough woman, Chas found her to be tedious and a little classless.

"Mayor White, what a pleasure." He shook her hand gently and gave her his customer service grin. "We are one of the sponsors of this remarkable event. Rossi Real Estate is always happy to help our community in any way we can."

The mayor put her index finger up to the side of her nose. "I'm on to you. You're here to look good. But you succeed, like always." She laughed at her own joke and raised her glass to him.

He raised his glass as well and they both drank. Ready to avoid awkwardly standing there, Chas's eyes went to the first person to his left. "If you'll excuse me, Mayor, I need to speak with Mr. Thomas here."

He nodded and stepped to the side, putting his arm around Fred Thomas, one of the canine officers with the police department. "Fred, how are things going?" He led the man away from the mayor for a few steps.

Caught unaware, Fred stammered. "What? Fine. How are you?"

Chas released his hold on the man and clapped him on the chest. "Great to hear, Fred. Say hello to the family for me. If you need a new house, give me a ring." And Chas walked away toward other people he knew.

It was then that he saw Hana enter, followed by her friend Lana. Lana? Something like that. A man was also with them, but he was more attentive to the friend than Hana. Good, not a date then.

A deep purple dress hugged Hana's curves in all the right places. Little shimmers of light bounced off the dress, making her practically glow. Her hair hung perfectly straight down her back, stopping right at the curve of her hip. Chas's pulse quickened as Hana laughed at something her friend said. She gathered her hair and pulled it over her shoulder, exposing the cutout back of the dress.

It felt like all the air was knocked from Chas's lungs when he saw her toned and flawless back. No tan lines showed from the neck to her lower back. She turned again and Chas noticed just how modest the front of the dress was compared to the back. It was like Hana was two people. A conservative, polite, demure woman on the outside and a flirty, fun, vivacious woman kept back from public view.

The thought of such perfection in one woman made Chas's feet move toward her without his brain inviting them to. He was drawn to her, simple as that. It could not be helped. Maybe it was a sign that she was the one for him.

"Oh, Chas, how nice to see you tonight." Hana beamed as he approached. "You remember La'Anna. And this is her husband, Rob."

Chas turned the charm on, shaking everyone's hand. "La'Anna, a pleasure. Rob." But he returned his attention to Hana. "As always, you are stunning."

The light in her eyes held his gaze. "Aren't you sweet? You look great yourself." She glanced around the room decorated with tons of glitz. "Do you have a date?"

The comment was like a sucker punch. It shouldn't have been, but it was. "No. No, I'm here to represent the company, so I thought it best to arrive solo." But I could be convinced to leave as part of a duo. Best not to voice that yet.

"My invitation didn't include a plus one, so I thought I'd better come alone. But that's fine. I actually have a basket in the auction and I'm making a donation, so I'll be making the rounds myself." She lifted her chin, the pride evident.

Chas extended his arm to her and winked. "Want to schmooze with me?"

She stepped forward and took his arm. "Gladly." She waved to her friend, but then looked around the room again before settling her gaze back on Chas.

Together, they approached mostly people Chas knew. He always introduced her and she made charming small talk with everyone. It felt right having her by his side. She was petite, but a powerhouse, commanding attention everywhere she went. People were interested in her and respected her. Many of the women knew her name and read her books, even a few guys said they had read her work.

After a turn around the room, the lights flickered and someone announced it was time to take seats for the meal and presentations. Before they went inside, Chas pulled Hana aside.

"I need to tell you something before I lose my nerve." He held her hands in his.

She knit her brows together, her dark eyes searching his. "What's going on? Is everything okay?"

Ignoring his pounding heart and the urge to vomit, Chas tried to smile. "Hana, I have loved every minute I have ever spent with you and I would like to do so on a more permanent basis. You are the embodiment of perfection and I can see a future with you. I don't know if you're talking to anyone else, but I would like to be the one and only."

A little gasp came from Hana's lips. "Are you... Are you asking me to be your girlfriend?"

Chas blinked. "I suppose I am. I want the chance to woo you, to spoil you, and to see where this might go." The pounding was like a roar in his ears. He could feel sweat beading on his back and the knots in his stomach tightened.

A baritone voice interrupted them. "Sir, you and the lady need to find your seats, please."

Ready to explode, Chas's eyes went wide. Didn't this idiot waiter realize this was an important moment?

Hana went from having her hands held by him, to holding his in her own. "It's okay. We can talk about this later when there are no interruptions. Okay?" Her eyes crinkled as she looked at him.

The smile bolstered Chas and he nodded. They entered the dining room and found their place cards. Chas was at table three, while Hana had been placed at table two. At least they were relatively close to one another.

What Chas did not expect was to see Pace McCoy in all his smugness send Hana a wave and a warm smile upon seeing her.

Hana took her seat next to his parents. She didn't realize she was with his parents, but Pace supposed she would find that out soon enough. He sat across the front table with his sister, brother, and the board members for Soft Paws. A small podium with the Soft Paws logo affixed to the front sat off to the side.

Unable to help himself, Pace made eye contact with Hana and waved. While this was their fourth gala, having Hana here gave Pace a sense of calm. He was not a fan of these fancy events, but they worked to bring in the money needed.

Pace's father made his way to the podium. An older version of himself, Pace watched as Gerry cleared his throat to get everyone's attention. "Ladies and gentlemen. I am honored to give a blessing for this event and this meal If you would please bow your heads."

Pace knew he could be listening to his father, but his gaze was fixed solely on Hana. She wore a purple dress that made her look like royalty. Her head was bowed while his father prayed, and she pressed her lips together. She was entrancing.

A light movement to the left made Pace look away and he spotted Chas Rossi checking his watch. Then his gaze went from his wrist to Hana. It wasn't a passing glance, he was watching her. Did they know each other? Pace felt his pulse quicken and his palms get clammy.

The sound of a hundred people saying, "amen," distracted him and when he looked back, Chas was chatting pleasantly with a woman to his right. Maybe the gaze at Hana meant nothing. Pace hoped that was the case.

Servers came from the back, carrying trays of salads. A few wandered with drink pitchers refilling water and tea.

Pace turned to his sister, the mastermind behind the whole thing. "This gets better and better every year, Em."

She looked out over the crowd and clasped her hands together. "Doesn't it? And if your numbers are right, we will make a profit over seventy thousand, right?"

"If all goes as it should. The auction numbers were looking great, and the ticket price covered the catering." Pace hated dealing with the numbers, but that was his job. "We have some incredible things in that auction."

Emmie looked away from him. "I saw that Hana put something in."

Truthfully, Pace hadn't paid attention to who had put things into the silent auction. "She did? What?"

Laughing, Emmie leaned in closer. "The first is a copy of her new book series, including lunch with her. The second isn't an auction item, but she paid the adoption fees for four dogs so they can go to their forever families."

The pang that hit his heart was fast and furious. She had paid for four adoptions? That both amazed him and didn't surprise him in the least. She was a generous woman who adored their four-legged friends. With a look in her direction, he saw Hana chatting happily with the Joneses, some of their biggest supporters.

After the meal was wrapping up, Quent stood and made his way to the podium. "As the main veterinarian for Soft Paws, I want to thank you all for helping support this wonderful organization. It's not easy giving attention to twenty dogs, a few cats, and the occasional rabbit or sugar glider. Not to mention cleaning up after them, feeding them, and trying to find them forever homes. I know I, as well as Doctor Frederick and Doctor Sanders, have come to love the way the McCoy family takes care of their residents.

"But as you know, it's not cheap. Medications aren't cheap. Food, bedding, heat, and air are all costly things. And it's with your generosity we can keep serving the pets of the Upstate who need a home." He paused and clapped, creating a rousing round of applause.

"I would like to thank our corporate sponsors now. These companies all donated over five thousand dollars directly to Soft Paws." Quent pulled a piece of paper from his pocket and read off a list of ten sponsors. Each had already been sent thank you cards, tax-deductible paperwork, and their logos were being added to the side of their building.

"This year we had two diamond sponsors who went above and beyond with donations of ten thousand dollars." The crowd gasped and Quent paused for effect.

This was the part Pace dreaded. Many times, sponsors who donated so much thought they could then dictate how the company was run. But if they had read through the donation paperwork they signed, they would see that it gave them no rights whatsoever.

"Please give a round of applause for Holcombe's Pet Food and Rossi Real Estate."

Knowing he had to, Pace stood and applauded toward Holcombe's representative, Ginger Holcombe. He gave a nod to Chas Rossi. While it was the elder Rossi who had signed the check, Pace knew that Chas was the one there to smile and wave. The entire room was on their feet in a standing ovation.

It was then Pace saw Hana turn to Chas and put her hands over her mouth in surprise. She scooted over to him and hugged him and he was more than ready to welcome her into his arms. They looked cozy. Too cozy.

So, the looks between Chas and Hana before the dinner weren't coincidental. Blood boiled in Pace's veins, though he tried to remind himself Hana was not his. Yes, he had kissed her once, but they weren't dating. He had no right to feel the way he did.

It was Pace's turn to speak and he took his position, trying to block Hana and Chas from his mind. "Ladies and gentlemen, my brother, sister, and I have been running Soft Paws as an official non-profit for seven years now. This is our fourth gala and I'm blown away by the generosity this city has for our animal companions. While I am not one to usually enjoy dressing up, I do enjoy seeing your beautiful and generous faces.

"If you did not notice it earlier, out front is a table with information on the dogs and cats we currently have in our facility for adoption. If you're so inclined, take a look and see if adding one of them to your family is the right move for you.

"We have about ten minutes before bidding on auction items closes. so if you had your eye on something, please make sure you bid on it now." Pace stepped away from the podium and kept an eye on the timer of his watch.

With minutes to spare, Pace himself went to the tables and wrote in a few last-minute bids. When the alarm went off, he, Emmie, and Trey quickly scooped up the bid papers. They went over them quickly then Pace returned to the podium.

"I now have the pleasure of introducing my older brother and my baby sister, who will go over the winners of tonight's auction. Please welcome Trey and Emmie McCoy." Pace clapped and hugged his sister when she approached. Trey shook his hand heartily – he was putting on a brave front in the wake of his breakup with Caroline.

They carefully went over each item, announcing the winning paddle number for each lot. Excited cries went up with the winner of a Myrtle Beach vacation went to Mrs.

Potter. And groans of disappointment were heard when a brand new Coach bag went to Blanca Rodriguez.

Trey pulled up the next paper. "We have item seventy-two, donated by best-selling author Hana Willis. A set of her newest trilogy and a lunch date for the winner and her. Our winning bid was $252 from paddle number twenty-three."

A knowing grin spread across Pace's lips as a few sighs signaled losses. But he was paddle twenty-three and he had been determined to win. He had bid more than fifty dollars over the last number in an effort to claim the prize. The lunch, that he would insist on paying for himself, was all he was interested in. The books would be donated to the library. Or maybe he would keep them.

Hana approached after all the winners were read. "I didn't see anyone step up to claim my books. Is everything okay with them?"

Emmie piped up. "Oh, everything is great. The winner just didn't want to reveal himself in front of everyone." She turned to Pace and winked. "Isn't that right?"

Leave it to his sister. Pace didn't know what to say, so instead he turned bright red and shrugged.

"You? You paid $250 for books I would have given you anyway and a lunch I would have gone on without you having to bid for?" The realization hitting her, she shrunk back a little and looked down. "Pace, that's so kind. But it's your own program you're giving to."

He looked at her and lifted her chin with his finger so they were looking eye to eye. "I know. I would have put it into Soft Paws anyway. But I..." He swallowed hard but his mouth stayed dry. "I wanted you to know you're..."

Hana took his hands in hers. "I understand. And we do need to talk about...this. Maybe you can come for lunch tomorrow to my place? Bring Moses."

He nodded and kissed her cheek. "That sounds perfect. I will see you then. Text me the address."

Her inky eyes sparkled at him. "See you then."

Every ounce of hope in Pace's body was brimming to the surface as he watched Hana wave and walk off toward her friend.

Oh, Hana was in trouble all right. She liked both Pace and Chas, and it seemed they both had feelings for her. La'Anna was right. She needed to be honest with them both or they would all get hurt in the process. This was nothing like the books she was writing. If she was putting her characters through this madness, she was a sadist. No more love triangles in her books.

She approached La'Anna and Rob as they exited the gala. The pair had won football tickets to a Clemson game and Rob was a little more excited than La'Anna.

"Not in the mood for football?" Hana laughed as Rob was still going on and on about getting the tickets.

"I like it well enough, but not to this level." La'Anna laughed at her husband's shouts of excitement. "But he's happy. This is going to be his birthday gift."

Hana pulled La'Anna to the side. "I wanted to ask you... How do I tell these two guys that I like them both and that they're not my only suitor? Because you were spot on with how they both feel."

"Suitor? Girl, what century are you in?" She waved her hand in dismissal. "That's not the point. Listen, what you didn't see was those two men shooting death glares at each other all night. They know each other and there's bad blood there already, Hana. Tread carefully."

Bad blood? She hadn't seen them give each other looks throughout the night, in fact, when Chas was announced as a diamond sponsor, Pace had given him a nod. But, of course, they would be diplomatic in public. Both were above pettiness. Though this would throw a twist in her own plans. Would telling them about each other cause one to back down? It would make things easier, but Hana knew she liked them both and wanted to see where things went.

"I guess I have to be forthcoming. Pace is coming for lunch tomorrow. Did you hear how much he paid?" Hana rubbed her hands back and forth, needing the comforting motion. "And Chas asked me to be his girlfriend."

"Wait. Pace won your stuff?" La'Anna's mouth dropped when Hana nodded. "And Chas seriously asked you to be his girlfriend? Like a twelve-year-old would?"

"Not quite like a twelve-year-old. He asked if we could be exclusive. But then we got interrupted. I have to tell him I'm not sure. And I don't know how to do that, L.A." Hana bit her lip and worried her hands back and forth more.

La'Anna grabbed her hands. "Stop fidgeting. And you are sure. You're sure that right now you can't be exclusive. Do not lie to these guys, Hana. You will end up being the one hurt and I can't see that happen. Right?" La'Anna raised her eyebrows, wanting Hana to agree with her.

"Yes, yes, you're right. Oh my gosh, I feel like one of my book characters. Maybe Rose, she was in that love triangle with Hunter and Oliver. And it didn't go well for her, either. This is torture." Hana put a hand to her forehead. "Am I hot? I think I'm feverish."

Looking over Hana's shoulder, La'Anna squeezed her hands. "You're not feverish, but your first test is right now. Be strong, call me after you talk to him." She kissed Hana's cheek and rushed off to catch up with Rob.

Turning, Hana saw Chas slowly approaching her. She swallowed hard and hoped she said the right words.

Chapter 11

"Chas, there you are. I didn't see you inside." Hana's stomach did flips and she could feel her mouth go dry. She knew her voice sounded off, higher pitched. "Did you win anything?"

He straightened the cuff of his tuxedo jacket as he looked upon her. "I won a few things, but I missed out on what I wanted most."

Please don't be the books and lunch. She squeezed her eyes shut. "What was that?"

"Your books and a lunch with you."

Of course. Hana bit her lip and opened her eyes. She giggled, but it came out stiff and phony. How was she supposed to do this? She had never really dated before, especially not since getting out of school. She hadn't had time. What would her characters do?

"Oh, Chas, you know you don't have to make a bid to have lunch with me. And I'm happy to give you books. Or would they be for your mom?"

He stepped closer to her, his gaze locked on hers. The look on his face said volumes more than anything else. It said he wanted her and he wasn't going to take no for an answer. "Now that we're alone, how about continuing that conversation? Want to grab coffee?"

Wandering to a bench, Hana sat and patted the spot next to her. "Let's chat here. It's a lovely night and I'm still stuffed. I think the gala raised a lot of money for Soft Paws and you being a diamond sponsor... Chas, that's amazing."

Chas remained standing in front of her. He crossed his arms. "That's my father's doing. He's always had a soft spot for animals."

Hana noticed he seemed closed off, and his tone led her to think he was quite upset. "Are you not an animal lover as well?"

Shaking his head, he was truthful. "Not like my dad. Or you. Or Pace McCoy."

Behind Chas came a voice. "Talking about me?"

The knots in Hana's stomach drew tighter and she held her breath. Was this really happening here? She forced a smile onto her face. "Pace. What a wonderful event. Congratulations."

Chas rolled his eyes. "Not now, McCoy. This is a private conversation."

Hana knew it was time to come clean with them. She had to be honest and telling them both at once seemed like a great idea to her. Only, she didn't know how they would react. "Actually, Chas, I need to speak with you both. Please."

Pace approached, stopping a few feet from Chas, creating a triangle between the three of them. How ironic.

A wish for the right words popped into her head before she spoke. Hana inhaled deeply. "Chas, I think you're wonderful, and I really enjoy it when we run into each other. But I told you before I'm not looking to date and I'm not ready to be exclusive with someone right now. And Pace..."

"What's the story with you and McCoy?" Chas interrupted, he turned to glare at Pace.

Hana hated confrontation and this was getting to be too intense for her. Sweat rolled down her back and she felt her stomach churn. She didn't look at either man, she couldn't bear it. "We're friends. Well. Maybe more. We see each other at the dog park, Lulu really loves Moses. And he's been kind enough to help me with a book I'm working on. We've really gotten to know each other and..."

"He's the reason you don't want to be exclusive." It wasn't a question.

Both men looked at her as she nodded. It was true. She had growing feelings for both Pace and Chas. They were sweet, generous men in their own ways, and yet they were completely opposite from one another. Neither said a word as they looked at her.

Hana felt tears prick her eyes. "He is. I enjoy spending time with you both, and if one day that leads to something more with either of you, then that's awesome. You both know I haven't been looking for a relationship and I'm still not. I like to spend time with you both. As friends. If that's a deal-breaker for either of you, I understand."

Silence permeated the air as they all digested her words. Hana looked from Chas to Pace, trying to read their expressions. Pace ran his hand through his hair, making it stand on end. It was a move that made Hana's heart pound. Chas, for his part, was in his power stance with his arms crossed and his feet apart.

After a minute of silence, Chas wandered a few feet, but then came back and stared Hana down. "Hana, I have never met anybody like you. You bring out the fun side of me that I thought was just about gone for good. Work is my life, but I think I can finally say I found someone who makes me want to do more than work. So I'm throwing my hat in the ring. I will fight for a chance with you."

The hungry expression that lit on Chas's face made Hana feel warm and gooey inside. His hair fell over his face, giving him a look of vulnerability Hana wasn't used to seeing. Chas turned his attention to Pace and Hana slowly turned as well.

Jaw set, Pace jammed his hands in his suit pockets. She was used to seeing him casual in jeans, so the scruffy cheeks paired with a formal suit made Hana giddy. Finally, he spoke. "Hana, you are amazing. And my feelings for you have been growing, I'll admit. But listen. I am not going to get into a knock-down-drag-out fight with Rossi. I'm sorry, I'm not. Either we're meant to be or we're not."

The shock Hana felt was overwhelming. She blinked several times, trying to process what he said. While she didn't want anyone to fight over her, the notion that Pace wasn't willing to try made her heart hurt.

"Ha. Then I'm the winner." Chas turned to Hana and held out his hand. "Hana, I promise you will be happier than you ever thought possible. I will spoil you. McCoy has always been a loser."

That was it, then. Pace didn't want her or at least didn't want to fight for her. Hana looked at him before turning away.

But then Pace took a step closer and pulled his hands from his pockets. "Hana, I do like you. But I can't give you the lavish lifestyle Rossi can. Nor would I want to. I won't fight, but I'm also not giving up. You are not a prize to be won, but a woman with a choice to make."

Tears threatened to fall and her heart nearly exploded. Giving up wasn't in his plan. He was doing things in his own way. It was how Pace did most things, differently. In fact, Hana realized, both were doing things their own way. Chas was competitive and would do anything to win. Where Pace was more passive and wanted things to happen naturally.

Hana appreciated both ways of doing things. At times she was a go-getter who couldn't be stopped, but she also liked to slow down and let things happen as they would. But she didn't know how it would turn out with both of those approaches battling one another. At least one side was battling. The other...well, she wasn't sure.

Having his heart in his throat wasn't a feeling Pace was familiar with. Never before had a girl made him feel the way Hana made him feel. He realized that whatever it was between him and Amanda, it certainly was not love. Not that he was sure this was love either, but at least he knew it was something.

Having Chas Rossi in the mix, however, wasn't something Pace had seen coming. He didn't know Hana had ever met the man, let alone had known him long enough to develop feelings for him. Pace wanted to be angry, but they weren't dating and he had no right to feel possessive. But of course, he did. Fighting for Hana's affection was Pace's first thought, but it wasn't his style and he knew he couldn't match Chas's version of fighting for a girl.

He had taken a more passive approach. He wouldn't fight for her, but he was not going to give up either. He would simply spend time with her, enjoy that time, and see what happened. And this was his first chance to do so at his auction-won lunch.

He prepared for his lunch with Hana and fought the urge to dress up the way Rossi would have. Hana liked him for who he was. Pace shook his head. He was best off in his well-worn jeans. This time, though, he had paired them with a plaid button down. His hair was badly in need of a trim and it stuck out all over, and the stubble on his face was at least three days old. Clean-shaven wasn't his thing.

A simple mix of daisies, carnations, and a few other flowers he didn't know made up a sweet bouquet to present to Hana. Pace took a deep breath, wiped his hand on his jeans, and knocked on the door.

He looked down at Moses. "Be polite." He wasn't sure if the command was for the dog or for himself.

The now familiar sounds of Lulu's squeaking came from behind the door and Hana swung it wide open. Moses bounced inside and hunched down on his front two legs so he was closer to Lulu. For her part, Lulu jumped up and down with excitement, her little tail wagging.

"Hello, Moses. Good to see you." She laughed at the pair. Then she looked to Pace, her almond eyes almost dancing. "Pace. Come in."

He presented her with the flowers, suddenly feeling inadequate. "I went with flowers that reminded me of you. Unassuming, sweet, gentle." The temperature in the house suddenly rose about ten degrees and he worried he would have sweat stains within minutes.

"Oh, they're perfect. How did you know Gerbera Daisies are my favorite?" She inhaled their fresh scent. "If you want to go straight to the back and open the door for the dogs, my yard is fenced. I'll put these in water."

Pace went to the sliding door and pulled it open, Moses and Lulu chasing each other around in circles. Clearly, they were now best of friends. What did that mean for him and Hana, though?

He sat on the picnic table that occupied the small patio and studied his surroundings. Hana's house was small and adorable, in a row of similar little gingerbread-style houses. The sunny colors and simple decor screamed Hana Willis.

"Pace? Can I get a hand?"

He stood and followed the voice inside to a modest kitchen. He was surprised in such a tidy house to see a messy kitchen. Bowls were all over the counter, the sink was full of pots and pans, and Hana stood proudly in the middle of it.

"Sorry for the mess. I haven't gotten to the cleaning up part yet. But that's okay." She placed two plates piled high with food on a tray. "Can you carry the drinks? I hope Sprite is okay."

He grabbed the two tall glasses fizzing with soda, chuckling at her choice of beverage. "Sprite is perfect." He followed her back outside to the table.

She set the tray down and presented him with one of the plates, setting the other on the opposite side of the table. When she sat down across from him, Pace moved so that he was next to her. The blush on her cheeks couldn't be hidden and it bolstered his confidence.

"Um, this is bulgogi, it's a type of beef barbecue." She pointed to the meat on the plate. Then to some sort of rice mixture. "And this is bibimbap. It's my favorite. I hope you like them."

Pace picked up the chopsticks that were across his plate. "I'm sure I will, Hana. Thank you." He picked up a piece of the beef and tried it with Hana watching him intently. It melted in his mouth, a perfect blend of spices on the tender meat. "This is outstanding."

Her shoulders instantly relaxed and she let out a big breath. "Oh, good. I'm so glad you like it."

They ate in relative silence, watching the dogs run around. At one point Hana went inside the find a large bowl to fill with water for Moses, but otherwise, they enjoyed the peaceful company.

When the plates were empty, Pace stood to take them to the kitchen. "It's only fair that I help wash up."

Hana put her hand on his arm. "Oh, no. I insist. I have a dishwasher I'll load in a while."

Sitting back down, Pace could feel the awkwardness creeping into the day. The pups must have sensed it as well because they both came close and laid down for an afternoon snooze in the sun.

She tucked her hair back and bounced her knee. Her eyes stayed fixed on the wooden table. "Pace, I hope all of this with Chas isn't... I mean, I feel terrible for liking you both. But I appreciate your honesty. You have one of the purest hearts I've ever encountered."

"Well, I was a little surprised. Okay, a lot surprised. But we're not dating. It's not something we ever discussed, though I feel like things are moving forward with us. If you're not ready to be exclusive, I get it. We can have fun hanging out like this without any pressure." He put his hand on her knee to show he meant what he said, even if he did wonder about it himself.

Her face was pained. "I don't want you to be upset with me. I'm just not sure."

He stopped her and looked into her eyes. "Hana, really it's fine. We have never said we were a couple. I don't know that I'm ready for commitment myself, though I think you're the most extraordinary woman I've met in a long time. I'm not going to fight dirty, but I'm not going to completely give up on seeing you."

"Thank you, Pace. I have been fretting over this all day." She picked up her drink and took a long swig, setting the cup down with a thunk. "I completely agree with that sentiment. I'm not ready for a full-on commitment at this moment. One day, sure, but..."

"Not today. It's fine, Hana." Pace stood again, picking up the dishes. "Now, let's wash the dishes the old-fashioned way. It's more fun."

She followed him into the kitchen and together they washed the dishes, covering their arms in suds and blowing bubbles on one another. Laughter rang out through the house and carried outside down through the neighborhood.

Operation woo Hana was about to begin. Chas would not let Pace McCoy, or any man for that matter, win her over. He would give her lavish gifts, take her on spectacular dates, and spoil her the way a princess should be spoiled. He'd even get that scruff ball of hers a fancy dog collar. It wasn't merely about winning. It was about winning Hana. He didn't know what it was about her that was so entrancing, just that she was all he thought about. Her face, her voice, her laugh, the way she tilted her head when she asked a question. It was all so endearing and sweet and sexy at the same time.

Chas had never been a ladies' man. He'd had his share of dates and even a serious girlfriend a few years back, but nobody made him feel as alive as Hana. And he didn't want to spoil anybody but her.

The lunch McCoy won at the auction should have been long over. He pulled down Hana's street and spotted her little coupe in the driveway, but next to it was an older, faded truck. It had to belong to Pace. A check of the clock showed that it was well past three in the afternoon. A scowl came across his face.

Leaving the dozen roses he had gotten her in the car, Chas looked inside the front window. Movement out the backdoor caught his attention and he snuck around the side of the house. Chas peered over the fence and saw Pace throw a ball. A huge beast of a dog ran after it, Hana's little one trailing behind. He didn't see Hana right off, but he didn't want to get caught.

"I guess I need to become a dog person." Chas went back to the car, grabbed the flowers, and laid them on the front step. He backed up and nodded. "You got this."

Back in his car, he drove to the pet store. He looked through all the fancy dog accessories. The shelves were lined with collars, bows, scarves, and clothes. There was even dog nail polish.

"Can I help you find something?" A smiling teenager stood at his side.

Chas started to dismiss her, but then he stopped. "I need a gift for a dog." He felt ridiculous saying such a thing.

The girl looked confused. "Your dog?"

He scoffed. "No. It's, um, my girlfriend's. A small dog."

"How small? What kind of dog?"

What kind of dog? He had no idea. "Small. Jumps a lot. Looks like the dog from The Wizard of Oz." He nodded. Yes, that was what kind of dog it was. A Toto dog.

The awkward smile told him the girl thought he was stupid, but he didn't care. "So a small terrier. About ten to fifteen pounds?"

He nodded.

"And if it's your girlfriend's dog, you want to impress them both. I have just the things." She grabbed a basket from around the corner and started loading it up.

In went a pink satin collar with a bow. Then what Chas could only describe as a party dress followed. The girl rounded onto another aisle and Chas followed her. She picked up a squeaky stuffed taco and a bag of small treats.

She handed the basket to Chas. "You don't want to overdo it, but this says you care. Play with the dog. It will give you big brownie points."

"Um, thanks?" He looked from the girl to the basket. The girl led him to the register and checked him out. Almost fifty dollars later and Chas was ready to pamper Lulu instead of Hana.

Back at his apartment, Chas tossed the bag on his kitchen table to wrap later. Maybe he should text Hana, let her know he was thinking about her. But when he pulled his phone from his pocket, he saw that she had already texted him.

HANA: ARE YOU WORKING TOMORROW?

The next day was Sunday, and while Chas usually worked every day, he didn't have anything on his calendar aside from his weekly lunch with his parents.

CHAS: NO, BUT I AM HAVING LUNCH WITH MY PARENTS AT THE GREENBRIAR CLUB. YOU COULD JOIN US IF YOU'RE INTERESTED.

HANA: I ONLY HAVE TWO WEEKS LEFT WITH MY SISTER, SO I'LL PROBABLY HAVE LUNCH WITH HER. BUT THANK YOU. I WAS WONDERING IF YOU WANTED TO JOIN LULU AND ME FOR A WALK THROUGH FALLS PARK IN THE AFTERNOON.

Falls Park was a place where people could see and be seen. It was a huge draw for locals and tourists alike with a beautiful garden, a suspension bridge with a stunning overlook of the Reedy River. It was a wonderful date spot.

CHAS: I WOULD LOVE TO. WANT ME TO PICK YOU AND LULU UP ABOUT THREE?

HANA: THAT WOULD BE WONDERFUL. SEE YOU THEN.

The urge to ask about Pace was strong, but Chas knew he needed to be the bigger man. Bringing it up would only make him look petty.

Chapter 12

It wasn't like Pace to feel so possessive over anyone outside of his immediate family, but here he was, feeling like he needed to defend his territory from the enemy's attack. As he left Hana's the day before, a dozen long-stemmed red roses were laid outside her door. There hadn't been a name, but he knew who had left them. Which meant Chas Rossi had been to the house while he was there. How much had he seen? What part of the afternoon had he stumbled upon?

Hana had picked the flowers up, looked around, and not said a word about them. His simple daisies didn't begin to compare with the roses, though he took some comfort in knowing the daisies were a little more Hana's style with bright colors and easy beauty without the stuffiness and formality of roses.

She would choose him because she wanted to. If she wanted to. Not because he had thrown punches or spent the most money.

He pondered all this as he drove Moses in his truck, the engine rumbling, to the dog park. Going for a run always helped him clear his head and gave Moses much needed exercise. His apartment wasn't exactly conducive to owning a Boxer, but it worked. Moses spent a lot of time at the rescue, wearing a harness that said he was a working dog and not for adoption.

Early June was the perfect time to be outside. It wasn't too hot, the humidity hadn't descended like a wet blanket over the city, and the mornings were still crisp enough that working up a sweat felt good.

He started throwing the ball for Moses and having him retrieve it. Each time it was brought back to his hand, Pace would pet and praise the dog.

"You're so good with him." A leggy brunette approached him, her own Boxer in tow. She motioned to the leash and then to the ball. "May I?"

Pace nodded and the woman released her dog, a brindle female. Moses jumped and danced around with her. "That's Moses. I'm Pace." He stuck his hand out to her.

"Ginny and Willow." She shook his hand, matching him in firmness.

Unsure which name went with which female, he could only nod. He threw the ball and both dogs chased it down, Moses getting to it first. They ran back up and it was deposited at his feet.

"Do you come here a lot?" She turned to him and checked him up and down.

He did not give her the once over as she had done to him. "Most days, before I go to work." He threw the ball again, this time the brindle getting it and trotting back over, leaving Moses wondering what had happened.

"Willow and I live about ten minutes away and come here several times a week." She stepped closer still.

Ah, so Willow as the dog. That made her Jenny. Or was it Ginny? Pace shook his head. He was trying to think, not make small talk with someone. He threw the ball again and Moses brought it back, this time, though he kept it in his mouth.

"Looks like we're done throwing the ball."

She looked at the dogs and shrugged. "Oh well, what are..."

He interrupted her, wanting to cut her off before she invited him to something. He wasn't interested. "I'm going to get a quick run in before I head to work. It was nice to meet you, Jenny."

The look of confusion on her face told Pace she wasn't used to being given the cold shoulder. "Oh, it's Ginny."

But Pace had already hooked Moses up to his leash and started off in a jog. Yes, he had been rude, but sometimes it was best to stop things before they ever started.

As they ran, Pace made a mental list of things he needed to do in the coming week. Payroll at Palmetto Magic, pay bills both there and at Soft Paws. First, he needed to have Norman the mutt's teeth looked at, and then schedule for the new female that came in to be spayed. Emmie would write even more thank you notes to the patrons from the gala. He needed to talk to his vendor for the bar. And then he needed to see Hana.

He hoped she would come work at the bar that afternoon, though she didn't usually stop by on Sundays. Those were her family days, he already knew. But still, he wanted to see her. Texting her was an option, but he didn't want to seem desperate. But maybe saying he had enjoyed the day before and the food she had made would be good.

He paused and let Moses lay in the sun for a minute. He pulled up Hana's name on his texts.

PACE: I HAD A LOT OF FUN YESTERDAY. MOSES SURE ADORES LULU. AND YOUR FOOD WAS DELICIOUS!

It only took a minute for her to text back.

HANA: THANK YOU. IT'S FUN TO HAVE SOMEONE TO COOK FOR. AND LULU IS STILL WORN OUT FROM PLAYING WITH MOSES YESTERDAY. WE'LL HAVE TO DO IT AGAIN SOMETIME.

The heat that spread across his body couldn't be helped.

PACE: ABSOLUTELY.

He pocketed his phone again and rubbed Moses's head. "Let's go, boy."

After their run, Pace headed to the rescue where Moses napped and he cleaned out kennels. If he was already dirty, he might as well get all the dirty chores done.

Quent arrived as he wrapped up. His best friend had been a constant in his life for twenty years, and while him dating Emmie had initially put strain on their relationship, it quickly recovered when Pace saw how much Quent adored her.

Walking to the quarantine area, Quent bent low to one of the dogs. "Are you checking on Norman?" Pace looked over to the older mutt and watched as his tail wagged.

Quent nodded and leaned back against the wall. "Yeah, I figured I'd get that done today while I had a spare minute. I also wanted to talk to you."

"Shoot."

"I know your dad will be against this, but I want to ask Emmie to move in with me." Quent looked Pace in the eye. "What do you think?"

Pace laughed and picked up his cleaning supplies. "You're right, my dad won't like that at all. But Emmie is twenty-six. She can make her own decisions." He hung the pail and scrub brush up after washing them. "But I will say that I side with my dad on this one. I know you've been dating for a good while now. Why not just make it official?"

Running his hand through his hair, Quent sighed. "I've actually asked her to marry me and she said she wasn't ready. I thought this might be better and help her get ready." He looked a little hurt, but there was a look of determination on his face.

Leave it to Emmie to turn down a marriage proposal. "I'll have to ask Em about that..." Pace chuckled. "Why wouldn't she be ready? She's crazy about you. And we all like you well enough. Like I said, she can make her own choices, but I know we would all prefer she not move in without at least a promise of marriage."

Quent pushed away from the wall and approached Pace. "Listen, man, you know I love your sister. And I will marry her if she'll have me."

Satisfied with the sincerity in his voice, Pace agreed. "Okay. I believe you. You can ask, but prepare for resistance from clan McCoy."

A firm nod was Quent's only reply. He turned to Norman and opened his kennel. "Okay, old man, let's check those teeth." Norman happily followed Quent to the exam room.

Stopping to get Moses from the office, Pace made his way home and into the shower. He wondered if one day he would want to move in with Hana. He thought they would have fun chasing the dogs around, cuddling on the couch, and cooking delicious food together. It could be a lot of fun. And for the first time in a long while, Pace had a solid hope for his future.

Lists and plans always worked for Chas. If something wasn't on his calendar, it didn't exist. He wrote out lists for his lists and Hana was much the same way, so he thought she would one day appreciate that he was making a list for how to win her over.

The flowers had been the first step. It irked him that he didn't get to deliver them himself, but he knew she would love them, and leaving them on the doorstep was romantic and mysterious. The next plan had been asking her out for an official date, but she had beat him to it. He liked her initiative. Of course, he would invite her to dinner at Pomegranate after their walk, he'd already made the reservations and included the dog. They could go back to her place and either stay there or she could secure the dog and come back to his house for a nightcap.

But first, he had to get through lunch with his parents. Again. Chas strode into the club and spotted them at their usual table. The overly friendly host greeted him and pointed his parents out. Chas just nodded to him. Their usual server brought a sweet tea to him the second he sat down, as if she was waiting for him.

"Chas, darling, what are your plans today? Not working again on a Sunday, are you?" His mother patted his cheek as he leaned in for a kiss.

He took pleasure in announcing his plans. "I actually have a date this afternoon, Mom. With Hana Willis."

As expected, his mother was delighted. She clapped her hands together and almost squealed. "Oh, good. I'm glad you have an up and comer for a girlfriend. Is her father one of the Charleston Willises? I bet he is."

He rolled his eyes at his mother's assumption, but it didn't matter anyway. The server took their orders and Chas turned to his father.

"Dad, did you see hear that the Parker Millan house was going up for sale? I think the Westleys would love it." It was always best to talk business with his father.

"Set it up, Chas. I have to get back on the campaign trail. Are you running for mayor in the next term? You need to submit your forms." Chuck drank from his water glass and Chas watched as his father's hand shook slightly.

Chuck Rossi had been the mayor of Greenville and he expected his only son to follow each and every one of his footsteps. From the real estate business to running for mayor, Chas had to do everything as his father had and in the timeline his father wanted.

Feeling bolstered, Chas looked to his father. "I don't think so, Dad. I don't really want to run for mayor. You know I'm dedicated to the company, but I'm ready to live my own life now. Running for mayor isn't in my plans now or down the road."

Chas squinted, ready for the barrage of words his father would hurl at him. How he needed to do more, be more. Chuck Rossi did not disappoint. He spent a solid five minutes explaining how life worked to Chas as if he was a child who hadn't gone to college or expanded their business by thirty percent in the past few years.

It would have made sense to get up and leave, but Chas couldn't do that to his mother, so he sat and tuned his father out. Used to the tirades, Marcie also tuned Chuck out, instead preferring the company of her phone.

When their food came, they ate in silence. The food was bland and overcooked, though it might have been the sour mood Chas was now in.

As she dabbed her mouth with her napkin, Marcie looked from her husband to her son. She leaned in close and hissed through her teeth at them both. "You two are like huge pouting babies. Chuck, let the boy live his own life. He's thirty. Chas, it's about time you stood up for yourself. Be mayor, don't be mayor, do what makes you happy." With that, she stood, grabbed her purse, and went off towards the ladies' powder room.

Chas stood and leaned on the back of his chair. "You know, Dad, if you were encouraging instead of demanding, things could have been a whole lot different between us." He turned and stalked off, leaving his father sitting alone at the table.

He drove home and sat in his driveway for a few minutes. He owned a spacious four-bedroom home in a coveted neighborhood. Bought for a song, Chas had flipped it and decided to live in it when he opted to sell a client the home he had been living in at the time. It was the fourth house he had lived in over the last five years, so nothing was personal. He kept it showroom ready at all times just in case it was the perfect house for someone else.

He was ready to put down roots, though. A house that would be his for the next fifteen years or more. A place to raise a family, to hang pictures on the wall, to put up a Christmas tree each year. He even wondered what it would be like to own a dog or cat.

Inside, he changed into khaki shorts and a moisture-wicking button-down. Casual wasn't exactly his strong suit. He attempted to muss his hair, but after glancing in the mirror, he quickly changed his mind and brushed it back into style. There was a place for everything and everything in its place - including his hair. After grabbing the gift bag for the dog, he headed toward the west end to Hana's house.

When Hana the doorbell rang, Hana hesitated before answering it. Was she ready for this? Dating two guys? Chas had been the one ready to fight for her. The look of bloodlust on his face when she told him about Pace was both sexy and a little scary.

She answered the door and Chas stared at her, his mouth slightly agape. "You look amazing."

Knowing she must be blushing, she covered her face with her hands. "Hello to you, too. And thanks, but I'm not exactly dressed to the nines." She stood back so he could enter the house.

As he turned to face her again, she pulled her hair back and secured it with a ponytail holder. His expression was one of pure amazement and she wasn't sure why. It made her feel a little self-conscious and she looked down. It was then she noticed the gift bag in his hand.

"Oh, um, I got a gift. But it's not for you." He held up the expertly wrapped gift bag.

She felt the smile melt off her face as she knit her brows together. "You brought a gift but I can't have it?" Who was it for if it wasn't for her? Why would he bring it to her house?

Flustered, Chas shook his head. "No. It's for Lulu. I got Lulu a gift. A few actually." He handed the bag to Hana.

He had gotten her dog a gift? Hana was blown away. She quickly sat down and called to Lulu. "Look here, Lulu. Chas got you a present. Let's open it."

She tossed the tissue paper to the side and dug into the bag. She pulled out an adorable doggie dress and a matching collar with a bow. Then came a toy taco. Lulu immediately went into play mode and bowed down, wagging her tail.

"Oh, you like the taco, huh? Here you go." She tossed the toy across the room and Lulu ran after it, picking it up in her mouth. She carried it back, looking quite proud of herself. "Oh, Chas, this is so sweet, really. Thank you so much."

He stuffed his hands into his pockets and shrugged. "It's no problem. I thought she might like them. And you, maybe."

Hana rose up and kissed Chas on the cheek. He blushed the way a ten-year-old boy would and she thought it was completely adorable. For such a strong businessman, he really was shy in the romance department.

She took his arm and looked from Lulu to him. "Why don't we let Lulu stay here to play with her new toy? We can walk along Falls Park on our own." She winked at him and checked that Lulu had some water before grabbing her phone and depositing it in her pocket.

Lulu was going to be a bit of a buffer between them since Hana was nervous about their first official date. But the nerves had melted away as soon as she opened the door for him. Chas was a gentleman to the core and the gift for Lulu had been that extra little something that earned him brownie points.

After they parked in a street-side garage, Chas was at her door to open it for her within seconds. It reminded Hana of her parents. Her father always opened the door for her mother and the act of chivalry was one that Hana always loved to see. He held out his hand for her to help her out of his car.

"Thank you so much." She knew she blushed a little but didn't try to hide it.

Chapter 13

Never in a million years did Hana think she would be on a date with someone who had been named the bachelor of the year before. Chas was a perfect gentleman, opening doors for her, always watching out for her, interested in every word that came from her mouth. It was endearing, but also a little too much at times.

"What do you like to do for fun?" She stopped as they approached the suspension bridge over the Reedy River Falls. "So far you've asked me all about my family, my publishing journey, my interests. What about you?"

He stopped next to her and put his hands in the pockets of his pressed shorts. "I really don't. I've taken dates to events before, but I've never really dated anyone seriously And I don't go out for fun very often. The last time was probably in college."

Giving him a side-eye, Hana took a guess. "Frat boy? I'm thinking not AGR..."

Chas leaned against a railing next to her. "Frat boy? Yes. Of course. Pi Kappa Alpha legacy. I was president my senior year."

He didn't seem surprised that she had pegged him as having been in a fraternity. Chas looked quite proud to have been the president of his chapter, and from what Hana knew, presiding over things was what made Chas Rossi tick.

"And you went to Clemson?"

He nodded. "I did. As did my father and my grandfather. Go Tigers."

Hana continued walking and Chas followed. "Did your sister go there?"

Shaking his head, Chas said she had gone to Converse College like their mother. Apparently, family legacy meant a lot to the Rossi clan. They talked about their experiences in college. Some were similar, and others were wildly different. Hana hadn't been in a sorority and she didn't attend mixers. That was all Chas knew outside of football and classes. Hana had been in literary societies and book clubs and knew the library inside and out.

Digging deeper, Hana wanted to know about Chas's life decisions. "What did your parents think when you followed in your father's footsteps? I bet they were proud."

The snort that came from him was quite audible. "What did they think? Do you mean what did they plan? I was told I would be a business major. I was told I would then double up and take my real estate classes along with my regular coursework. There was no choice for me." He shook his head.

"What?" Jaw dropped, Hana could hardly believe her ears.

"My life has been planned out from the moment the doctor told my parents 'It's a boy.'" His deep eyes met her own and Hana reached out to touch his arm.

"I can't imagine, Chas. I'm sorry they've dictated your life." Her voice was soft, barely audible.

"It's okay. They're wonderful parents. Really they are. I've had everything I ever wanted. The very best of everything. And everything they did, it's because they thought it was the best." He rubbed his eye briefly and Hana worried the conversation was making him emotional.

She linked her arm through his as they crossed back off the bridge onto solid ground. "What would you have been if you had been given more autonomy?"

He turned to face her. "That's just it. I don't know. Probably exactly what I'm doing now. But maybe I'd be happier about it. maybe I wouldn't have pushed myself too hard and I would have done more for myself by this point. That's why..." He trailed off.

"That's why? What?" She laughed nervously.

The smile he gave her was dazzling. "That's why I'm doing this now. I'm not considering my parents first. I'm doing what makes me happy. And that's you, Hana."

He pulled her close and she accepted his embrace. He smelled like expensive cologne – leather and sandalwood – mixed with something that left her feeling heady and almost intoxicated. Chas wasn't perfect, not by a long shot, but he was showing her his vulnerabilities and his hang-ups, and that was honesty Hana appreciated.

After that, the topic changed to a more pleasant one. At least, more pleasant for Hana. They talked about Lulu and how Hana had gotten her. They talked about how Chas had always wanted a cat but his sister was allergic. Once he was on his own, it had never happened.

"You know, there are cats at Soft Paws who would love to be your companion." Hana tugged his sleeve thinking they could go to Soft Paws right that moment.

"You know McCoy and I don't get along. Why would you suggest I go there?" Chas scowled and shook his head.

"Because it's not about you and Pace. Or me. It's about a sweet kitten that needs a loving home. And I happen to know that there's a litter of five kittens ready to go." Hana bit her lip as she looked to him.

He crossed his arms. "I'm not home much."

She inched closer to him and smiled. "Cats don't need constant attention like dogs do." She hopped a little as he considered her words, shaking her shoulders and grinning like a, well, like a Cheshire Cat.

"I'll think about it." With that, he lowered his head and kissed her softly on the temple.

It was an innocent enough gesture, one some might see as absentminded. But Hana read into it. The intimacy, the comfort, the trust. It was all there, in Chas's simple kiss. And it made Hana's stomach knot up and take flight as if a hundred butterflies had suddenly broken free of their chrysalises.

The rest of the afternoon passed quickly. Too quickly for Hana's taste. But she had promised to go to dinner at her parent's house to honor Jenna and her upcoming wedding. Chas drove her home, seeming disappointed at the end of their date. But he remained a gentleman through and through, even walking her to her door and planting a chaste kiss on her cheek before retreating to his car.

❧ ✿ ☙

When his phone rang, Pace answered it without looking at the name on the screen. "Hello?" There was a pencil in his mouth, so it came out more garbled than he had planned. He removed the pencil and continued punching numbers into the computer so he could make his order the next day from his supplier.

"Pace?" A familiar feminine voice filled his head and made him stop mid-entry.

"Hana? Hi." Why did his palms feel sweaty and his knee start bouncing?

She stammered a moment. "I, um, well. You're going with me to my sister's wedding and I thought maybe you would want to join us for dinner? It's okay if you can't. I know it's short notice - we're eating in about an hour. More Korean food, though."

Standing, Pace ran his fingers through his hair and stretched his shoulders. Was she inviting him to meet her family? "This is a family dinner?"

"Oh, um, it is. Again, you don't have to come with me. But I thought it might be nice to meet everyone now before they bombard you at the wedding." She laughed and Pace thought he would do anything to keep that laugh going.

Did he want to meet her entire family? He supposed he would anyway at the sister's wedding, which was coming up quickly. Then Pace wondered why Hana invited him and not Chas. Shaking his head, it didn't matter.

"You know what? Sure. I would love to." Truthfully, the thought scared him half to death. Meeting parents and siblings? That was terrifying. But if Hana had invited him, he wanted to go. "I should probably change first. Do you want me to pick you up?"

"I'll pick you up, that way you don't have to rush. But we're casual. I know they'll really love you." A sharp inhale came through the phone.

"Hana? You okay?"

There was a pause before she answered. "Oh, yes. I'm sorry. I just. I don't want to pressure you or anything."

She was so dang sweet, Pace felt like a moon-eyed teenager. "You're not. Promise. I'm at 319 Urban Way." He was sure she could hear his little dance through the phone.

"See you in a bit." With that, she hung up.

Pace shut his computer down. Ordering could wait until the next day. "Come on, Moses. Let's hurry home." Moses stood and stretched, his tail wagging. "I'm excited, too. But you're not seeing Lulu today."

Within forty minutes, Pace had raced home, changed clothes three times before settling on a blue gingham button-down and his favorite jeans. He wet and combed his hair, but it sprung up even curlier than usual. When a knock sounded at his door, he shrugged at himself in the mirror.

He met Hana outside and realized they matched. She was wearing a knee-length dress that perfectly matched his shirt. "Did I tell you I was wearing this shade of blue and not realize it?"

Hana laughed. "Wow. I promise I wasn't spying on you. But we look awfully cute together." She pulled out her phone and cozied up to him. "Smile."

His arm wrapped around her instinctively and she snapped a photo of them together. He watched as she looked at the photo then at him. Her eyebrows raised and she grinned wide. Pace thought she looked incredibly happy and he realized he was as well.

"Ready? Want me to drive?" He grabbed his keys from his pocket.

"You don't know where you're going. I'll drive." Her keys were on a bracelet around her wrist, which she lifted and jingled. "And that way you're captive and can't run away." A sassy wink came his way and she giggled.

At her parent's house, Pace was quickly put at ease by her family. They were casual and relaxed, even with the extra person thrown into the mix. There had been a little trepidation about going to a family night, but Hana had either prepared them well or they were truly a relaxed family.

"McCoy, right? Is your father Gerry?" Hana's father Mark invited Pace to sit on the couch.

"Yes, sir. He sure is." Pace hoped that was good.

Nodding, Mark pursed his lips. "I've met him a handful of times over the years. Stand up man, your father. And a great Christian family."

"Oh, yes, Hana mentioned that you are a deacon at your church." A lump formed in Pace's throat. He wasn't a regular church-goer and he knew where this line of questioning was going.

Hana came to the rescue at that moment. "Pace, come meet Will, my sister's fiancé."

All too eager to avoid the firing line, Pace stood. "Excuse me, Mr. Willis."

Nodding, Mark gave him the go-ahead. "Call me Mark. We'll chat later."

Hana leaned into him. "You looked like you needed saving. Sorry."

"Don't be. He cares about you and who you're around. That's a good dad." He avoided looking back at Mark, though.

They chatted with Jenna and Will for a few minutes before Min said dinner was ready and they all went to the dining room table. Enough food to feed an army was laid out and Pace was introduced to Alex and Nari, Hana's other two siblings who had been in the kitchen helping out.

After a prayer, food was passed around the table and conversation flowed. Pace ate food he had never seen before and he loved every bite. The mix of Korean food with traditional American fare gave him an odd level of comfort as the flavors melded and mixed on his plate.

Hana's father Mark had an easy smile and looked like a wonderful family man. He was a down-to-earth guy who clearly loved his family. He doted on Hana's mother, winking at her and finding ways to gently touch her arm or her shoulder. They sat side-by-side, unlike Pace's parents who had to be at the heads of the table. Here it seemed people grabbed whatever spot they wanted. On this occasion, Nari sat at one head and Will at the other.

He looked to Hana as she laughed at something her brother said and he wondered if she was the one he would spend his life with. Then he blinked a few times as his entire body froze. The thought surprised him and scared him. But the frozen feeling melted and turned into a spreading warmth. He wanted to reach out to her and take her hand, but he refrained. He wasn't sure what was going on between them, but he was willing to give it a shot.

Realizing there was no time like the present, he went ahead and reached his hand out under the table and took hers. Her small hand fit snugly into his and without looking at him, she turned her hand and entwined her fingers with his. Not sure what she was feeling, Pace's mind was screaming for him to kiss her. Clearly, this was not the right time, but he took her easy acceptance of his hand as a good sign.

"Hana, Jenna, you get to help clean up since Alex and Nari cooked." Min placed her napkin on her plate and nodded at her oldest two children.

Without hesitation, Jenna stood and began gathering plates.

Hana turned to Pace, bit her lip, and squeezed his hand, running her other hand over the back of his fingers. "I'll be back in a few minutes. I promise they won't bite." She stood and released his hand, grabbing half-empty bowls of noodles and chicken.

"We do bite." This came from Alex, who was snickering as he put his plate on top of another. "It depends on how much we like you if we bite hard."

Nari burst into laughter. "Yeah, the more we like you, the harder we bite." She placed her hand in front of her mouth as her eyes crinkled, the same way Hana's did. Nari was a younger carbon copy of her sister.

"You don't scare him like that, Nari." Min scolded her youngest child. "Why don't you go text someone?"

Happy with the excuse to get up, Nari jumped from the table and pulled her phone from her pocket, wandering from the room. Alex followed suit.

Across the table, Will shook his head. "They've never bitten me. They must hate me."

Will was a tall guy with straight hair pulled into a low ponytail. His face was clean-shaven though. Hana said he was a business manager somewhere, but Pace forgot where. Still, he was a nice guy who was easy to talk to and seemed to fit right in with the Willis family.

When the suggestion of a game night was made, Hana politely turned down the offer, saying she had deadlines to meet and articles to write. They said their goodbyes and left.

The ride home was silent, but when they pulled into Pace's parking lot, Hana turned to him.

"Are you scared off yet?"

"Do you want me to be scared off?" Pace unbuckled his seatbelt and turned in his seat to face her.

She shook her head. "No, I don't. When, when you took my hand under the table, I wanted to kiss you." In the darkening light, Pace could still see her turn pink.

It was time to take advantage of the opportunity. Pace leaned in, placed his hand on Hana's cheek, and pulled her close. He placed his lips on hers, tasting the exotic spices still on her lips. They spurred him into deepening the kiss and Hana responded by leaning in closer.

Pace didn't know what this thing between them was, but he was completely smitten and needed to know where it would end up. His heart might end up broken, but it was worth the risk. Without saying anything, he threw his hat into the ring with Chas's. He was going to fight.

Trying to win Hana's heart didn't mean Chas was going to stop also trying to win clients. If anything, it meant he was going to be trying harder. He wanted to make sure he spoiled her like the princess she was.

He strode into the office bright and early, ready to tackle the day. He whistled as he passed Barbara's desk. "You are quite chipper this morning, Chas." She winked at him.

"I feel it." He took the messages she handed him. He didn't need her to take the messages anymore with the invention of voicemail, but it lent a more personal touch that clients seemed to appreciate. They liked to talk to a person, not a recording. And Barbara was like an aunt to him, he liked keeping her employed.

"You have to get fitted for your tux today since you didn't get to the rental shop last week." Her keeping tabs on him reminded him of an aunt as well.

He had forgotten about the tux fitting for his friend's wedding. Chas owned a tuxedo, but this was a specific design, so he had to rent one that had been worn a hundred times before. The notion grossed Chas out completely. He was reminded that he needed a date for his old friend's wedding as well since Hana couldn't go with him. But whoever he took would have to know it was just for the night, nothing else.

"Barbara, is your niece still in town? The pretty blonde?" He leaned on her desk and flashed his teeth.

"Baylie? Yes, she's here all summer. I thought you were going after my favorite author." Hands to heart, Barbara batted her eyelashes and sighed.

"I am, but she can't go to my friend's wedding next weekend and I need a date. Free food, fun dancing. Maybe one of the other groomsmen will like her." He winked.

"My Baylie doesn't go home with random guys, Chas!" His secretary looked shocked.

"Oh, no, I didn't mean that." Chas tried to cover his tracks. He didn't mean to insinuate that Baylie was loose. "I meant she might meet the love of her life at this wedding. I'll even throw in fifty dollars for a new dress."

After tsking him momentarily, Barbara pulled her phone from her desk drawer. "I'll text her. I'm sure she would love to be seen on your arm. Greenville's most eligible bachelor." She giggled a little and her fingers flew over her phone.

In his office, Chas left the door open and sat at his desk. No sooner had he opened his computer when Barbara hollered at him. "Baylie said she can go. She's excited and understands it's a one-time date."

Leave it to Barbara to announce that to the entire building full of co-workers. He shook his head but smiled anyway. Barbara was like family, he could never stay mad at her. And they were all used to her meddling antics.

An hour later, Chas was preparing to meet clients at a potential home when the intercom crackled on his desk. "Sir. A young lady to see you."

He pressed the button, feeling like he was on an episode of Mad Men. "Can you see if Jason can talk to her? I'm getting ready to head out." He stood and shuffled through some papers.

"I think you want to see this one." The familiar giggle of Barbara's came through the door after she cut off the intercom.

Without warning, the door flung open and Hana came in, eyes wide. "Chas. I have to know something."

Chas blinked. She stood there in a pair of scalloped shorts and a frilly tank top, her chest heaving. "Hana?"

But before he could ask anything else, she crossed to him, wrapped her arms around his neck, and kissed him.

Not one to turn down such a passionate outburst from a woman he really liked, Chas kissed her back. If they had been outside, Chas was sure fireworks would have exploded around them. He pulled her closer and she molded herself to him.

After they stopped to breathe, Hana moaned a little. "Okay, that's what I needed to know." She stepped back from him.

The emptiness he felt without her in his arms was immediate. Chas felt the cold air rush around him and he actually shivered. "I am so confused."

She blushed and looked down at her feet. "I'm so sorry. I shouldn't have done that. But I like you so much, I needed to make sure that spark was there to go along with it."

Well, now he was intrigued. He crossed his arms and raised his eyebrows. "And?"

She laughed and it sounded like a golden melody in the air. "And it's there. It's confusing, but... Whoa, is it there."

"Good." He stepped to her again and kissed her lightly on the lips. "I would invite you to stay, but I'm about to head out."

"I can't stay. I have a meeting and this was on the way. I just... I had to stop." She tucked her hair behind her ear.

"I'm glad you did." He kissed her nose this time. He could get used to kissing her all the time. "Can I call you later?"

"Absolutely."

Chas placed his hand on the small of her back where it fit perfectly. "I'll walk you out."

It didn't escape his notice that Barbara winked at him as they passed her desk. "Goodbye, Barbara. I'll be back later."

Chapter 19

"I can't believe my baby sister is getting married tomorrow." Hana hugged her sister close. They were less than two years apart in age and had always been together. They had done dance classes, Girl Scouts, and gone shopping together their entire lives.

Not only was Jenna getting married, but she was moving away after the wedding. Will had a job in Chattanooga that would be starting two weeks after their wedding. They would honeymoon in Jamaica for a week, then spend a week packing and moving. While Chattanooga wasn't too far, it wasn't down the road anymore and Hana was bereft.

"Oh, Hannie. Don't start. Now you can pick one of your mega-hunks and settle down." Jenna turned to the mirror and blended her make-up expertly.

Hana was a dunce when it came to make-up. A little mascara and lip gloss were all she usually did. But Jenna had insisted on making her over for the rehearsal. Hana felt like she had ten pounds of make-up on her face, but if Jenna was happy she would endure.

"It's not about picking a hunk, Jen. Though they are both hunky." She furrowed her brow, picturing both Pace and

Chas in her mind. "I want to have a real connection with someone. I want to fall in love one time in my life." She looked at her reflection and puckered her lips before sighing.

Why did it feel like she was falling for two separate men? After kissing Pace in the car, Hana felt like she was melting into her seat. His hands were strong, his touch demanding without being rough. Hana felt butterflies and fireworks and all those giddy feelings. She thought surely the same wouldn't happen with Chas, so she had gone to his office and kissed him as well. Same butterflies. Same fireworks. Same hunger for more.

She knew it was attraction. Animal magnetism. She knew it was endorphins and adrenaline running through her veins. As a writer, Hana knew what lust was. But she didn't want lust. She wanted sparks that sizzled forever. The problem was she could easily envision that with both of the men who were tugging her heart in different directions.

"Hannie? Hello?"

Snapping out of her thoughts, Hana shook her head. Absently, she looked at her sister. "I'm sorry, Jenna. What?"

"You used to always get on me about daydreaming over boys. Now look at you. You're just ten years later than me." Jenna playfully batted at her sister. "I said the groomsman who is walking you down the aisle had something to be at tonight so he won't be here. Dad is going to stand in for him."

She nodded and shrugged. She hoped the groomsman wouldn't make a complete fool of her by not knowing what to do going down the aisle. But these were supposed to be college-educated men, Hana reasoned.

"What's the guy's name?"

"Will calls him Ace. I think it's a nickname, but I honestly don't know what for." Jenna tugged on her dress one last time. "Let's roll. I need to practice getting married."

The rehearsal went off without a hitch. The dinner was excellent, a mishmash of American, Korean, and Hispanic dishes stretched out across the length of Min's large room. Will's father was from Mexico and his mother was from Puerto Rico. Jenna said she was attracted to Will at first because she knew they would have beautiful children. Of that, Hana had no doubt.

After sleeping like a log, Hana woke up ready to go. When it was time to head to the hairdresser's place, Hana kissed Lulu goodbye and took off, knowing she would do everything she could to help her sister have a great wedding day.

Before throwing her dress on, Hana helped her sister wriggle into her giant marshmallow-like ball of a dress. Jenna was nothing if not a princess. The bejeweled sweetheart neckline gave way to more white tulle than Hana had ever seen. Risking messing her hair, she climbed under her sister's skirts to help straighten every layer as smooth as possible.

As she climbed out from under the oppressive dress, the coordinator came in announcing it was five minutes to showtime. She looked at Hana and shrieked. "You're not dressed! What happened to your hair?" She grabbed Hana's hanging dress and thrust it at her, "Put this on now while I find bobby pins!"

Hana pulled the dress over her head, further messing up her hair, and shrugged out of her maxi dress. Her mother zipped up the teal A-line dress as the harried coordinator came back with the hairdresser.

"We're supposed to be fussing over the bride, not the sister." The stern-lipped coordinator rolled her eyes at Hana and turned her attention to Jenna.

Hana turned so the stylist could fix her hair. "Sorry." She toyed with the groom's ring that she stuck on her thumb upon finding it sitting unattended. She would need to hand it to her younger sister before they went down the aisle.

Jenna took her hand and gave it a squeeze. "It's okay, Hannie. No biggie. A pin and some hairspray and you'll be fine. I saw Pace out there, he won't mind anyway." Jenna winked at her.

"Okay, it's go time, everyone else is in line." The coordinator barked orders to everyone. She hurried Hana into her place and gave everyone a last look-over.

Hana hardly paid attention to the man beside her until she offered her arm to him. "Sorry, I'm Jenna's sister, Hana."

"I know." She knew that voice. "Well, I knew you were Hana, I didn't know you were her sister."

Chas Rossi! The Ace of Will's fraternity, her absent escort, was Chas. "I – how – I don't..."

"I was thinking the same thing. I guess we should have compared bridal couple names when saying we both had weddings to go to. So you're the bride's sister?"

The music fired up and they were instructed to step forward. The coordinator dared anyone to speak with a flare of her nostrils. As they passed her, Hana whispered through a forced grin. "I am. How do you know Will?" She spotted Pace in the crowd, and his face fell to a scowl upon seeing her next to Chas.

"Will and I are old frat buddies."

"All Jenna knew was that you were called Ace." Hana wanted to shake her head in disbelief, but then the photographer snapped their picture. At least she was smiling.

"That's me. Um, did you bring a date?"

How long was this aisle? It felt like it stretched for miles. Hana was missing seeing her cousins and family. She answered honestly, "I did. You?"

"Yep." And then they parted ways, Hana going to stand on her sister's side, Chas going to the groom's side.

Hana watched as her sister and father made their way down the aisle. Tears escaped from the corners of her eyes and she had to blot them away as their father kissed Jenna on the cheek, whispered something, then kissed her again on the forehead. He placed her hand in Will's and stepped back. Hana kept her eyes on her father and she saw the pride and pain that step back caused. He would no longer be the main man in Jenna's life. Will Diaz would now take residence in that spot, and the idea nearly broke Hana's heart.

As the pastor spoke, Hana allowed her mind to wander. She looked out into the crowd at Pace. Their eyes met and Pace's expression turned happy and he raised his hand in a little wave. Knowing she could not wave back, Hana gave her flowers a little shake and raised her eyebrows to him. It must have struck him as funny because he hid his face in the program.

That caused Hana to risk a glance at Chas, only to find him not looking at the couple being married, but at her. Embarrassed, she gave him a weak attempt at a smile and wondered if he had seen her looking at Pace. He looked pleasantly back, but then he peered out into the crowd right where Pace was sitting. Chas's head cocked to the side a moment, but then he straightened up again and looked out onto the groom's side of the congregation. Hana assumed he was looking at his own date.

The pastor cleared his throat brought her back to attention. "The ring?" Nari was the maid of honor and she stood looking perplexed. Nari turned to Hana with alarm in her eyes.

Hana pulled Will's ring off her thumb and handed it to Nari. She had forgotten all about it. Nari blushed madly and quickly handed the ring to their pastor, who continued with the ceremony without missing a beat. Nari mouthed thanks to Hana who shrugged and crinkled her nose.

Within moments Jenna and Will were pronounced Mr. and Mrs. Diaz and with a kiss and many cheers they were married. Hana was again faced with Chas who offered her his arm and a warm expression.

"Always there to save the day, huh?"

A sigh of relief came from her lips. "I'm just glad I grabbed the ring when I saw it, otherwise it would still be sitting in our dressing room."

Outside, Hana and the rest of the bridal party waited to be called back into the church for the plethora of pictures that were to come. As she laughed over the forgotten wedding ring with others, Pace approached her.

And as he approached, Chas stepped up to her other side. She saw Pace glance above her, presumably at Chas, then as natural as could be he embraced her and kissed her cheek. It was a power play move, she knew. Pace hadn't expected Chas to be at the wedding. She would have to explain that she hadn't expected it either.

"Rossi." The look on Pace's face was pure possession. Over her. His shadowed jawline was tight and his grip around her shoulders was growing tighter.

Puffing his chest, Chas nodded. "McCoy, I wasn't expecting to see you."

Hana could hear alarm bells ringing in her head. She would not allow them to ruin her sister's day.

The coordinator was barking orders as everyone came into the reception site and Chas did not appreciate her demeanor. "Where is the bride's sister? We are behind schedule."

He looked around and spotted Hana approaching them. "There she is. Hana, over here!" He gestured to her and she quickened her step, flowers in hand.

She took her place by his side without a word or glance to Pace McCoy. He should have known she would bring him. It hadn't occurred to him before then, but of course she would take the other guy she was interested in. Tugging on his tux jacket, Chas resolved to remain gentlemanly regardless.

Each couple that was introduced did a funny dance like people used to do on the 70s show Soul Train. Chas quickly turned his thoughts to a routine for them. "Hana, I have a plan, just go along with it when they introduce us."

"What do you mean?" Her eyes widened as if in panic, but there was no time to explain.

The deejay's voice boomed into the microphone. "Next up we have bridesmaid and bride's sister Hana Willis being escorted by groomsman Chas 'Ace' Rossi."

Before she could protest, Chas hoisted her up on his shoulder and held her by the knees. Hana screeched in surprise but stayed steady as he spun her around and the DJ played an up-tempo song.

"Looks like she's being carried in, not escorted, folks! Look at that." The deejay began to laugh and the crowd soon joined in, clapping to the beat.

Hana began to laugh along with the DJ and gave a loud whoop as the crowd cheered. Then the attention was turned to the maid of honor and best man and Chas stopped his dance moves. He moved to a quiet corner to help Hana off his shoulder.

Suddenly, she grabbed his head with her hands and squeezed her athletic legs over his shoulders. "How do I get down? I'm stuck!"

"You're not stuck. Hang on, I'll get you." Chas wondered how to get her down with her dignity still attached. The last time he had done this to a girl was in college, where he unceremoniously dumped her on a couch.

A chair appeared beside him with Pace McCoy at the other end of it. "Take my hands, Hana. You can slide off."

"I got her, McCoy, don't sweat it." Chas jerked to the left and Hana screeched again.

"I just want to get down." Hana's voice shook as she held Chas tighter.

A few seconds later she reached her hands out to Pace McCoy and she slid down with her eyes closed, landing gently on the chair.

"Are you okay?" Pace drew her in under his shoulder and Chas saw red.

"I'm fine. Thank you so much." She heaved a huge breath before turning to Chas. "That was so much fun, Chas! I've never made such an entrance before!"

Before he could reply, she turned back to McCoy, her date. "Jenna's coming! Come on, Pace, I want to see her." She took his hand and jumped off the chair then ran back to the dance floor in time to see the newlyweds run into the waiting crowd.

Chas went back to his own date, Baylie. She was young and blonde, a sweet girl who was as clueless as they come. Not serious relationship material. She was, however, fun evening material and he intended to have fun at this wedding. Especially if he had to watch Pace McCoy getting up close and personal with Hana.

Pace looked over to the girl he had seen following Chas around. She was a cute little blonde who resembled all the cheerleaders his classmate had dated back in school. She looked like she could still be in school. She was too busy taking selfies to notice the exchange between her date and Hana. Not a serious relationship, then, Chas was too competitive to back down from Hana anyway.

He watched as Hana went over to her younger sister. She smiled, but her eyes were still wrinkled with irritation. Soon they were called back for more pictures. Pace didn't mind waiting. He liked to people watch, especially when the person was Hana.

During the dinner, Pace noticed Will had tattoos on his arm. He hadn't seen them when they had eaten dinner together. He pointed them out to Hana.

"Oh, yeah, Dad doesn't like them, but Jenna thought they were hot." She laughed as a waiter refilled her glass of sweet tea.

A thought came to him. "What do you think of mine?" He smirked and reached out a hand to play with one of her long, loose curls.

A giggle erupted from her and the scent of orange and vanilla wafted up to his nose. "I like them. When I first saw them at Palmetto Magic I thought they were perfect on a gruff bartender. Do you have more?" Her eyes sparkled as they roved over his body looking for clues.

Pace had to admit, he liked her looking at him as a piece of meat to be devoured. He leaned in close and whispered in her ear. "Aside from the sleeve, I have a few. But you'll have to wait to find out where they are. They're not easily found in a suit."

The shudder that ran through Hana could be felt from where he was, inches away. He had to admit to liking her reaction to him.

"I've been thinking about getting one, actually." Her hand gently came to rest on his knee. "But I'm a big wuss."

Without thinking, he put his hand on top of hers. "I'll go with you and hold your hand if you'd like."

She looked at him, her eyes considering his words carefully. Slowly, she nodded. "I would like that very much."

"What kind of tattoo do you want?" His finger trailed up her arm, causing goosebumps to appear.

She inhaled sharply. "Something book related I think." Her dark eyes stared into his.

Their exchange of words was somehow intimate even though they were innocent enough. He turned her arm over and traced the vein that ran up to her elbow. "Where would you put it?"

"Anywh—"

"Hana! Come on!" A call broke their spell. Nari was calling to her and Hana blinked several times.

A shy smile was cast his way. "Duty calls. I'll be back." She squeezed his hand and got up to join her sister.

Within seconds, Chas sidled up to him. "You're not going to win."

With a roll of his eyes, Pace growled. "Hana is not a trophy to be won, Rossi. And you cannot win if I'm not competing with you."

Chas scoffed at him. 'What do you call this then?"

Pace stood so he was eye to eye with Chas. They were roughly the same height but with different builds. He would not pick a fight, even though he was sure he was stronger than pretty boy Rossi. And while they were both vying for the same girl, Pace refused to compete as if Hana was a race.

"I call this being out on a date with an astonishing lady. You appear to have your own date over there." He gestured to the table where the blonde girl sat waiting.

"Only because Hana couldn't go with me. We didn't realize we were going to the same wedding." Chas rolled his shoulders back and stuck out his neck.

Shaking his head, Pace chuckled. "Again, Chas, do you want Hana, or do you want to win? Because I don't care about winning or losing to you. I just care about spending time with the girl I enjoy kissing."

Yes, it was a dig, but Pace didn't care. Chas needed to get out of his face before fists began to fly, and the last thing Pace wanted to do was cause a scene and make Hana upset. Both of them tightened their fists, but Pace knew he wouldn't be the first to throw a punch. He wanted to make sure Hana knew Chas had hit first.

Chapter 15

As Chas stepped forward, Pace prepared for a fist in his jaw. Before that could happen, though, Hana stepped between them. "Chas, I think Will needs you. Now." They all three stood staring for a moment, each looking at someone different.

"Now, please." Hana put her hand on Chas's chest and while she didn't push him, Pace could tell her arms were locked into position, keeping him at bay.

Relaxing, Chas readjusted his hair, fixed a teeth-baring grin to his face, and turned to see the groom. He sauntered off as if nothing was wrong.

"I didn't need you to save me." Pace scratched his beard and jammed his other hand in his pocket.

"I wasn't saving either of you." She looked at him, her eyes narrowed. "I was saving my sister's wedding from a fiasco. Now, you are my date and I would like to dance. Please."

After a cleansing breath, Pace nodded. He bowed to her and offered his hand, which she readily took. "I would be honored to escort you onto the dance floor, Miss Willis."

Her body was tense as they began to dance slowly around the floor. Pace wrapped his arms around her, pulling her closer. Softly, he began to sing along with the song and he could feel Hana's muscles relax.

"You're a great singer." She ran her fingernails over the back of his neck, causing shivers to run down his spine.

"Only if I whisper sing slow songs from twenty years ago." He chuckled, then sighed. "I'm sorry about that with Chas. I swear I had no intention of causing a scene."

The tension returned to her arms. "I'm glad I saw you when I did. When I see two men with fists, I'm not taking chances. And over what? Me? How ridiculous. I'm just your average American girl." Then tension traveled down her spine, her dance steps growing stiffer and stiffer.

Pace pulled her chin up so she was looking him in the eye. "Hana, don't you realize you're not just some average girl? You are kind to everyone, you love animals, your laughter could light a room." He knew he was gushing, but it didn't matter. He was completely smitten.

Whoa. He was completely smitten. The realization made him stand taller and pull her closer. He inhaled the scent that lingered over her.

She tried to lower her gaze, but he wouldn't let her, holding his finger firm under her chin. "Pace, that's so kind of you. I have to tell you, I think much the same of you. And you run the rescue and your own business. You're like the perfect dinner roll."

The perfect what? The quizzical look on his face must have said it without words because Hana laughed.

"The perfect dinner roll is firm and crisp on the outside. It protects the warm, soft center. That's you. Firm outside and soft inside." For effect, she squeezed his bicep. He flexed under her fingers. This time she did look away, but not before he caught her biting her lip.

The song ended and they returned to their seats. Pace offered to get Hana a Sprite from the bar and she happily agreed. As he walked across the reception room, he was stopped by Hana's brother, Alex.

"Did I see you and someone else ready to come to blows over there?" Alex's brow was furrowed and his arms crossed. He wasn't a large guy, but he was still intimidating.

Honesty was the best policy, so Pace nodded. "Yes, I'm sorry. We don't get along and didn't realize the other would be here tonight. I promise it won't happen again. I won't ruin your sister's wedding day."

Alex licked his lips and nodded. "That other guy, Chas, is the realtor, isn't he?" When Pace nodded, Alex shook his head. "I heard Hana say he was interested in her. If it makes any difference, I'll be lobbying for you. I've never seen her look so happy."

Pace followed Alex's gaze to Hana, who was now chatting with an older woman and laughing hysterically. The sight of her laughing made Pace's heart hammer in his chest and his mouth go dry. He scanned the room for Chas, who was now dancing with his date, but his eyes were glued to Hana as well.

"I better get her that Sprite." Pace scowled and walked away from Alex, who nodded in return. Pace didn't want to leave Hana alone any longer than he had to for fear that Chas would swoop in. But, he reminded himself, he was not going to fight dirty. He would have Hana choose him because she wanted him, not because he needed to win.

He returned, Sprite in hand, just as Chas had sat his date back down and turned toward Hana. Pace handed her the drink and put his arm on the small of her back, gently turning her away from Chas's direction.

"Did you have someone to let Moses out while you were gone? My next-door neighbor offered to let Lulu out for me. She's an older woman and Lulu loves her." Hana's eyes shone as she spoke.

He had completely forgotten about having someone care for Moses. He was a good dog and never had accidents in the apartment, but the poor boy still needed to go out. "Absolutely. I asked Emmie to let him out. I'll text her and make sure she remembered."

He pulled his phone from his pocket and fired off a text to Emmie begging her to walk Moses around the block really quick. Seconds later, a text came back with a thumbs-up emoji.

When he looked back up, Hana was chewing her lip and picking at her fingernails. "Pace, I know this is silly, but I would love to share a photo of the wedding on my social pages. It helps with reader engagement. Can I share a photo of the two of us? Or would that make you uncomfortable?"

A photo of them together on her social media? "What, um, what would you say? About me?"

She shrugged. "I guess that you're my date. I don't have to, though. I can maybe ask Alex to pose with me." She looked across the room for her brother.

Knowing Chas would be all too happy to pose with her if asked, Pace quickly agreed. "Of course, I would be honored. Can you mention Soft Paws? Or not. That's poor form."

She grabbed his arm. "Oh, no, it's not poor form at all. I love that idea."

A passing-by cousin was roped into taking a photo of them. Hana snuggled in close to Pace, her hand placed protectively over his chest. As if on instinct, Pace covered her hand with his and put his other around her waist. They beamed and the cousin took several shots with Hana's phone. With a nod, Hana accepted the phone back and looked through the pictures.

"Which one?" They peered at the pictures. The last one was excellent, but as she scrolled to the first photo taken, Pace nearly gasped. He was still looking at Hana in that one and the look in his eyes told him way more than his head knew. He looked like he adored her. And he did, but this photo said so much more.

Hana looked from the phone to Pace, an unspoken question in her eyes. "I'm saving this one." Her voice was barely a whisper. "I'm saving it for me."

His nod was barely perceivable. "Send it to me."

She inhaled and held her breath for a second before exhaling. "I think the last one would be good to post for the world to see."

He could only mumble his agreement before he leaned down and kissed her.

***

Chas clenched his jaw as he watched Pace lean down and kiss Hana. He flared his nostrils like a bull seeing red. He grabbed Baylie, who yelped a little but stood up from her seat. Without a word, Chas hauled her to the dance floor right in front of Hana and Pace.

If they wanted to put on a show, he could as well. He pulled the girl close so their bodies were pressed together. Baylie needed no prompting, she held her body against his and put her head on his shoulder.

Risking a glance, he saw Hana's jaw drop. Chas swore under his breath. He wanted to show Pace up, not make Hana think he was interested in the girl cozied up to him. He couldn't shove the girl off of him, so he gently tried to put some distance between their bodies.

Instead, she held on tighter. "Chas, you're such a great dancer." Baylie tilted her head up and batted her eyelashes. Her deep green eyes sought to meet his.

Pace pulled Hana away from the floor and they disappeared from sight. Chas felt panic rise in his throat. He couldn't lose her. Not over something stupid like a rivalry with McCoy.

"I'm sorry, Baylie, but I have to go. Give me a few minutes and I'll take you home." He left her standing on the floor as he took off after Hana and Pace.

Trying to be sneaky, he stopped to say hi to Will's parents. No sign of Hana by the food. Next, he clapped a fellow fraternity brother on the back. But before the guy could talk to him, Chas had wondered again. He saw a teal dress float out the back door. That had to be Hana.

He waited a minute and then snuck a look outside. There she was, her hands roving all over Pace, his face lowered to hers. Chas was disgusted and broken. Had she led him on all this time? Had he really lost her to Pace McCoy?

Dejected, Chas turned and leaned against the wall by the door, his eyes closed. He was a huge idiot for thinking he had a chance with someone like Hana Willis. She was smart and successful, kind to everyone, a perfect match for him. Why didn't she see that?

"Chas, have you seen my sister Nari? She looks just like me but younger and taller." Hana stood next to him, but was facing the room, scanning it for someone.

"How would I know? If you weren't so busy sucking Pace's face off, you wouldn't have lost her." As much as he wanted to turn around and punch the wall, he knew causing a scene wouldn't do anyone any good.

Now Hana did look at him, and it was not a pleasant expression. "Excuse me? I did no such thing. Yes, we kissed a bit ago, but I wouldn't call that sucking his face off." Her hands were on her hips as she glared at him.

"Don't lie to me. I just saw you outside, hands everywhere." He pointed to the door.

Hana was through it in an instant. "Nari! What are you doing?"

The couple was still outside kissing and now Hana was beside a pair of extremely embarrassed teenagers. Sure enough, Nari looked almost identical to Hana but was a shade paler and an inch taller.

She pulled Nari inside but stopped at Chas. "I want to talk to you and Pace together in just a minute, but first I need to take care of this one." She whipped her head around to her sister, who was bright red with tears swimming in her eyes. Again, she yanked on her sister's hand and they disappeared into the crowd.

It wasn't Hana that had been making out with someone. Chas felt instant relief until he realized he had completely messed up. Again. He was too good at putting his foot in his mouth. He had to apologize to Hana before she brushed him off for good.

He wondered if he could get Baylie back home before Hana wanted to talk to him. He should have never brought the girl as a date. But when Chas looked to where she had been sitting, she was gone. He spotted her red minidress on the dance floor with the bride's brother. He guessed that would also be Hana's brother. They were pressed close together, swaying to the music. Baylie laughed at something the guy said.

"I guess she's okay, then." He would never tell Barbara that her niece was being so brazen. But then again, Baylie was all of twenty-two and he remembered being more carefree at that age.

He sat and downed a glass of tea in one gulp. He could have used something stiffer, but he knew he needed to be responsible and he needed to be clear-headed to talk to Hana later. Pace was talking to an older couple who had to be Hana's parents. How did he know them? Had he met her parents? Why hadn't she introduced him to her parents?

When Baylie didn't come back to him after dancing with the brother, he sat by himself and watched the crowd. Then he pulled out his phone and answered a few emails. He was about to pull up the MLS when Hana approached him and folded her arms, looking at him expectantly.

He stood and pocketed his phone as if he had been caught by a teacher in class. Sweaty palms would not be good, so he tried to wipe them inconspicuously. "I am so sorry, Hana. I saw them outside and thought it was you. She looks like you, especially through a tinted door."

"I get that. And honestly, I'm glad you knew where she was because she did not need to be kissing that boy. But that's another matter." Hana huffed. "Right now, I need to talk to you and Pace." She turned on her heel and walked off to a quiet corner where Pace stood waiting.

Chas didn't know what was going on, but he had a feeling he would not like it one bit.

When they all stood within a few feet of each other, Hana looked from man to man. "First off, I need to say that I feel like I have missed out on my sister's entire wedding because I've been too busy watching you two. Now, that's not your fault. I didn't know Chas was in the wedding and you two had no way of knowing the other would be here."

She paused, trying to find the right words. Both Chas and Pace stood with hands in their pockets, stern looks on their faces. When Hana wrote love triangles they didn't go like this. She vowed to herself never to write one again because it wasn't fair to any of her characters.

"I can't do this anymore. No more fighting over me. No more. I have chosen." She took a deep breath.

"Hana, I—" Chas started.

"Stop, Chas. Just stop. I chose myself. I'm picking myself. I'm not desperate for love. I don't feel the pressure to get married and all that right now. So why am I torturing myself?" Tears pricked her eyes and she flexed her hands. "I really like you both, but this is also not fair to you two. Chas, you have a lovely date, who seems to have opted to dance with my brother because you're following me. And Pace, I haven't given you the proper attention a date deserves because I've been too busy trying to help Jenna and then trying to make sure you and Chas don't get into it."

"So you're not picking either of us?" Pace cocked his head to the side and rubbed his jaw.

"That's right. I'm afraid we're all losers in this war. You two are both fabulous men. You're both generous and kind and successful in your own ways. You're both like fairytale princes, a hero any woman would love to have. But this princess has to choose herself right now. I'm sorry."

Hana looked from Chas to Pace, hoping she wasn't making the biggest mistake of her life. But for her own sanity, she had to stop the nonsense. She had to untie the knot that had been in her stomach for weeks.

Without a word, Pace stepped forward, kissed her on the cheek, and backed away. He turned and walked off. When he pushed through the front door, phone to his ear, Hana turned to Chas.

Never one to be silent, Chas opened his mouth, closed it again, then huffed. "I made a fool of myself and I am sorry for it. I hope we can still be friends. You are a wonderful woman, Hana Willis." He nodded but didn't approach her before turning to walk toward his date. He spoke to Alex and the girl, who both nodded, and then he too disappeared into the night.

Hana sank into a nearby chair, her heart feeling broken and her mind too confused to think. This was nothing like the books she wrote with happy endings. This was heartache tenfold.

"You sent them both away." Jenna's voice came over her.

"I did. I said I couldn't do it and I had to choose myself." Hana wiped a stray tear as she looked up to her younger sister. "Am I a fool?"

Rubbing her back, Jenna made motherly noises. "No, sweetie. Not at all. In fact, I think you're the wisest person I've ever met. Choosing yourself is always the right thing to do."

"You look like an angel, Jenna. I love you."

Jenna sat and hugged her tight. "I'll always be your guardian angel, Hannie. Just remember to do what makes your heart happy, then everything will fall into place."

<h1 style="text-align:center">Chapter 16</h1>

It had been two weeks since Hana had decided not to pick either Chas or Pace. Her sister had loved on her for a few minutes before heading off on her honeymoon and now it was moving day for Jenna and Will. The family had gathered at Jenna's apartment with the moving truck full to the brim. Hana had managed not to cry over her sister's departure. She would save those tears for the quiet of her own home.

"Now, you have the recipe book I gave you so you can make bibimbap yourself?" Min fussed over her daughter, choosing to mother her instead of cry.

Jenna stopped, box in her arms, and a tender look crossed her face. "Umma, you know I can't cook. But I heard there's an excellent Korean restaurant close by."

Hana had to laugh. Their mother's love for traditional food and making that food had not been passed down to Jenna. Sure, she loved to eat it, but she was not a cook by any means. Neither was Hana for that matter, but she tried. The cooking genes had gone primarily to Alex and Nari.

When hugs were passed around, Will hugged Hana first. "You know, he misses you."

She knew Chas missed her. She missed him, too. But she would not let thoughts of Chas or Pace get in the way of saying goodbye to her sister. "I know. And I will miss you. And kind of hate you for taking my sister so far away."

"It's only a few hours. Come see us in the mountains." He laughed.

"We have mountains here." He pouted, but only for effect. Hana liked Will, he was a good guy who adored her sister. "Be safe."

He nodded and moved on to give Nari a hug.

Jenna had hugged everyone before finally coming to Hana. She willed herself not to cry as Jenna stretched out her arms to hug her. But the tears came anyway. They rolled down her cheeks, one after another. When a sob escaped, she let them flow freely. "I'm sorry. I didn't want to cry."

Pulling back, Jenna showed her her own wet, tear-streaked face. "I know. But we do it all together, don't we?"

"But you're leaving me now." Hana sniffled.

Jenna brushed tears from Hana's face. "I guess we all have to grow up sometime. I love you, Hannie."

"I love you too, Jennie."

Jenna kissed their mother one last time and hopped into the car she would be driving behind the moving van. She rolled the window down and waved as Will pulled onto the road ahead of her.

Beside her, Alex wrapped an arm around her shoulder, Nari on his other side. "One down, three to go." He patted them both and released them, shouting for pizza as he walked.

"It's his way of showing grief." Nari shook her head.

"Asking for pizza?" Hana laughed through her tears. She knew Alex would miss Jenna, but as a young man, he didn't show the way she and Nari did.

Back at her house, Hana decided to take Lulu for a walk around the neighborhood. She had avoided the dog park for the past few weeks, not wanting to run into Pace and Moses there. Lulu loved the attention of passers-by and especially enjoyed the little girl who had run into the road to meet her. Hana had started walking down the sidewalk in front of her house so the girl wouldn't run into the road again.

As they walked, Hana reflected on the last few weeks. She had broken up with both Pace and Chas, had her sister move away, and had missed a deadline with her publisher. Thankfully they had extended it for her. Again. But they wouldn't keep doing that. She was only as good as her last book and she needed to get another out before her name was forgotten.

She had a loyal fan base, but a good number of her books went to first-time readers. She knew she wasn't Mark Twain or Jane Austen or Maya Angelou. She would not go down in the annals of literature. But Hana was okay with that. She brought a smile to people's lips and an escape from their day-to-day, and that was her goal. To give them an alternate world to live in for a few days.

Resolved to finish the first draft of her new novel, Keeping the Keeper, within two weeks, Hana jogged Lulu home and opened her computer. This was where her research with Pace had come in. Of course, she had modeled the hero, Jackson, after Pace. Jackson was short on words, rugged, and outdoorsy. But then she had given him a few very Chas-like qualities as well. He was a perfectionist, generous, and had great hair.

It would be hard to finish, but she could do it. She had to. She grabbed a bag of cashews and got to work, losing herself in the words on the screen. Her heroine, Daphne, was about to march away from Jackson in disgust when Hana's phone rang.

Absently, she answered. "Hello?"

A man cleared his throat on the other end. "Sorry to call. But I don't know what to do with a kitten."

"Chas?" Did he say he had a kitten? They had talked about him getting one a few weeks before, but she couldn't see him going through with it.

"Sorry, yeah. I got a kitten this morning and I don't know what it needs. I am a little overwhelmed." The sound of a tiny kitten's mewls carried through the phone.

The cry was heart-wrenching. "How old is it?"

"I don't know. I got it from some woman online. She was giving them away and I thought why not. But it's really small and I'm in over my head." The utter panic in Chas's voice made Hana jump from her seat.

She couldn't leave him and that poor kitten struggling, so she closed her computer and told him she could be right over to help him. This had nothing to do with their attraction, she told herself. And everything to do with helping a friend and an innocent animal that might be too young to be away from its mother.

She hopped in the car and raced over to Chas's house.

Babying things was not in Chas's nature. He hadn't been around many human babies and even fewer animal babies. Yet still, he was now bouncing and rocking with a tiny orange kitten that had finally fallen asleep in his arms. It had been fun for about ten minutes after he got it home and then it went onto his rug and peed on it, then began to cry mercilessly for what seemed like hours. In reality, it was all of a few minutes. He knew because he had checked his phone.

All Chas could think was that he needed a carpet cleaner and earplugs. In a moment of panic, he called Hana and begged her to help. When she knocked on his door, he carefully opened it, still rocking and bouncing.

Hana's eyes were wide as she watched him move rhythmically while he opened the door. "What have we here?" Her voice was soft and high-pitched as she approached Chas. Well, the kitten.

"It's finally asleep, but I have no idea what to do with him. Or her? I don't even know." He felt heat rise on his face and he couldn't believe he was embarrassed that he didn't know how to care for a minuscule cat.

Eyes flitted from cat to human as Hana assessed the situation. "Well, let's start with what we have." She looked expectantly at Chas. When he didn't answer she asked again. "What do you have?"

"A cat." Wasn't that obvious?

Hands went to hips like lightning. "What else? Food? Water dish? Litter? Anything?"

"No. Should I order them on Amazon?" Chas already regretted the rash decision to bring home a cat without any preparation. It was so unlike him. That's what he got for trying to be spontaneous. A spoiled rug and a life depending on him for everything.

Shaking her head, Hana took the kitten from his arms. "No. You need these things. Now. Well, this morning before you decided to get a cat." She examined the tiny fluffball. "I'm not a cat expert, but I'd say he – or she – is about six weeks old. Just barely old enough to leave the mother. I would use a mix of formula and wet food for now, then change over to dry food in a while. You need a vet, too. But we can go to the store and get all the things you need for now."

The kitten woke up and immediately nuzzled into Hana's arms and meowed. It began purring and trying to suck on her finger.

With a look, Hana nodded to Chas. "You drive. Apparently, I'm a surrogate until you can get some real food." When she winced, she stopped him. "First, I might need some milk. Or half and half?"

Half and half was easily on hand, it was one of Chas's indulgences and thankfully wasn't flavored. Hana instructed him to put a little into a plastic cup and she carried it and the kitten to the car. Chas watched a moment as she dipped one finger into the thick liquid and it rolled down to the kitten's mouth. It suckled on her hand greedily. The poor thing was starving, Chas realized. He berated himself for not realizing he needed things right away.

"I'm sorry, Hana. Clearly, I was not ready for animal ownership." He drove to the pet store where he had purchased the gifts for that scruffy dog Lulu. "I can't thank you enough for coming to the rescue."

With the cup almost empty, Hana tapped out the last of it onto her hand. "You would have figured it out. And you'll be ready. Don't worry. Soon this little thing will adore you. I can't tell if it's a boy or a girl, though."

Chas had tried to figure it out himself earlier but had no idea what he was looking for, so the mystery remained.

Thirty minutes and way more money than he thought necessary later, Chas was ready for the world of cat ownership. Someone at the pet store said all orange kittens were boys, so Chas felt it was time to name the thing. Nothing came to mind, though.

"What should I call him?" He looked to Hana who was still cradling the kitten in her arm.

She looked at the kitten and tilted her head. "Well, there are a lot of famous orange cats you can name him after. Garfield, Morris, Hobbes." She looked to Chas.

With a shake of his head, he pulled into the driveway of his house. "No. I don't want something expected. I want unusual."

He could only guess what she was thinking because she was quiet as they brought the kitten and all his new accessories into the house. "I'm just going to get you set up, then I have to go. I am supposed to be working and am on a deadline." She eyed him as she put the kitten down on the floor.

Immediately, the cat pounced on a dust mote that floated through the air. He ran around awkwardly for a second before catching sight of his own tail and trying in vain to turn around to see it again. Chas chuckled and thought maybe he could get used to a companion after all.

After asking for directions to a bathroom, Hana carried a bag with her down the hall. Chas had thought she needed to use it, but now he was curious.

"What are you doing?"

"Setting up the litter box." She held up the bag as if that explained it. "Would you prefer somewhere else?"

The idea of cat litter in his bathroom made him feel ill, but he guessed it was the appropriate place for it. "Where else might it go?"

"Laundry room?" Her answer was nonchalant, as if everyone kept cat feces with their clean clothes.

With a rapid shake of his head, Chas agreed to the bathroom. It was better that way. Keep all toilet issues together in the same room. Maybe he needed to install a cat door to the bathroom?

The kitten leaped after Hana and followed her to the bathroom. The twelve-year-old inside him thought to name the kitten something bathroom-related, but he thought better of it. His mother would never get over him naming anything after something like that.

With the food and water set up in the kitchen, Chas was feeling rather proud of himself. He had gotten a kitten, and with help, had provided for its needs. After a few minutes, Hana reappeared, the kitten still hopping after her. Her phone was in her hands and Chas heard his phone ding for an incoming text message.

"I sent you the name of a local vet I recommend. She will treat you and not-Garfield just fine." She put her phone back in her pocket.

"Hopalong." Chas blurted the word out as Hana was opening her mouth.

She paused. "What?"

"His name. Hopalong. He was hopping after you like a frog. So I'll call him Hopalong." Chas grinned and looked down at the tiny kitten. The name suited him.

"Okay then. Well, you and Hopalong have a nice evening. I need to let Lulu out and get to work." She grabbed her keys from her bag, then looked at him with a sad expression. "It was nice to see you, Chas." There was hesitation in her voice and she stopped at the doorway.

Everything in his being wanted to tell her to stay. Everything told him to grab hold of her and not let go. But he didn't. He needed to respect her wishes. And maybe one day things would happen again. With Hana or someone else. He wasn't sure. But Chas knew the right person would come at the right time. He just hoped it would be Hana Willis.

"Goodbye, Hana. Thank you for helping." He stayed put and waved while she waved back and let herself out.

Chas scooped up the kitten and scratched his head. "Okay, Hopalong, it's me and you. Let me know if you need anything." Hopalong mewled and began purring in response.

⚬——— ᴡ ———⚬

Wallowing was not Pace's style. But his brother was excellent at it. After being dumped by Caroline, Trey had become proficient at drowning his sorrows to the point of needing to go to rehab. The family took turns sitting with him in the evenings, at the direction of the counselors on staff, to talk to him and remind him that he had a lot still to live for and that booze wasn't the way to solve his problems.

After owning a bar for a few years, Pace was used to people trying to drink their blues away. And he was used to knowing when to cut them off. The problem had been that Trey wasn't drinking at Palmetto Magic, he was drinking in his living room with nobody to cut him off. He had gone to rehab willingly for twenty-eight days to try to get dry.

A chessboard was set up in the common living area where a few residents watched television and one young lady read a book. They all looked perfectly normal to Pace, but then he knew that addiction knew no boundaries. He had sat at the chessboard so when Trey came in, he joined him at the small table.

Without a word, they began playing – Pace with white and Trey with black. They had learned to play when they were children at their grandfather's house. They were evenly matched and often played at home now as well. After a few moves, Trey made a noise as if he was annoyed.

"What's eating you?" Pace wasn't ahead of his brother, so it wasn't the game causing the scoff.

"Caroline hated chess. She hated everything I did. And now look at us. Two McCoy men who have had broken engagements. What's wrong with us?" Trey made his move, pushing his bishop diagonally across the board.

Pace hadn't thought about them both now having broken engagements. But Trey was correct. "I don't think there's anything wrong with us, Trey. I know Amanda wasn't the woman for me. And I hate to say it, but it looks like Caroline wasn't the one for you. There's someone out there for you, though." Pace moved his knight and hoped his words were comforting. It was something he would say to one of his patrons.

Another scoff came from Trey. "I guess you found your someone else with that writer girl?"

The game forgotten for the moment, Pace looked at his brother. "I haven't talked about it since it wasn't relevant to you, but no, actually. Hana and I broke up. Broke up? I don't know that we could break up since we weren't technically dating, but regardless. We're not seeing each other anymore. She chose herself over me and Chas Rossi." Shaking his head, Pace still couldn't believe what had happened.

It didn't help that Hana hadn't been in the bar, either, for the two weeks since the wedding. Pace missed seeing the joy in her eyes and having her ask him questions. He now thought of Sprite as Hana's drink and he felt a pang whenever someone ordered one. And then he felt stupid for feeling that way.

"Good for her." Trey made a move that Pace didn't pay attention to. "I think that's what Caroline did, too. And really, we all need to choose ourselves and do what's best for us."

Wise words from a man who had hit rock bottom. Pace nodded and looked at the chessboard. He didn't know what move to make next.

"Choose yourself, man. Nobody completes you except you." Trey had tears running down his cheeks, which surprised Pace. Trey wasn't a crier. "I was fired from the church and I think I'm done with traditional ministry. Dad will be so mad. I think...I think I'm going to become a counselor and work with people who have addiction."

Whoa. That was a big decision. Pace's eyes widened and he leaned forward, reaching his hand out toward his brother. "Are you sure, Trey? It's not an easy life. And Dad won't be upset. I think he'll be really proud of you."

Trey stretched and yawned. "I'm choosing me for once. Not what Dad wanted for me. Not what was expected. I'm going to do what I want to do, and I've wanted to do this for years. I told Caroline I didn't want to be a pastor anymore and that's why she left. She chose herself." With that, Trey picked up his King and tucked it in his pocket. He stood and walked off, giving a backward wave to Pace as he went.

Mouth agape, Pace sat still for a minute to see if Trey returned. He didn't. With no reason left to stay, Pace stood and left the center. In his car, he thought about what it would look like to choose himself and go after what he wanted.

He had already done the unexpected by taking over the bar. He managed the rescue, which was something he had chosen for himself. Pace was a typical middle child who had to fight to be heard and compete with his siblings. Because of that, he had learned to forge his own way in the world.

In many ways, Pace had chosen himself already. But he knew he often gave in to the expectations of others. Maybe this was his chance to step outside of the box and chase what he wanted. And he knew precisely what he was going to go after.

Chapter 17

Hana was determined to not call Pace about a part of the story she was stuck on. She didn't need his help. She could call any bartender in town and ask them how they would handle a certain situation. But they would all think she was absolutely nuts. Pace would know exactly what she was talking about and how to answer it without her having to explain the entire story plot.

She was also determined to not call Chas about his kitten. Surely he called the veterinarian and set up an appointment for Hopalong. He would know to scoop the litter, right? And change it every so often? She didn't need to follow up with him, either.

"Ugh, why can't I think straight?" She looked to Lulu who did not have an answer for her. She looked at her computer again and decided throwing it against the wall would be a bad idea, so she closed it instead. "I need a change of scenery. Want to go to the park, Lulu?"

Knowing the word park, Lulu's tail began to wag rapidly. She danced in little circles around Hana's feet, urging her to stand and head toward the car. They hadn't been at the park in weeks, and Hana knew her pup missed it.

"We can do it. We can go to the park and not see Pace and Moses, right? It's not like we ran into them every time we went there." She was more trying to convince herself than her dog, who probably had no idea what she was prattling on about.

At the park, Hana scanned the grounds for the familiar gait or bark of Moses. He would be easier to pick out than Pace. Not seeing any sign of either, Hana let out a deep breath. She unhooked Lulu and let her run over to a poodle she had seen a time or two before. They were mismatched friends, but Lulu seemed to love the larger dogs. Hana waved politely at the poodle's owner and hovered a few feet away from the playing pups.

The reminder to not look for Pace kept running through her head. She would not turn in a circle to see if she found find him. She would not roam every corner of the park to see if he was anywhere within its boundaries. Hana was absolutely not going to check Pace's Instagram to see if it gave any hint as to where he was.

"Not today, Satan!" She nodded for effect.

"Sorry, what?" The poodle's owner cocked her head to the side and looked at Hana.

"Oh, sorry, nothing." Hana waved and ducked her head, an embarrassed titter rolling its way up her throat. Afraid she would burst, she called to Lulu and retreated with her to a bench where Hana poured some water out for the dog.

Then she heard it. The bark of a Boxer. Moses's bark. And she could simply feel Pace come into the area. How, she did not know, but she felt it. Without moving her head, she glanced left and saw Moses and his boundless energy run through the trees.

Did she scoop Lulu up and hide? Did she accept that Moses and then Pace would find them? Hana felt like a guilty teenager who had snuck out of the house and been busted. She had no reason to feel like that, so while her inner self went through the turmoil of what to do, she sat, trying to be as cool and collected as possible.

Within seconds, Moses jumped in front of her and barked at Lulu. Lulu, thrilled to see her friend, began jumping about. Hana had to laugh, the pair did love each other. Pace stopped several yards away, clearly unsure what to do. He waved and Hana returned the gesture.

After a minute, she finally waved him over and patted the bench next to her. As he approached, she offered an olive branch. "No reason we can't be friendly."

He sat as far away from her as he could. "Of course. How have you been?" His words were halted and his body was stiff.

As her stomach turned flips, Hana reminded herself to breathe. "I'm good. Working on a tight deadline, but we both needed some fresh air. You?" She realized her posture was also stiff, so she tried to relax, rolling her shoulders back.

"I've been good. Dealing with Trey right now. He's in rehab and has decided on a career switch." Nervous laughter filled the air. "Our father was not amused, but Trey said he's finally choosing himself."

That was what Hana had said when she cut things off with Pace and Chas. She didn't know if Trey had known about that speech, but she was glad he was finally stepping up for himself. "I'm sorry he's in rehab. Emmie told me about it."

"You talked to Emmie?"

She shrugged. "We got to be friends. We chat on occasion." Was it wrong to tell him that? She wasn't sure.

"I just didn't know. She didn't tell me that." He stood and whistled to Moses. "We should get going."

Her mind raced with thoughts to keep him there with her. "Actually, since you're here, I have a question for you. For the book. If you don't mind?" She rubbed her hands on her thighs and wished she had worded that better, but it was too late.

After giving Moses a pat on the head, Pace sat again. "Shoot."

She explained the direction the story was going and asked him what a true bartender would do in the situation. After a moment of thought, Pace told her a story about a time that exact thing had happened to him and how he had reacted. By the end of his story, Hana knew exactly what her character would do.

"Can I use your situation as inspiration for what my character does?" She looked at him and blinked several times. It wasn't batting her eyelashes per se, but it also wasn't not batting her eyelashes.

With a shrug, Pace agreed. They chatted for a minute more, before Hana realized she was dangerously close to outright flirting and she didn't want to lead Pace on.

"I should get going. Now that I have an answer, I can finally finish that scene. Thank you, Pace." Her voice was soft and she didn't look him in the eye. She scanned the park for Lulu and whistled to her. "Lulu!"

Lulu, followed by Moses, trotted back to their bench, tongues wagging. They both sat side by side, waiting for instructions. "It's time to go, Lu. Tell Moses goodbye."

Realizing how silly she sounded, Hana chuckled and clipped the leash on Lulu's collar.

"It was good to see you, Hana." Pace also clipped on Moses's leash. "I miss seeing you at the bar. You know you can come work anytime."

Hana's eyes fixed on him and went over his stand-on-end hair and his reserved smile. His scruffy jaw flexed as she studied him. "Thank you, Pace. We'll see."

With that, she clicked her tongue and flicked the leash and Lulu began toward the exit, Hana trailing behind. She told herself not to look back at Pace, but she couldn't help herself. She looked back. And there he stood, in the same spot, watching her go. Hana quickly turned, face flushed, and quickened her step.

As she walked, she imagined what her characters would be doing when she got her fingers back on the keyboard. What her bartender, Jackson, would say to the woman at the bar while the heroine, Daphne, was within earshot. How Daphne would react. She was certain they would not act like the completely awkward ninny she had just become with Pace.

Really, Hana. You're the writer. Shouldn't you know how to handle these situations? Daphne huffed at her. Even her characters were giving her a hard time.

At home, she argued with herself, or maybe it was Daphne, more. She was not interested in Pace. Or Chas for that matter. Except she missed them both. She realized the unfairness of the situation she had put them all through. Leading them both on and confusing herself in the process. It was best to maintain distant yet friendly relationships with both of them. Chas had the kitten situation settled and now she could finish her book and never write about bartenders again.

There was really no reason for her to talk to either one again. That thought caused her to sit abruptly on her couch and breathe deeply. What a sad predicament she had led herself to.

After running into Hana at the dog park, Pace was even more determined. Hana was the woman for him, he knew it. When he walked into the park that morning, he could feel her presence well before he could see her. Didn't that count for something? It had to.

But he knew it would take time, and he had plenty of other things to keep him busy. Tending to Palmetto Magic was at the top of his list at the moment. He had spent a lot of energy on keeping it purely a bar without a lot of fussy foods and whatnot. But with the neighborhood it was situated in, it was becoming harder and harder to maintain that position. There was a steady stream of people coming in and asking for a full menu.

When a chef with a laundry list of credentials came in saying he was looking for a position in the city, Pace really considered making changes. He scheduled a proper interview with the young chef and called around to see what changes would need to be made to create a trendy dining establishment. The time to grow up a little had come and Palmetto Magic was growing up with him. He could cater to a more high-end clientele, but he didn't want to put out his regulars, so Pace was trying to solve how to make that work.

As he looked over his numbers and a floorplan of his space, his phone rang.

It wasn't a number he knew, but he felt prompted to answer anyway. "Hello?"

A gruff voice on the other end greeted him. "Mr. McCoy? I'm Bruce Owens, I own the space next to your bar. I'm looking to sell and thought I would offer it to you. Your grandfather and I had worked out a right of refusal agreement years ago and I'm honoring that."

The space next door wasn't large, maybe a thousand square feet. It was a long, narrow space that had been a photography studio when he was a child and was now a mostly empty florist's space.

They chatted for a few minutes and Mr. Owens named his price. It was well under the market value given the current market and Pace knew he would be a fool to pass it up.

That's when an idea came to him. He could make the smaller space a dedicated bar and use his current space for an upscale dining area. The front would be a perfect place to open a walkway and they could easily add a door from the kitchen into the bar space.

With a promise to talk to his financial advisor and get back to Mr. Owens within the week, Pace's body hummed with excitement. Just as he had been thinking it was time for a slight shift, one was presented to him.

"I should call Quent." His best friend would tell him to go for it, he knew. And Emmie would also be thrilled. "Then, I should call Hana. She'll be so excited."

He stopped and his smile was replaced with a sneer. While Hana might be excited for him, the news didn't affect her at all. Why would she care? Still, he opted to text her before calling his sister.

PACE: I WANTED TO SHARE THAT I MIGHT BE EXPANDING PALMETTO MAGIC AND TAKING OVER THE SPACE NEXT TO US. I'VE BEEN THINKING ABOUT EXPANDING THE RESTAURANT SIDE OF THINGS AND THIS OPPORTUNITY JUST PRESENTED ITSELF.

There, that sounded professional and friendly without making it sound like he wanted her input. Which, naturally, he did. He wanted Hana to be excited for him.

HANA: PACE, THAT'S AWESOME. I HEARD ROBERTSON'S FLORIST WAS GOING OUT. I DIDN'T KNOW YOU WERE THINKING OF GOING BIGGER.

PACE: IT'S BEEN A NEW THOUGHT. INSTEAD OF RUNNING THIS BUSINESS BECAUSE I HAVE TO, I'M GOING TO RUN IT BECAUSE I WANT TO. I CAN MAKE THIS A GREAT PLACE FOR THE WEST END.

He watched those three little dots dance across his screen as she typed. Pace held his breath as he waited.

HANA: IT'S ALREADY THE BEST SPOT ON THE WEST END. BEST WINGS AND NACHOS IN THE UPSTATE. I THINK IT'S A FABULOUS IDEA. CONGRATS!

Bolstered by her encouragement, Pace called Quent to tell him and see what he thought. He was smarter than anybody should be and always gave it to Pace straight. And he was sure Emmie was there with him, so he could get her opinion as well.

When he answered, Pace launched into telling him what was going on.

"Do you want to expand? I had no idea this was an idea you had." Quent's country accent came through. Emmie's voice was in the background asking questions.

"It's barely a thought in my head, but then this came up. I think this is what I'm supposed to do." Pace jumped up from the couch and paced the room. Moses paced with him.

The phone made a staticky noise as Emmie grabbed the phone. "I only have one question. You know I have to ask it." Emmie's voice was terse and Pace could picture her mouth crinkled to the side.

"Shoot."

Not one to hem and haw, Emmie blurted out her question. "If you put more effort into Palmetto Magic, what about Soft Paws? I know it's a selfish question, but I have to know."

With a groan, Pace cracked his neck from side the side. "It's something to consider. Hopefully, more space and more sales means more money and more staff. But until that's going smoothly, I will have to step up. But believe me, I do not intend on shirking my duties to Soft Paws. I know we had two more people volunteer recently, so hopefully there are more hands on deck there, too."

Emmie was quiet a moment before piping up, drawl coming through loud and clear. "Pacey, it's going to be great. We will figure it out and everything will happen as it's supposed to. I know it. I am so excited for you."

From behind her, Quent's voice came through the phone. "I think it's a great idea. It's about time you put your passion into that business."

Maybe, just maybe, he could really do this. Pace sat down and grabbed Moses around the neck. He would make it happen.

⚜

Chas would have been happy never having anything to do with Pace McCoy again, yet here he was representing Bruce

Owens, a retail space owner, selling to none other than Pace McCoy. At least, Chas thought, he didn't have to deal with Pace too much. While the thought to halt the sale crossed his mind, it would be unethical and he could potentially lose the sale, so he swallowed his feelings.

He had tried to talk Mr. Owens into hiking the price up. But the man was adamant on the price he had told McCoy, saying he was going to honor his agreement with an old friend. Chas had to say that keeping one's word was an admirable trait and he dropped it after the old man told him that.

In his office, Barbara came in with a plate of sugary sweets. Chas certainly had a sweet tooth, so he chose a small cookie and waved away the rest. "Thanks, Barbara."

"You know, my son is signed up for the Reedy Race. How's your training going?" She looked at him sweetly, like a concerned grandmother.

Training had been nonexistent because Chas had forgotten about it completely. He cursed under his breath. "I can't believe I forgot. When is it?"

"Two weeks." Barbara grimaced. "But you're in good shape, Chas, you won't have a problem."

Not have a problem? It was a 10K, so Chas was sure he would have a problem. If he hadn't paid a pretty penny for the race and a sponsorship spot, he would back out. Rolling his eyes, he stretched and stood. No more cookies for him.

"I guess after work I'll be going for a run." He laughed, ushered Barbara from his office, and closed the door behind her. "Oh, I'm going to hate this."

After work, he put on a t-shirt and shorts and laced up his running shoes. They were tight and heavy. Chas much preferred his work shoes. He knew that was a little odd, but it's what he was used to.

He started off at a mild jog. It was muggy out and the humidity made his shirt cling to him immediately. He wasn't a fan of running shirtless, so he endured. He thought about running through downtown, but the crowds would prevent a good pace, so he stuck to the outskirts. Several men and women were also out walking and jogging through the city. A few sped past on bikes and Chas had to swerve to miss a young mom with a stroller.

Storefronts and restaurants blurred as he picked up the pace and found a steady rhythm of his feet hitting the pavement. Music from the early nineties blared through his earbuds, pushing him on. Chas turned a corner and a giant, but familiar, face glared at him from a store window.

As Chas was distracted by the window, he did not see a park bench directly in his path. He collided into it and flipped over it, landing on his back. The wind was knocked out of him and pain radiated from his left leg. Stars danced in front of his face for a moment while he tried to focus on the simple act of breathing.

A female voice came to him. "Are you okay? Sir?" Cool hands gently touched his forearm. "Sir? Wait. Chas Rossi?"

Great. The last thing Chas needed was to be recognized by John Q. Public. As he struggled to look toward the voice, the image that had caused his accident came into view. A six-foot-tall poster of Hana's face and one of her books smiled prettily out over him, mocking him.

A woman moved into his line of sight. "Mr. Rossi? Remember me? La'Anna? I'm Hana Willis's friend." She came into focus, her face not familiar but also not unfamiliar. Chas had met her before and seen her on Hana's social media accounts.

"Right. Yes." He struggled to move himself to a sitting position but pain shot through him and caused him to collapse back down. "I think I might need some help."

"I'm going to call for an ambulance. Be still." She placed her hand on his arm again as she pulled a phone from her bag.

"Oh, no, I'm fine. I just need help getting to standing." Chas once again struggled to sit up.

With the phone to her ear, La'Anna shook her head. "No, you need a hospital. Your leg looks broken. Please be still."

Broken? Chas tried to concentrate on his legs. Pain coursed through his entire body, but yes, his leg was the worst. He could only think that he had smacked it into the bench. The small crowd that had gathered had broken up a little, but a few people still lingered, waiting to see what became of the man who had flipped over a park bench.

Hana's friend did not accompany him to the hospital, but she did give her account of what she saw to the EMTs. She had been coming out of the bookstore—the one with Hana's face in the window—and had seen a man run shin-first into a bench and flip right over it. He hadn't blacked out and he had been alert.

Chas almost wished he had blacked out. He was certain this woman would report back to Hana that he had had a huge accident with a bench. On the plus side, he wouldn't have to run in the race anymore. A broken leg was a perfect excuse to sit it out but still show up to present the medal to the winner.

While he sat in the hospital, he told his parents what had happened. His mother was sympathetic and clucked over him like a mother hen. His father, however, was a different story.

"Well, son, what distracted you enough to make you completely miss an eight-foot bench in front of you?"

He could never tell him that it had been the face of Hana Willis, gorgeous lips, eyes, and hair, that had caused his brain to completely lose all function. While his father loved his mother, he doubted Chuck Rossi would ever understand.

Chapter 18

With the purchase of the additional space completed, Pace had more than enough to keep his mind reeling. Poor Moses was not getting his exercise days like he wanted and Pace felt bad for the big dog in the little apartment. When he was at Soft Paws, he let Moses free in the dog run. He kept the others in line easily enough.

But Pace couldn't bring Moses into Palmetto Magic, it would violate all the codes and he couldn't risk any infractions with the new launch coming soon. Thankfully, his original space was staying as it was, the new doorway would be added last, and then both sides would be joined. Down the road, he hoped to take the bar out of the larger space to open it up for more tables or to become a stage for local musicians.

It was the dog days of summer where everybody felt like they were going to melt into a puddle and Pace was no different. He met with his contractor bright and early before doing some paperwork in his office. Then he planned to grab Moses and head to Soft Paws. There weren't enough hours in the day to get everything done. And when something was on a deadline, everything was on a deadline. A short one.

While he went through his inventory and order forms, a knock sounded on his office door. Nobody else was in the building aside from the construction workers, so he assumed it was his contractor needing more decisions made.

"Enter."

The door cracked open. "Pace?"

It was not his burly contractor, but the sweet, honeyed face of Hana Willis. Pace forgot all about his orders and stood as if dumbfounded by her presence.

She entered the room and hid something behind her back. "I wanted to stop by and thank you for all your help. And show you what you helped me with." She pulled a book from behind her back.

"Your book is ready?" For some reason, he thought the process was a lot longer.

She shook her head. "No. This is a mock-up so I can see the margins and cover and check for errors and whatnot. The actual book won't be out until December. But I wanted you to see it." The book was passed to him and Pace hefted it in his hands.

The front cover featured a couple sitting at a bar much like his own. They were headless in the photo, which Pace did not understand, but he didn't question it. Flipping the book over, the back cover mentioned the characters' names and their issues and how they were both afraid of falling in love.

"Unsure what to say, Pace flashed her a smile. "It looks really good. Congratulations, Hana."

She grabbed the book and opened it. "I thanked you in the acknowledgments. And mentioned Palmetto Magic. You might see an increase in traffic here."

Sure enough, he was named. He read it aloud. "'Special thanks to Pace McCoy and Palmetto Magic in Greenville, South Carolina for the expertise and all the Sprite. I couldn't have created this story without you.'"

Heat crept up his neck and he rubbed his hand over it to cover the redness. "Hana, I don't know what to say. Thank you."

She bit her lip in the special Hana Willis way. "Well, it's a good thing you're expanding. I'm happy for you, Pace."

"Thank you. Likewise."

She nodded and looked down. "I guess I should be going. I have a few things to get done, but I saw your truck here and thought I'd show you the mock-up." She put her hand on the doorknob. "See you around, Pace."

"Yeah." He tried to think of something else to say to her, but nothing came to mind and she disappeared, closing the door behind her.

Pace struggled through the rest of his ordering, distracted by the thought that Hana would think to include him and mention Palmetto Magic in her book. If she was a big name in South Carolina and getting more well-known with each book, it could mean a big boost in sales for him after its launch. Then he had an idea. He pulled out his phone and typed a text to her.

PACE: CRAZY IDEA. WHAT IF YOU HAD YOUR BOOK LAUNCH PARTY HERE?

He tossed his phone down on his desk but watched it and waited for it to ding with a reply. After thirty seconds with no response, he went back to his computer and finished his work. He would be back that evening to work the bar since

Jake had asked off for his son's birthday and nobody else volunteered to work his shift.

At Soft Paws, Pace put Moses in the dog run with the other large dogs. He greeted the volunteers and did quick chores before going inside to update the website. He loved putting a big "adopted" banner over the photos of the animals who had found their homes. Adding new dogs or cats – or on this day a group of fancy rats – always made his heart heavy. He realized without new animals, Soft Paws would be no more, but that was the goal.

He assisted a young newlywed couple in choosing a younger pup as their first pet. "Fur baby" was what the girl had said. It was a term he knew from Emmie, but Pace couldn't quite get behind the notion of the expression. He adored Moses, but he wouldn't call him a "fur baby." Still, the couple fell in love with a scrappy mixed breed who was still young enough to play but old enough to be housebroken. Pace waved them off and happily marked Grover as "adopted" on their website.

He had been distracted enough to forget about his offer to Hana until his phone dinged with a text message.

HANA: SERIOUSLY? THAT WOULD BE AMAZING. I WAS GOING TO DO IT AT MOM'S, BUT AN ACTUAL BAR WOULD BE PERFECT. ARE YOU SURE?

Pace didn't care if he looked over-eager in replying straight away. The Cheshire cat grin on his face would have given him away to anyone who saw him and he could feel his stomach begin to turn a somersault.

PACE: OF COURSE, IT'S A NATURAL FIT. I CAN EVEN CREATE A DRINK IN YOUR HONOR. THE HANA.

HANA: AS LONG AS IT'S SPRITE BASED.

PACE: NATURALLY.

HANA: I'M TEXTING MY AGENT RIGHT NOW AND WE'LL GET IT SET UP. THANK YOU, PACE!

PACE: YOU'RE MORE THAN WELCOME.

Pace pocketed the phone again and began to whistle as he went back out to the kennels and swapped the big dogs for the little guys. Moses followed him as he went to the cat enclosure to check on things in there before taking Moses home and heading back to the bar.

Yes, hosting the launch for her book about a bartender was a natural fit. Just like he thought the author was a natural fit for him.

***

A cast and a job that required a lot of walking did not go hand-in-hand. At least, Chas reasoned, it hadn't been his right foot. Then he wouldn't be able to drive, either. Working with crutches as he showed houses was a pain in the rear. Thankfully, his clients were understanding, but it put him in a sour mood every day he had to hobble through houses that were unfamiliar to him.

"How much longer are you in the cast?" His client, Don Clarkson, raised an eyebrow as Chas struggled to stay upright.

Forcing a friendly expression, Chas shook his head. "Another week, then I get a walking boot." He hated that idea, but at least he could ditch the crutches. "It's all good, though. What matters is finding you the right home to retire in. If you look over here, I think your wife will adore this sun-filled bedroom."

He maneuvered through the small home as best as he could, thankful it was already empty. The Clarksons had been loyal clients, having used him as an agent five years prior when they moved to the area from Ohio. Now they were retiring and ready to downsize.

When the tour finished, he met Clarkson back at his office to make a formal offer on the golf course home with a view of the seventh tee. With this sale, Chas would be on target to top his summer sales goal, so that made him chuckle with delight.

The leg break had put a damper on his plans to woo Hana, but she had texted him when she heard of his accident. She had offered to make him a meal and bring it over, but he had missed her when she dropped it off. His mother had met her at the door and assumed she was a restaurant delivery person. She had been mortified to learn she had given a five-dollar bill to her favorite author as a tip.

When he had texted Hana to both apologize for his mother and thank her for the food, she had simply laughed it off and said it would be a great bit in one of her books. And she would be sure to thank Marcie Rossi for the idea. Chas still needed to return her baking dish to her.

He hoped to return it in person when she would be home and he could bring her her favorite caramel macchiato as a thank you. Chas played the whole scenario in his head. He would hand her the drink, with one in his own hand for him. She would invite him in and he would oblige. Lulu would be wearing one of the frou-frou things he had gotten her and Hana would gush about how sweet he was. She would realize that she loved him and they would live happily ever after.

Okay, maybe it was jumping the gun a little bit, but he at least hoped she would invite him in and they could have a nice time discussing literature and the latest movies to come out.

With his daydream still in his head, Chas stopped by Hana's favorite coffee shop on his way home from work and got her a caramel macchiato and a hazelnut latte for himself. He pulled up to her house and realized he couldn't use crutches and carry both drinks in his hand.

He had not thought this through properly.

Thinking quick, Chas opted to ditch the crutches. After all, it was only a few steps from his car to the door. He could make it if he hobbled carefully.

Chas held a drink in each hand and closed the car door with his hip. He stepped carefully, knowing that his left leg was much heavier and taller given the thickness of the cast. Then he remembered the baking dish. It was in the backseat. He could not hobble, carry the drinks, and the dish. What had he been thinking?

He cursed under his breath.

"Chas? You okay?" Hana's voice came up behind him from the road.

He turned and plastered a mile-wide grin on his face. She walked up with Lulu on her leash. Hana wore a tank top and running shorts that showed off her muscular, tanned legs. Chas's mouth went dry.

"Chas?"

Finding his voice, he nodded. "Oh, yes. I'm sorry. I was returning your baking dish, and I got you a drink as a thank you. But I realized I can't carry all of this at the same time and keep my leg up. I'm not used to being so helpless." He also was not used to admitting his helplessness.

Hana took the drinks from his hands. "That's what friends are for. To help us not be so helpless. And to not mind when a little extra help is needed."

Chas grabbed the dish from the back seat, along with one crutch, and followed Hana and Lulu to the door.

She unlocked the door and held it open for him. "Come on in. I see there are two drinks here, so I am guessing you were hoping to sit down for a few."

Chas reddened. He didn't think he would be so transparent with his intentions. "I didn't want to assume, but I was thinking we could chat. I know your deadline to turn in your new book passed recently, and you have a new release coming out soon."

With the drinks on the coffee table and Lulu unhooked, Hana took the dish from Chas. "You have a great memory. I heard La'Anna was the one who came to your rescue after your accident."

"She's a real hero. She has a very calming presence." Chas was grateful for Hana's friend but didn't want to bring up the fact that it was her picture that caused him to break his leg.

"She had been in the bookstore helping them put up a giant poster of me in the window. La'Anna is great at helping me with some promotional stuff from time to time." Hana looked at him, but there was no malice or sarcasm in her voice. She was not mocking him or suggesting it was her photo that distracted him.

Still, Chas was not going to admit to anything. "Oh? I just know she appeared at my side after I wiped out. I sent her a card."

"She told me."

Ready to change the subject, Chas took a sip of his latte. "Is your drink okay?"

She raised the cup to her lips and drank. "Perfect. You know exactly how I like it." She took another sip before putting it back on the table. "So, seen anything good on television lately?"

They discussed the merits of a new show they had both seen and laughed over the character's misfortunes. It was nice having someone to discuss the mundane with. Chas didn't have many close friends with how busy he kept himself.

After about a half-hour, Chas said he should get going. He didn't want to overstay his welcome. The goal was for Hana to appreciate and want his company even more.

"Oh, how is Hopalong doing?" Hana giggled as she walked him to the door.

"He's great. I really like having a cat. I was worried for a day or two there, but he's been great company for me, especially now." Chas indicated to his leg. "Hopalong loves to watch TV."

"I'm happy for you. And Hopalong." Hana opened the door and Chas stepped through it. "Thank you for the caramel macchiato. And the conversation."

"Anytime, Hana. Seriously, anytime."

It didn't escape Hana's notice that she was still looking for ways to talk to and spend time with both Chas and Pace. At least she wasn't looking for a romantic link with either of them. That's what she told herself. She was too busy writing romance to be looking for romance.

Yet as she and La'Anna sat on her couch to watch movies and eat ice cream as some much-needed girl time, Hana couldn't help wondering how her best friend had known Rob was the one for her.

"Spit it out, girl." La'Anna folded her leg under her bottom and huffed as she looked at Hana.

Taken aback, Hana blinked a few times. "What?"

"What's the question? I see it forming on your lips, Han. You are itching to know something."

How did her best friend know her so well? After nearly twenty years as friends, the pair knew each other's ins and outs very well, but Hana always wondered how La'Anna could see inside her brain.

Leaning forward, Hana studied her friend. The petite powerhouse was kind to all but also knew how to throw down with the best of them. La'Anna was a force to be reckoned with if someone stepped between her and someone she loved. "How did you know Rob was the one for you?"

A perfectly arched eyebrow shot up. "Book research?"

"Personal." It was no use trying to hide her thoughts and feelings from La'Anna.

"I thought so. Still mulling over the business hunk and the fur-loving hottie?" La'Anna angled her body toward Hana and dug her spoon into her pint of Ben and Jerry's. She took a bite as she stared Hana down.

Hana sighed and put her ice cream down. It was freezing her hands. "They have names. But, yes." She thought of the two men, placing them side by side in her mind.

Chas and his classic good looks, chiseled jaw, and impeccable way of dressing. He was generous, always surprising her, and was more modest deep down than she would have ever thought given his status around the city.

Then there was Pace and his unconventional handsomeness, his contented face, and his relaxed attitude.

He was passionate about animals and his family and he was quite open with her about things.

"I have no reason to see either of them anymore, yet I find myself finding ways to get in touch with them. And now Pace is going to throw a launch party for me. And Chas adopted this adorable kitten that I want to cuddle all day." She grabbed a pillow from the couch and hugged it close, burying her chin into it.

The no-nonsense look came across La'Anna's face. "That's business and a kitten. And while both are great, neither has to do with the men involved. Pace has a manager you could deal with and there are kittens all over the city you could cuddle. Why do you want these men?"

Hana knew whining wouldn't help, but she couldn't help the groan that came forth. "I don't know. They're both charming and sweet and kind and successful. And I love spending time with them both. But I need to know how you know when someone is right for you."

Before she answered, La'Anna took a bite of her ice cream and winced as she swallowed. "Brain freeze." She made a series of hilarious faces as she tried to thaw her head. When she recovered, she put the carton down. "Honey, Rob is my best friend."

"Hey, now."

"You're my best friend, but Rob is my best friend, too. I want to do everything with him. And even if I don't, I want to tell him what I'm doing. I love to cuddle with him and do nothing. I want to come home to him and eat and talk about our day and it never gets old.

"I know we're still considered newlyweds, but you know we were together daily for a long time before that. And I still want him there day in and day out. I want him to be the first to know when something happens. And I want to grow old with him. I'll even wipe his butt when he's senile." She winked with the last comment.

Hana laughed. "Oh, that must be true love then. That's so gross." She thought about doing gross things for either Chas or Pace. "Yeah, I'm not there yet with either one. I guess I'm not thinking I need to marry one of them, but I want to see where it goes. And I don't know which one. Does that make me a horrid person, L.A?"

A warm smile came across La'Anna's face. Her friend moved to sit next to her and cuddled up close. She was quiet for a few seconds and Hana could only guess she was coming up with an answer or was going to tell Hana she truly was a horrid person.

"Honestly, it makes you human. I know you don't want to string either one along, and I commend you for it. But think about your future and who you want beside you at book signings and who do you want to support in their business endeavors. Who do you want to see you at your very worst and who will love you despite that?"

A picture started forming in Hana's mind. Who would she want to see her at her worst? And who could she support the most and who could support her in return? Both Chas and Pace were incredibly supportive and encouraging, but Hana had to admit that one was emerging as a front-runner.

A bemused look spread across La'Anna's lips. "I see you're figuring it out. Take your time, young grasshopper. Until then, let's watch the movie."

Chapter 19

There was not much time to focus on romance with deadlines looming. One book was slated to come out in a month's time and another was in editing purgatory. Hana both hated and loved when things got so hectic. She loved the rush of adrenaline and the highs of doing speaking engagements and promos. But she hated the sense of impending doom over whether or not people would actually like her book and she was not a fan of her editor or publisher sending scathing emails over how long she was taking.

It was all part of the business, Hana knew, but she still wanted things to go as planned and go without any hiccups. Who wanted hiccups? Nobody.

Still, as she stared at her computer screen needing to type out interview answers for a website, she found herself daydreaming. Her characters were often sweet, mixed-up people not unlike herself. They wanted success and love. But unlike her, they seemed to know who they wanted without a whole lot of thought. The hero felt the pull to the heroine, and vice versa. They were meant for each other because she designed them that way.

Real life didn't work like that. She was not created from thin air and made into the perfect mate for someone. And what if she went to the person she felt like she was made for and they didn't choose her in return? Or what if it didn't work out? Or what if she had chosen wrong?

But then, what if she had chosen right? That was almost as scary as being wrong.

Hana stood from her computer and Lulu stood and danced around her feet. "I'm just getting a drink, Lu. We'll go out a little later, okay?" She crouched down and scratched Lulu behind the ear and kissed her head.

With a can of Sprite in hand, she sat back down and tried to clear her head. Work needed to be her priority. She answered the interview questions, always a variation of the same few questions, and send them off to Kendra. Checking her schedule, she had a podcast interview that afternoon but was free otherwise.

"Come on, Lulu. Let's go for a walk." She finished the Sprite and tossed the can into her recycling bin. Lulu jumped up and danced herself to the door where her leash hung.

They enjoyed a walk toward the shops where Hana thought she might get herself an iced coffee and Lulu a little pup treat. Walking always cleared her head and provided some much-needed exercise for them both.

"Lulu!" A voice called out from behind them.

The little girl, Violet, was on her bike coming up the sidewalk. Hana saw the girl's mother with a large retriever on a leash several yards behind them.

Hana stopped so the girl could approach Lulu and pet her. She was always wary of the child since she had run across the street, but she was a sweet girl who was gentle with

Lulu. As the girl sat on the sidewalk, Lulu rolled over on her back so Violet could give her belly rubs.

When the girl's mother caught up to them, Hana reintroduced herself.

The woman, whose name Hana could not recall, shook her hand. "I remember. Violet talks about Lulu a lot still. I know she wanted a smaller dog, but my husband isn't a fan of them."

"It's a good thing they come in all sizes. I've seen your daughter while walking from time to time. I just live over on Elmwood Drive." Hana pointed in the direction of her house.

"Really? You're one of my favorite authors, you know." The woman reigned in her dog, who wanted to jump and play with Lulu.

"Thank you so much. I'll have a new one out soon, actually. You can find details on my website." Hana smiled at the lady and absently petted the golden hair of the larger dog.

"Thank you so much." The woman checked her phone and told Violet they had to get going. "It was nice to see you again."

The girl stood but crossed her arms and pouted. "But I want to play with Lulu. I hate Rocket."

Not wanting to get caught in that family discussion, Hana said goodbye and quickly moved on down the sidewalk. She felt bad that the girl didn't get the dog she wanted, but to say she hated that sweet Lab was a little extreme.

She and Lulu sat outside at her favorite coffee shop, enjoying their cool treats. Lulu sunned herself while Hana stayed in the shade checking her Instagram account. Her following was modest compared to some, but she was happy with her forty-thousand followers and her little blue checkmark.

"How are you, Hana?"

The voice was familiar and Hana didn't need to look up to know who it belonged to. "Good afternoon, Chas." She covered her eyes to see him better.

Tall and handsome in his button-down and blazer, Chas wore a schoolboy grin across his face. "Beautiful day."

Hana patted the spot across from her and Chas sat. "It is, and you look quite happy."

He leaned forward. "I just closed a huge deal. I don't usually like to discuss my commissions, but I know you won't judge me. I made almost fifty thousand on this deal."

Fifty thousand dollars on one real estate sale? Hana was in the wrong business. She knew Chas was a powerhouse in the industry and not everyone had that kind of income, but that was as much as many people made in a whole year. If it wasn't for her freelancing and working for her mother, she would be below that amount. Authors did not make a ton of money.

She tried to hide her shock, but she knew her eyebrows raised. "That's incredible, Chas. Congratulations. Don't spend it all in one place."

His expression changed. "I could spend it all on you in a heartbeat."

Now the shock did register on her face. "I hope you're kidding. Nobody, least of all me, needs that kind of spoiling. But I can give you the names of my favorite charities if you want to donate some. And save for your retirement."

The look on his face remained serious, giving Hana butterflies. His brooding eyes bored into hers and goosebumps came up over her arms as he spoke again.

"Believe me, I have plenty saved for a future family and my retirement."

Hana swallowed hard and nodded. "That's, that's wonderful Chas." An alarm on her phone chimed and the trance was broken. "Oh, I need to get back. I have an interview in a bit."

Chas stood and waited for her to stand as well. "Good luck with your interview, Hana. I'm glad I ran into you today."

"Likewise, and congratulations." Hana's voice was soft as she bid Chas goodbye and she and Lulu began the walk back home.

A chill ran over her as she turned back to see Chas heading in the opposite direction. Hana felt more sure of her choice now and a smile of joy crept across her face.

⚜

Construction knowledge was not Pace's forte. He could manage a business or a non-profit like nobody else, and he knew how to mix drinks, but knowing the difference between pieces of wood and tools wasn't in his wheelhouse.

His father, however, knew all the tools and could hand you the right thing without thinking. It was a big relief when his father offered to come check things out. Especially since Gerry McCoy was still unhappy about his son running a bar. But he did like the idea of a dedicated dining area and a separate bar area and told Pace as much.

After a thorough inspection, Gerry clapped Pace on the back. "It all looks good, son. Everything's up to code, they're using good materials. I'm glad you went with McMillen for your contractor."

Pace chuckled. "Well, he is from the church and he's giving me a good deal." He poured a Coke for his father and passed it to him.

After taking a long drink, Gerry's face turned serious and he picked at his fingernails. "Did you know Emmie was moving in with that man?"

"That man? Dad, you've known Quent for years. This should be no surprise to you." Pace shook his head. His sister had announced her move in with Quent a few days before.

After his talk with Quent earlier, Emmie had been asked to cohabitate and she had agreed as long as Quent didn't ask her to marry him for at least six months. She had been all too excited when she called and told Pace her good news. It would seem, however, that their parents were not quite as thrilled.

With a scowl on his face, Gerry stared Pace down. "He said he's asked her to marry him and she said no. So why jump to this? And how could Emmie agree? It's living in sin."

It was a delicate line to balance, trying to support both Emmie and his dad's stance. Pace licked his lips and shifted on his feet. "Dad, Emmie is an adult. She's twenty-six, not sixteen. She needs to make her own decisions and that includes making her own mistakes. But, for the record, I don't think she's making a mistake."

Gerry hung his head and wrung his hands. "Just wait till you have children, Pace. The worry doesn't end when they turn eighteen and go to college. Trey had gone rogue since his breakup with Caroline, you encourage people to become drunks, and now Emmie is the proverbial cow giving it away for free."

Shock didn't adequately convey how Pace felt with his father's comments. "Seriously, Dad? I get that you will always worry about us and want the best for us. But wow. Trey is still doing ministry but is following his calling. As am I. I don't encourage drunkenness. I do my best to prevent it. I've even prayed with customers before. And Em? I will not be repeating your words to her. Or to Mom. You made your choices and now we get to make ours. You and Mom have done a great job, but right now, I think I need some space."

With that, Pace threw up his hands and walked away from his father before he did something like punch the man. Father or not, his words were beyond scathing. He slammed the door to his office and sat at his desk. Then he stood and walked the length of the room. He emitted a low growl and wondered if he would put his fist through the wall if he punched it.

The phone ringing in his pocket made him jump and his heart race. he pulled it from his pocket to silence it, but when he saw Hana's name he calmed immediately. How did she have that effect on him?

"Hello?" His voice was gruffer than he intended. He imagined he sounded like the Beast from Beauty and the Beast.

"Whoa, hello to you, too. Is everything okay?" Hana's concerned voice came through the phone.

"I'm sorry, yeah. I'm just fuming over a comment my dad made." Pace raked his hand through his hair and leaned on his desk. "What's up?"

A slight hum came through the phone before Hana spoke. "Oh. Parents, it seems, are fallible humans just like we are. Sorry he upset you, though." She paused, but Pace didn't speak. "I wanted to ask about the book launch party, but it's not a big deal. I can wait. Or I can text you."

Talking to Hana would be the highlight of his day, but he was in no mood to make polite chitchat. "Text me your questions, if you don't mind. That way I can make sure I get the right answers for you when I'm in a better mood."

"Absolutely. I hope your day improves, Pace."

He couldn't help himself. "Hearing your voice made it much better already."

She giggled lightly and Pace could imagine the blush that crept up her tanned skin. "Oh, you're a flatterer, Pace McCoy."

They hung up and Pace had to admit that he did feel better after speaking with Hana, even if it was only for a minute. He emerged from his office to see the crew still hard at work and his father nowhere to be seen. But there was somebody else standing at his bar he never expected to see.

"Chas. What can I do for you?" Pace approached him warily.

Chas kept a blank expression, but pulled something from his pocket. "I'm bringing by something from Mr. Owens. He forgot to give you this extra set of keys and also tell you that there's a small safe in the back apparently. He said it was there before he bought the building." Chas slid a few keys on a keyring across the bar to him. "That would be the tiny skeleton key, there."

Pace stopped ten feet from Chas where the keys had stopped. He picked them up and studied them a moment. Two regular door keys and one little key that looked like it belonged to a little girl's diary were on a ring. "Did he mention where this safe would be? I haven't seen it."

"Bruce only said in the back." Chas shrugged. "So, you're going to make this a real restaurant?"

Pace nodded. "Restaurant here and a bar on the other side where the florist was." He did not offer to show Chas around.

With a nod, Chas turned a full circle and looked around. "It looks nice."

Pace narrowed his eyes. Chas was being nice to him without anyone else around? What was his game? "Thanks."

Then with a nod, Chas narrowed his eyes. "I talked to Hana the other day. She brought me Korean food when I broke my leg."

Oh, this was the game they were playing? Pace spun the keys on his finger. "Yeah, her bibimbap is amazing, isn't it? She's made it for me before. In fact, I just got off the phone with her."

The smooth face across from him steeled and Chas's expression turned dark. Even though Hana had chosen herself, it seemed both he and Chas were still circling in the bull pen. Knowing Hana, she was likely just being friendly and not thinking the two bulls were still seeing red. Pace stared Chas down and Chas reciprocated.

But without another word, Chas gave him a nod and headed for the door, a single crutch under his arm. He pushed through and into the daylight without a backward glance. Pace pocketed the keys and shook his head. Maybe he needed to put Hana in this mysterious safe.

❧

"Chas, you have an appointment with Jamie Huntington." Barbara burst into his office unannounced to tell him this.

Her face was lit up like a Christmas tree.

Chas wracked his brain since clearly the name meant something to Barbara. Who was Jamie Huntington? He had no idea. Shaking his head, he finally just asked. "Who?"

Barbara sat down in the chair across from him. "*The* Jamie Huntington. She was Miss South Carolina a few years back and then she was Miss America. Don't you remember? And now she has her own cosmetics company that is made right here in the Upstate. She wants you to help her find a retail space."

The name still meant nothing to him, but a former beauty queen with a business certainly intrigued him. He had listened to Hana and donated some of his earnings from his last big sale to a good cause. One that would display his name for the world to see. Another high-profile sale could not only boost his business but also help Hana to see how successful he was.

He had not set out to tell Hana last time that he had earned a hefty paycheck from a big sale. Most were modest and kept him afloat, albeit with nice things. But the big ones were always exciting for him and renewed his passion for his work. Seeing Hana afterward was icing on the cake and Chas had been pleased with her reaction.

One of the things Chas liked about Hana was that while she was impressed with things, she didn't gush or treat him any different. She was humble and modest despite her own successes. After helping her buy a house, Chas knew her annual salary and he also knew she worked hard to earn it. If only he could convince her to be with him, she wouldn't have to work so hard.

When it came time to meet this Jamie Huntington, Barbara ushered the woman in as if she was a queen. Well,

Chas chuckled, she was a type of queen. Former pageant queen or not, the woman was lovely with auburn hair and large doe eyes.

After introducing himself, she tilted her head to the side. "Do you remember me?"

He hadn't even known her name until a minute ago. His brain worked overtime to think of how he might know her, but it came up blank. "I'm sorry, I don't think I do."

She threw her head back as she laughed. "That's okay. I wouldn't expect you to. We went to high school together. I was two years behind you, but we had some of the same classes."

"I'm sorry I don't remember. Surely I would have noticed you." He leaned forward in his chair.

She didn't blush, but she did look away momentarily. "Oh, probably not. I was incredibly awkward and gangly. Definitely an ugly duckling. I didn't come out of my shell until you were long gone."

Ready to make a sale, Chas flashed his sales smile and sat up straighter. "Well, I definitely see you now, Ms. Huntington."

Chas chatted her up, learned what she was looking for, and used his computer to show her a few options in storefront spaces. All the while, he was thinking he should try to talk Hana into getting a retail space and opening a bookstore. Bookstores, however, were a dying market with online sales these days. But coffee houses with bookshelves would be an incredible business venture. And he knew she enjoyed her coffee drinks.

"Mr. Rossi?"

Snapped back to attention, he blinked and felt his cheeks redden. "I'm sorry, you were saying?"

She tapped her long, pink fingernails on the table while she stared him down. "What's the square footage difference between the place on Poinsett and the one on Church Street?"

He shook his head to clear it. "Only about three hundred square feet." He pulled his computer back to him and began typing. "But look at this one on Queen. Aptly named. It's about the size you want and the rent is under your budget."

"Rent? I don't want to rent, I want to buy." Jamie rolled her eyes.

She was annoyed with him, Chas could tell. But he didn't know why.

While he wanted to make the sale, her demeanor was a little harsh. He flashed her his million-dollar grin and placed his folded hands on the desk. "Of course. But if you would allow me to continue. I happen to know the owner of this building and he mentioned selling to me a few times if he found the right buyer. You, Ms. Huntington, might be that person."

He showed her the space online and she took an immediate liking to it. After chatting a little further and promising to call her within the hour to arrange showings, Jamie left his office, her black stilettos soundless on the carpeted floor.

As he looked up the number for the Queen Street building's owner, Chas considered the beauty queen. "That's a woman who knows what she wants and doesn't take no for an answer." She reminded him of his own mother and he laughed at the thought. Marcie Rossi would simply love Ms. Huntington.

With meetings set up and Ms. Huntington scheduled, Chas returned to looking at the space on Poinsett. His thoughts once again went to Hana and the notion of opening a coffee shop with a bookstore. They could open it together and call it Sips and Pages or something equal parts cheesy and darling.

Without thinking, he fired off a text to Hana to see if she'd be interested in his idea.

Chapter 20

Hana hated deadlines. She appreciated them, she respected them, but man did she hate them. And it seemed that no matter what she did she could not get ahead of them. Her brain was muddled and nothing could clear it. Usually, a walk with Lulu or hanging out with her family would spark that desire to get to work, but lately, she was struggling.

Leaving Lulu at home, she headed to her mother's house. Maybe some of Min Willis's stern talking and comfort food would give Hana the kick in the pants she needed.

In the driveway, she found her sister outside washing her car. Nari waved a sudsy hand but did not remove the headphones from her ears. Hana waved back and went inside, sure she would find her mother outside in the garden if Nari was outside as well. The matriarch of the family liked to impose outside time on her children and forced them into the fresh air as often as she could.

Hana couldn't complain. It was those forced days outside that helped her to appreciate nature and go on her long walks downtown. Now Hana loved to be outside.

"Umma? Mom?" She kicked off her shoes and put her bag on the desk by the door. She walked through the house, it had not changed in a decade.

"Out back." As expected, Min was in the backyard, weeding her garden. "Come out here, Hana."

At the porch door, Hana slipped on her father's sandals and stepped outside into the sunshine. Without being invited, she knelt down and began pulling weeds alongside her mother. Maybe the labor would help her clear her mind.

"Why are you not working? Are you not the best author in the country?" Min's style of encouragement was unique, to say the least.

"I'm not the best in the country, Umma. Just popular with readers. But I feel stuck." As if it knew her plight, the weed she yanked on held firmly to the soil. With another tug, Hana freed it from the dirt.

"Your story is stuck?"

Hana paused. Was her story stuck? No. Her story was coming along nicely. When she sat down to write, it flowed through her fingers willingly. It was her that was stuck. She told her mother as much.

"So, you're stuck in life. Why?" Min didn't look her way but kept pulling weeds. "You were not stuck in the spring, what has happened to make you feel stuck?"

Tears filled her eyes as it hit her what was bothering her. And she felt like a ninny for it. "La'Anna and Jenna got married. I feel... I feel left behind. And like I'm not good enough. And I'm not looking for a husband, but I feel like everyone around me is getting married so why not me?"

Hana sat back and swiped under her eyes, knowing she was smearing dirt on her face but not caring. Ever since she had helped plan the weddings of the women she was closest to, Hana had felt like love would be around the corner for her. She knew it didn't work like that, but she still held that hope in her heart. And then she met Pace and Chas and everything seemed to fall into place.

Except, maybe Hana wasn't falling in love with them, she was falling in love with the idea of love. Which was why she had chosen herself several weeks before and told them she needed to stop playing with a love triangle. It didn't mean she couldn't be friends with them, but she definitely needed to stop looking for one of them to suddenly fulfill all her romantic needs.

With a fistful of weeds in her hand, Min turned to her daughter. "Every aspect of our lives needs weeding from time to time. We need to remove the negative things that choke out the beautiful." She tossed the weeds into the pile. "Right now, you need to weed your mind. Figure out what needs to go and release it. You're freeing it from you and you're freeing you from it."

How was her mother always so wise? Hana leaned forward and kissed her mother's forehead. "Thanks, Umma."

Min nodded, her eyes crinkling as she did so. "I didn't tell you anything you didn't already know. You simply needed to hear it in someone else's voice."

After spending time with her mother and sister, Hana went home feeling lighter. She knew what she needed to do. She even knew how to do it. She needed to bite the bullet and get it done, which she would do after taking Lulu for a quick walk.

Except, when she got home, Lulu wasn't at the door. "Lu? Where are you?" She went to the bedroom to make sure the door wasn't closed with Lulu on the other side. All the doors were open inside. "Lulu?"

Panic rose in her chest. Hana turned in a circle and looked in the backyard. The door was unlocked and open just a crack. It wasn't enough for Lulu to get out, but Hana knew. That was how she had left the house. Running outside, Hana scanned the fence. Sure enough, the gate was swung wide open.

Hana went to the gate. "Lulu! Come on, Lu!" She whistled. Nothing.

Next door, Hana's elderly neighbor got her attention. "Oh, sweetie, your pet sitter came by and took Lulu for a walk."

Pet sitter? "I don't have a pet sitter, Mrs. Reynolds. Who was it?"

The woman put a hand to her lips. "Oh, I didn't get her name. Pretty young girl, about your height I'd say. But I didn't have my glasses on. She said she was taking your dog for a walk."

"How long ago was that?" Did someone dognap Lulu? Why? Sweat beaded on Hana's forehead and her legs would not hold still as she paced the yard.

Slowly the woman thought and Hana wanted to scream at her to think faster. "It was before I watched my show, so, maybe an hour or so I guess."

Did she call the police for a missing pet? Why didn't she have video surveillance set up? What was she supposed to do? She did what any young woman would do in an emergency. She called her father.

Her father said he would meet her at her house right away and to call the police while she waited for him. This did seem like a case of dognapping. With shaky hands, Hana called the police and told them what had happened. They were going to send an officer over right away.

Knowing she needed to get the word out, Hana texted all her contacts in the city.

HANA: SORRY FOR THE MASS TEXT, BUT LULU IS MISSING. SHE WAS DOGNAPPED BY A YOUNG WOMAN RIGHT FROM MY HOUSE. MY DAD AND THE POLICE ARE ON THEIR WAY OVER. PLEASE, IF YOU SEE A DOG THAT LOOKS LIKE LULU, LET ME KNOW.

She included a recent photo of Lulu in the text. Then she took to social media and shared the photo saying that her beloved pup was missing.

Text replies came in rapidly. La'Anna said she would head to the shelter right away. Her brother offered the canvas the neighborhoods around hers.

PACE: I SENT THIS ON TO ALL MY RESCUERS. WE'LL FIND HER, HANA. I'M HEADING TO THE DOG PARK WITH MOSES RIGHT NOW AND WE'LL LOOK.

HANA: THANK YOU! LULU LOVES MOSES!

CHAS: I'LL OFFER A REWARD FOR HER RETURN. IF SHE WAS TAKEN, THEY MIGHT WANT A RANSOM.

ALEX: RANSOM FOR A DOG?

CHAS: HANA IS WELL KNOWN WITH A LOT OF FANS. SOMEONE MIGHT WANT TO EITHER TAKE ADVANTAGE OF HER OR JUST HAVE A PIECE OF HER. A REWARD IS SET AT $5,000 BUT I CAN GO UP.

HANA: OH, I CAN'T THANK YOU ENOUGH FOR THAT.

She should decline the offer of reward money, but Lulu was her life. She would take it if it meant getting her home. Hana would pay Chas back.

A separate text came from Pace.

PACE: WE'LL PUT HER PICTURE UP ALL OVER THE CITY. DON'T WORRY, HANA. WE'LL GET HER BACK. MOSES IS FRANTICALLY SEARCHING FOR HER.

Good ol' Moses. Hana sighed as her father and a police cruiser showed up at the same time.

Dognapping seemed a likely possibility to Chas. Hana was well-known all over the southeast and people knew she lived in Greenville. She walked the dog all over town and he had seen how some people fawned all over Hana and Lulu. While he didn't understand the appeal of stealing a dog, he did understand wanting a piece of something you felt passionately about.

Offering the reward had been an impromptu decision on his part. He knew Hana loved that dog and while he wouldn't offer that kind of reward for Hopalong, he would want to get his cat back, so he knew Hana had to be frantic.

The urge to go to Hana's house was strong, but if her father and a police officer were there, he would only be in the way. He opted instead to canvas the area around her house. He drove down her street at a snail's pace, looking left and right for the little wiry dog. He knew Pace McCoy was at the dog park, so he didn't head in that direction, instead he thought to head towards the area pet stores. If someone had recently acquired a dog, they would need supplies, right? That was something he had learned after bringing Hopalong home.

He pulled into the one he had bought the gifts for Lulu from. He showed the picture to the girl at the counter. "Have you seen this dog today?"

The girl looked at the picture. "No. Is that your girlfriend's dog?"

Chas looked at the girl again. It was the same girl who had helped him before. "No. Um, yes. Same dog. But she was dognapped earlier today. If you see her, will you call me?

He handed the girl one of his business cards. Please, she's desperate to get her dog back. The dog's name is Lulu."

The girl nodded. "Of course. I'm so sorry. I hope you find her."

Chas wished he had posters to hang. Then an idea came to him. Instead of going door to door, he would go to his office and put out a blast to all his clients. Maybe he could get an emergency billboard put up. If a deranged fan took Lulu, he would use his clout and his reach to get her back.

He rushed to his office and slid into his chair, flinging his computer open. He typed out a quick email to every business he knew, every former client. He included the picture of Lulu and made sure the five-thousand-dollar reward was prominently displayed.

Then he called the billboard company he worked with to see if they could get Lulu's picture put up right away.

"I need my ads changed. Immediately. Like within ten minutes." He tapped his foot and fiddled with a pen on his desk.

"Mr. Rossi, we can arrange a change for tomorrow. It will cost you a few hundred dollars, though." The woman's voice was slow and uninterested.

"No, I need it done now. There's been a kidnapping." His voice was raised and he slammed his hand on the table.

"A kidnapping?" The rep became interested all of a sudden. "Of course, sir. Who was taken? Can you send me a photo?"

Finally. He should have led with that. "The name is Lulu Willis. She's a little terrier. I will email a picture right away."

"I'm sorry, did you say a terrier? As in a dog? Your dog has been kidnapped and you want me to have employees stay late to program changes to your ads? And go through the expense? For a dog?" The rep laughed.

Heat rose in Chas's body and he balled his hand into a fist. Maybe she was a fan of Hana's. He would try that angle. "Listen, lady, this is Hana Willis's dog. She's a famous author. There's a five thousand dollar reward."

The slow, relaxed tone returned in her voice. "Mr. Rossi, I don't care if it's Kim Kardashian's dog. Email me the info and it will go up tomorrow by ten. That's the best I can do for you. We'll bill it to your account."

He started to reply with a string of curse words, but the woman had hung up. Her boss would be hearing from him later on. He couldn't believe her audacity.

Several email messages had come through. Many people said they would keep their eyes open for the dog, and a few with unhelpful ideas like checking the dog park. Who would take a kidnapped dog to the dog park? McCoy was wasting his time by looking there.

* * *

Moses ran around the park in circles. Every time he came back to Pace, Pace would tell him to go find Lulu. Moses knew the name of his little best friend, so he would run out, his ears perked up, looking for her. He returned each time looking confused. It was clear she was not at the park.

Pace had called Emmie right away and told her to keep her eyes open at the rescue. La'Anna said she was checking shelters, but Pace hoped that was a dead end. Why would someone steal a dog only to surrender it?

No, someone had taken Lulu with the intention of keeping her or getting ransom, as Chas had said. Pace hated to admit that Chas was probably right, but this wasn't about them. This was about Hana and her getting Lulu back.

Pace couldn't imagine if Moses was lost. He would also be frantic. He tried to think like a dognapper. If he had taken a dog, what would he do? He would hide out somewhere quiet. The dog would be staying inside, and if he took it out to use the bathroom, he would stay hidden.

The big question was if someone had gone with Lulu on foot or had a car. If it was a car, it would be harder. But if the person had walked off with Lulu on a leash, maybe Moses could track her down.

He fired off a text to Hana.

PACE: ARE THE POLICE STILL THERE? I HAVE AN IDEA.

HANA: THEY JUST LEFT, BUT MY DAD IS STILL HERE. CALL ME AND TELL ME.

He dialed her number and she picked up before it even rang.

"What's the idea? The police weren't too helpful aside from saying they would keep an eye out." Her voice was high-pitched and it sounded like she'd been crying.

"Do you have any idea if they took her off on foot or had a car?"

Hana took a deep breath and Pace could hear the shakiness in it. "My neighbor Mrs. Reynolds said the dog sitter had come, then she said the person, a female with a ponytail, had taken Lulu for a walk on a leash. But Lulu's leash is still here. So I think they went on foot at least for a bit."

Pace told her his idea of having Moses try to follow Lulu's scent. Loving the idea, Hana told him to bring Moses over right away. They hung up and Pace got Moses into the truck to head to Hana's neighborhood.

Mr. Willis opened the door for them and Pace greeted Hana's father. "This is Moses. He's Lulu's buddy. I think maybe he can sniff her out. Or at least a direction."

Moses went straight to Lulu's bed, sniffing for her. Pace went to Hana and wrapped her in a tentative hug. "He remembers your house. That's good."

He relished the feel of Hana in his arms, even if it was just for a moment. Her hair smelled like orange and cloves and Pace couldn't help but to lightly kiss the top of her head. He hoped she didn't feel it.

Moses went to the back door and whined a bit. Hana broke free from Pace's embrace and went to the door, opening it for him. Pace noticed the look Mark gave him. It was a mix of curiosity and approval. He must have seen the kiss on Hana's head.

Grabbing Moses's leash, they all followed the dog out in the backyard. Sure enough, Moses went right for the gate, which was now closed. Pace patted Moses on the head. "Let's see where he goes."

Hana squatted down to Moses's eye level. "Moses, I need you to find Lulu, okay? Please?" As tears swam in her eyes, she stood and opened the gate.

Pace held firmly to the leash. "Find Lulu, boy. Where is she?"

Moses tore from the gate, nearly yanking the leash out of Pace's grasp. He ran to the front yard and sniffed a bush. Hana and her father followed close behind. Head up, Moses took off to the left of the house to the front of Mrs. Reynold's yard.

"What's this way?" Pace called behind him.

Hana jogged up to him. "This is the way we go all the time to the coffee shop. Lulu and I travel this way all the time." As Moses strained on the leash, Hana stopped. "He's just following an old scent, Pace. He doesn't smell her now."

Her father spoke up. "It's worth a shot, Hannie. It's better than sitting around worrying."

They continued to follow Moses's lead. Sure enough, he turned down the road Hana said they took to her favorite coffee shop, through a neighborhood very much like Hana's. But about halfway down the street, Moses began to turn circles.

"What's going on? Why did he stop?" Hana watched Moses intently.

Pace looked around. Had Moses lost the scent? "I don't know. Maybe the scent dropped around here." He turned, following Moses's darting to and fro. Moses turned back a few paces but then returned to that spot. "Find Lulu. Where is she?"

Moses sat, clearly having lost whatever scent he was following.

"I'm guessing either she was put into a car or was picked up and carried from here." Mark scratched his head as he, too, turned in a circle looking around. "We're between houses, there are cars all up and down the street. I don't know."

Hana ran her hands in circles over one another and cracked her knuckles. "So that's it?"

Pace stood before her and looked her in the eye. As much as he wanted to, he didn't touch her or pull her into his arms. It wasn't his job. "It means we know she went this way. Maybe someone in this neighborhood has a video doorbell that saw something. Or maybe one of them actually saw Lulu being walked down the road. We make posters and pass them out."

Her father came up behind her and put his arm around her protectively. "Pace is right. We'll get posters made. I think Nari was already working on that. We'll make sure each house here has one as soon as possible. If someone took her, they won't hurt her, sweetie."

They headed back toward Hana's house, and Pace was very aware of Moses's pulling. But he never wanted to break from the exact path they had taken. Pace encouraged the Boxer to find Lulu several times, but he stayed true to the path he was on.

Back at Hana's house, Mark got a call that sure enough, Nari had made posters and was heading over with them. Pace agreed to stay and grab a few, he would post them wherever he could.

"Thank you, Pace, for coming over. Just seeing you and Moses makes me think we'll get her back." Hana wiped under her eyes, which were puffy from tears.

Pace took her hand in his. "We will get her back. Like your dad said, nobody wants to hurt her. They will either ask for money, and Chas is making his reward known to the world, or they want a piece of something you love because they love you."

This time he didn't fight the urge and pulled Hana in close to him. She rested her head on his chest and Pace thought he might burst with how he felt about her.

"Thank you so much." With an unsteady breath, she pulled back and gave him a tearful smile. Then she knelt down next to Moses and hugged him tightly. "Thank you, Moses. You're a hero."

Hana kissed Moses on the head and Pace felt a little jealous of his own dog.

Mark came to stand by his daughter. "We'll be in touch. Thanks for your help."

Pace shook his hand. "Any time, sir." He meant it, and he felt like Mr. Willis knew he meant it.

Chapter 21

While Moses stayed in the truck with the windows cracked, Pace knocked on every door on the north side of the street. He asked everyone who answered if they had seen Lulu, and if they didn't answer, he left a flier in their door. Nobody had seen her.

He got to where Moses had stopped earlier. "Where are you, Lulu?" He turned a circle, studying each house nearby.

They were little cookie-cutter houses in faded pastel colors. Front yards were almost nonexistent and the back yards looked small. Many were fenced, but not all. Children's toys littered the lawns of a few houses. Nothing stood out as being the home of a potential dognapper.

Pace approached the next house on the row and knocked. A woman answered. He held out the flier to her. "Excuse me, I'm looking for this dog. Have you seen her around the neighborhood?" He opted to not claim Lulu was stolen. "We think she came this way and are hoping someone saw her."

The woman studied the picture. "Oh, she's familiar. Comes this way often? But I haven't seen her in a day or two. The last time she was with that cute girl with the black hair."

"That would be correct. But you haven't seen her today? She came up missing this afternoon." Pace shook the paper for emphasis.

"No, afraid not. But I think the next door neighbor has one of those door cameras. Maybe check with him." A noise behind her caused the woman to turn. "Sorry I can't help more." She shrugged and closed the door as a child's voice came yelling from inside the house.

Pace wasn't sure which next door she had meant. He had tried the house to the left with no answer, but he had left a flier. Next he crossed the yard to the house on the right and knocked. While he waited, he noticed a camera on the doorbell. He held the picture up to it.

"I'm looking for a missing dog. Have you seen her?" No answer came. He left the paper in the door and went back to his car to check on Moses before continuing down the way.

After canvassing the road and knocking on every door, Pace sat in the truck and thought where he could go from there. The dog park was a good choice, as were several businesses nearby. He started with the businesses on the other side of the neighborhood. He posted a flier at the coffee shop and outside a yoga studio. He handed a few out to people walking their own dogs.

After posting a few at the entrances of the dog park, he and Moses went home. It was getting dark and there wasn't much more he could do. He called Emmie on his way home to see if she had any leads.

"None of the vets I asked today had seen her. I'm guessing she's microchipped?" Emmie sounded like she was in the car, her voice was echoing.

"Yes, she is, thank goodness. Poor Hana is beside herself. I wish there was more I could do." Pace parked in his spot and Moses followed him out of the truck. "I have a few more fliers left, but I must have passed out close to a hundred."

On his way inside, he tacked one to the community board.

"You really care about her." Emmie's voice was soft.

"Of course I do, Em. I feel this connection with her I can't describe. I want to take away any and all hurt in her life." Entering his apartment, he flicked on the lights and Moses jumped right up on the couch looking sad. He missed his friend.

"What if you can't find the dog and fix this one?"

Pace held his breath. What if they couldn't find Lulu? They had to find her. "Romantically involved or not, I will hold Hana until she feels like she can surface again. But we will find her."

They chatted for a minute more before hanging up. Pace changed into pajama pants and sat with Moses on the couch, putting his arm around the big dog. He realized he hadn't eaten anything and stared at the fridge, willing it to send food over to him. When nothing magical happened, he made his way over to the fridge and rummaged through it, choosing to make a cold turkey and swiss instead of cooking.

As he sat back down, his phone rang. Hana's picture popped up on the screen. With his heart racing and a prayer on his lips, Pace answered. "Hana?"

Her voice was sad and she had been crying. "Sorry, Pace, nothing yet. I just, I can't settle. Usually, we sit on the couch and watch something before bed, and she's not here. And La'Anna can't come over and Jenna is gone." She trailed off as the muffled sound of crying came through the phone.

"Do you want Moses and I to come back over? He would love to cuddle with you for a while." Pace would love to cuddle with her as well, but he didn't say that.

She sniffled. "Oh, no, thank you. You're probably getting ready for bed. I just needed a distraction."

"What do you two watch at night?" Pace took a bite of his sandwich while he listened.

She giggled through the tears. "Oh, I can't tell you. It's too embarrassing."

Well, now he had to know what it was. "Come on, tell me."

She hesitated before blurting it out. "I love to watch Pepper's Pimple Poppers. It's so gross, but I can't tear myself away."

Gross, yes, but Pace had seen it before and it was certainly attention-grabbing. "Wow. Not what I thought you would say." He chuckled at the thought of Hana eating popcorn and watching someone's zits being popped.

A groan came through the phone. "Oh, see? You think I'm weird. But that's not all I watch. I also like cooking shows and I enjoy period dramas. Have you seen Reign?"

His sister had been obsessed with Reign a few years prior. "Oh, yes, I know all about Reign. Emmie made me watch several of them. Were you team Francis or team Sebastian?"

The worry started to disappear from Hana's voice. "Team Francis, of course. He was the heir to the throne and Mary loved him. Though the show was in no way historically accurate."

She filled him in on the inaccuracies of the show. Not that Pace cared that much, but it kept her mind off Lulu. Apparently, Hana was a Tudor era buff and knew all about Queen Elizabeth the first and her cousin Mary Queen of

Scots. Pace listened to her talk while he finished his sandwich and got himself a glass of water.

"Oh my goodness. I have been carrying on. I'm sorry." She took a deep breath and Pace thought he could hear the frown leave her face.

"You're quite the storyteller, Hana. You have a real knack for it. You should write a book or something." He laughed and listened to Hana laugh in return. He could listen to that laugh for years to come.

The laughter stopped suddenly. "Oh, I almost forgot she's not here." Her voice cracked. "I'm sorry. But thank you for the momentary distraction."

Never had Pace wanted to reach through a phone so much before. Being comforting wasn't his strong suit, but he would do anything to take Hana's pain away. "I wish I could do something tonight. But we'll get her back, Hana. Moses and I will go out again tomorrow and look. He knows something's not right."

"Thank you, Pace. For everything. I better get going."

They said goodbye and hung up. Pace held onto Moses and said a prayer that Lulu would be returned quickly.

At ten o'clock on the dot, Chas watched the billboard closest to his office switch to the missing dog poster with his reward. The dog's picture was easily one hundred times her actual size, but everyone in Greenville would see it. Along with the other seven billboards that rotated through with ads for Rossi Real Estate, the entire Upstate would know Hana Willis's dog had been taken.

He had posted his own number on the billboard, knowing people would call in immediately with tips. He didn't want Hana bothered with false leads. Sure enough, within minutes his phone rang with someone who sounded drunk saying they had seen the dog in an Uber not ten minutes before. Chas hung up on the man as he headed to his appointment with former beauty queen Jamie Huntington.

He met her on Queen Street and waved as she approached. "Ms. Huntington, it's a pleasure to see you again. I think you'll really like this spot." He got the key and unlocked the door for her.

She stepped through and studied the entry for a minute before turning to him. "I saw your billboard on the way over here. The missing dog. You are a fan of Hana Willis?"

He put his hands in his pockets. "She's a personal friend. Her dog was taken from her home yesterday afternoon." He went back to a set of light switches in the middle of the space and flipped them on for her. "There is plenty of room here for makeup counters, demo areas, and more."

Jamie cocked her head to the side and smirked as she sauntered toward him. "I'm a huge fan of her books. I would love to get her into my cosmetics line. She would be a perfect spokesperson with her flawless skin."

Unsure what her game was, Chas admired the woman's forward nature. She was a go-getter much like him, always thinking of the next step. But he knew Hana would not be interested in representing a brand of make-up if her dog was missing.

"Once she's found her dog, I can certainly arrange an introduction. Now, if you'll look back here you can see the beautiful natural light that comes through." He motioned for her to follow him and she obliged.

After several minutes they had toured the entire place and Jamie seemed unimpressed the entire time. She was hard to read, however, and Chas felt unsure of his next move with her.

"Did you want to see the other places? Or did you have questions about this location? I have information on the foot traffic here." He went through his briefcase and pulled out the information on demographics, passing it to her.

With hardly more than a cursory glance, Jamie Huntington put the paper aside with her purse and came up to Chas with a look of intention in her eyes.

Chas didn't have time to register what she was doing let alone respond before Jamie wove her fingers through his hair and kissed him. The shock that ran through his body was quickly replaced with the desire to deepen the kiss. He found himself pulling her closer. What man wouldn't want to kiss a former Miss America?

The thought of Hana kissing Pace came to mind and Chas broke away from her. Chest heaving, Chas watched as Jamie stepped back and smirked. She looked unphased while Chas felt like his mind was splitting open. He was trying to pursue Hana and here was this client kissing him.

"Not bad at all. I've wanted to do that since I first saw your picture online." She winked at him and ran her pink fingernails through her long hair to straighten it.

Breathlessly, he put his hand on the wall. "I... You're my client. I don't know..." He was making no sense. Probably because his brain had stopped working.

"Are you dating Hana Willis?"

"No. Not exactly."

She stepped toward him. "Good." Stopping a few feet in front of him, she picked up the paper again and looked over the area demographics. "I like this place. Let's see what we can work out."

Back at his office and with Jamie gone, Chas sat back in his chair and replayed the kiss in his mind. Women flirted with him and Chas was not immune to it. When he had been named the most eligible bachelor a few years before it came with its share of shameless flirting.

He had been so focused on Hana lately and everything good and lovely about her, the thought of flirting with or kissing or anything else with anyone else had completely left his mind. Resolved, Chas promised himself he would not allow Jamie to corner him again. He still wanted to pursue Hana.

Speaking of, he had several texts and emails from people about the dog. He read through each one carefully. Not a single ransom note came through and nothing else was useful. He decided he better text Hana and see what was going on.

CHAS: ANY WORD YET ON LULU?

HANA: NOTHING. IT'S BEEN ALMOST TWENTY-FOUR HOURS. NO RANSOM NOTE EITHER. I THINK THEY PLAN TO KEEP HER.

CHAS: THEY WON'T HURT HER. WE'LL KEEP LOOKING. SHOULD I INCREASE THE REWARD MONEY?

HANA: NO, YOU'RE BEING TOO GENEROUS AS IT IS. BUT I ADMIT I CANNOT THANK YOU ENOUGH. YOU'VE BEEN AN ABSOLUTE PRINCE.

CHAS: I HATE TO SEE YOU SO SAD. WE WON'T GIVE UP UNTIL LULU IS BACK HOME.

HANA: THANK YOU. I'LL KEEP YOU POSTED.

Hana went to bed for a second night without Lulu. There were no leads. Nobody had seen her. Nobody was asking for ransom money. Lulu had disappeared into thin air.

Climbing into her bed, Hana pulled a pillow to her chest and hugged it close. Lulu had been her companion for five years. She had dedicated a book to her. In the midst of changes, Lulu had been her constant, her confidante, and the thing that made her happy. Hana didn't know how to function without her beloved Lulu.

She didn't understand how none of her neighbors had missed someone walking her dog down the street. Lulu was a friendly dog who loved to approach everyone and anyone. Surely someone had seen her with a strange woman.

Hana fell asleep that night wondering where Lulu had gone. She slept fitfully, knowing there was something they were missing in the search.

The next morning, Hana went over to Mrs. Reynolds' house and knocked on the door. The woman invited her in. The house smelled strongly of mint and mentholated rub.

"Can I get you some tea, honey?" She motioned to the couch but Hana stayed standing.

"No, thank you. I wanted to ask again about the person who took Lulu. You said she was my height with a ponytail. Anything else?" Hana folded her arms and bit her lip. Surely the woman would remember something else.

Mrs. Reynolds closed her eyes and brought her hand to her face as she thought. "Her hair was light. Not quite blonde but light brown. No glasses. Your height. Oh. She did say hi to me. Her voice was higher pitched. And something on her sparkled. On her shirt maybe?"

A high-pitched voice and sparkles? How would that help her find Lulu? Was she supposed to ask everyone in the city to talk so she could determine the timbre of their voice? Did she need to go through everyone's closet to find sparkles?

"Thank you, Mrs. Reynolds. If you think of anything else, please let me know." Hana went to the door and opened it.

"I'm so sorry, sweetie. If I had known, I wouldn't have let her go with your puppy." The woman's eyes filled with tears.

Sighing, Hana went back to her neighbor. "It's not your fault. I'm glad you saw anything at all. It's helpful, I promise." Hana said goodbye and went back to her house.

She called La'Anna and told her what Mrs. Reynolds had added to the description of Lulu's dognapper.

"It sounds like a kid."

Hana sat up straight. "What?"

La'Anna listed off what the perpetrator looked like. "Someone your height. Hannie, you are not tall. Someone with a ponytail, a high-pitched voice, and wearing sparkly clothes on a Tuesday afternoon? It sounds like it would be a child."

Standing, Hana thought through what her friend was suggesting. "So not a play for money or a crazy fan." Then it hit her. "I know where Lulu is. I got to go."

"Wait! Where? How do you know?"

Hana grabbed Lulu's leash and her keys. "I should have realized when Moses stopped walking and lost the scent. It's because she was picked up. Not to go into a car, but to go into a house." She threw the door open and went to her car.

"A house? Do you need me to come meet you?"

"Nope. I got this." Hana sped off to the next neighborhood.

She didn't know how she was going to knock on a door and tell the people that their child had taken her dog. But she would do it. She hoped and prayed she was right and wasn't wrongfully accusing a little girl of stealing a dog.

Banging on the door, Hana called out. "Hello? Hello?"

A woman with circles under her eyes and a messy bun opened the door. "Yes?"

"I'm sorry if I woke you, but we met a while back at the dog park and your daughter took a keen interest in my dog, Lulu. Lulu is now missing and my neighbor said a little girl that matches Violet's description might have her." Hana bounced from foot to foot, itching to get inside the woman's house and search it.

"Your friend came by the other day asking about your dog. I'm sorry it's missing, but there's no extra dog here, just our Rocket." Her hands went to her hips and her tone was defensive.

Hana couldn't blame her. She would be mighty unhappy about the accusation as well. "Please, can I ask Violet?"

"She's at camp this morning, but I can assure you there hasn't been anything shady going on here. No extra dog barking, nothing. I'm sorry your dog is gone, but I don't know anything about it and I don't appreciate you accusing my child of taking her." She huffed and closed the door in Hana's face.

Feeling dejected, Hana went back to her car. She had been so sure the girl with the obsession with Lulu would have been the one to take her. Violet had long, honey-colored hair, was close in height to Hana, and seemed like the kind of girl to wear sparkly clothes.

She called La'Anna. "Back to square one. The mom says there's no small dog there, and the girl is at camp. She can't possibly hide Lulu, especially with another dog in the house."

"I'm so sorry, Hana. Lulu will turn up."

Chapter 22

As much as Pace wanted to spend the day helping Hana look for Lulu, he had work to do. He started the morning off at the rescue, cleaning kennels and going through adoption applications.

His sister came through the door as he waded through emails. "Any luck on Lulu?" Emmie wore a worried expression, her brows knit together.

With a shake of his head, Pace sat back in the chair. "No. Hana even texted me that she thought she knew where she was, but it was a dead end."

Emmie sat across from him. "Quent and I called every vet in the area and told them to check for chips on any animal that came through. But I'm afraid whoever took Lulu might have gone beyond the Greenville area."

His sister was right. The longer Lulu was missing, the less the chances were for her to be brought home. Clearly, someone knew where Hana and Lulu lived since they got into the house. But without a ransom note or some other demand, it seemed the culprit wanted to keep Lulu for themselves.

Standing, Emmie shot her brother a concerned look. "We won't give up looking. I know Lulu means a lot to Hana and I know Hana means a lot to you." She went to the door and looked back at him. "No matter what, Pace, be there for her."

Warmth spread from his lips down to his heart. "As long as she'll let me, I will be."

He turned back to his computer and trudged through emails and orders. He called a newlywed couple who wanted to adopt a dog before starting a family and set up a time for them to come see Princess Petunia, a young pug who was saved from a hoarder's home.

After letting the little dogs, Princess Petunia included, into the run, he said goodbye to his sister and headed to Palmetto Magic.

Construction was coming along nicely and everything was scheduled to be ready in advance of Hana's launch party - assuming she would still want to have it if Lulu wasn't found.

He had never realized just how much celebrity an author could have, but everybody who heard the name Hana Willis knew who she was. And not just from her books, but from articles in local newspapers and magazines, and from her kindness. That was one thing that always brought a smile to Pace's face - how Hana was known for her kind demeanor and loving personality. She was gorgeous, sure, but it was her beautiful character that drew him, and half of the world, in.

They had been over a guest list for the launch. Most were friends and family, her agent, local bookstore owners, and even a few people from local news stations. Pace felt lucky to be included on the list, along with his sister and Quent.

Hana had decided to make Soft Paws her charity of choice for the event, with donors receiving special merchandise from her and even a chance to name a future character.

He checked in with the foreman and gave the green light on the final stages of building. Once those were done, he would outfit the place to match the other side, get it stocked, and be ready to roll.

Back in his office, he just had to check in with Hana before getting into the nitty-gritty. He opted to call her instead of text.

"Hi, Pace." Her voice was low and gravelly.

He frowned hearing her sound so lost. "I'm guessing no news?"

She sniffed. "No. I realize she's just a dog, but she's my baby."

How could he comfort her? "I get it. Moses is my baby. I would be so completely lost without him." He paused, searching for the right words to brighten her outlook. "I know Lulu misses you terribly. What will you do when you get her back? We should plan a puppy party."

A sad giggle came through the phone. It was better than nothing. "I'd get her a steak as big as she is. And let her and Moses run around the yard doing zoomies together."

A steak as big as Lulu wouldn't be hard to find. "Thanks for including Moses in the party. We'll be celebrating soon. I just know it."

"Thank you. For everything." She sniffed again. "Oh, my mom is calling in, I better get that. I'll call you later."

"Bye." The phone went quiet.

After a few deep breaths and a prayer for Lulu to come home, Pace returned to his work. He paid invoices, readied a bank deposit, and ordered more barstools with electric blue seats.

After that, he went to the bar and readied for opening. His bartender was already there setting up and his cook was firing up the grill.

"Any word on when they'll be done next door?" His cook tied on his apron, a blue one with the Palmetto Magic logo on the top.

"I just ordered barstools and a few high tops. Hopefully, we can have a grand re-opening at the start of football season." The idea of a grand re-opening hadn't occurred to Pace until the words came out of his mouth, but it made sense. He'd have to put it on the calendar.

He needed to run a few errands, so he said he would be back and went out to the truck.

As the truck roared to life, a call from Emmie came through. "Pace you'll never guess what I just got a call about?"

Sucking in a breath, Pace squeezed his eyes shut. "Please say Lulu."

"Bingo. Not named, but I just got a call from a woman who said she found a dog in her basement and wants to surrender it to us. She described it as a 'Toto-type dog.' It's got to be her." Emmie was breathless.

"Did you get an address?" His knuckles turned white as he gripped the steering wheel, ready to turn in any direction.

A cackle came from his sister. "You bet I did. I said you'd be there in just a few minutes."

After getting the address and plugging it into his GPS, Pace raced toward the found dog. "Em. This is the neighborhood Moses took us to. The very house I went to and the woman brushed me off. I know it. The question is—did she have the dog all along?"

Emmie made a sound like she was choking. "Pace, come on. Don't jump to conclusions."

As he turned onto the very road he had been on several times searching for Lulu, Pace muttered under his breath. "I'm not jumping." He stopped in front of the house. "This is it, Em. The woman who knew Lulu belonged to Hana. She knows what Lulu looks like and who she belongs to. The dog's picture is all over the city. Something isn't right."

It took several deep breaths and Emmie's calming voice for Pace's emotions to level out. "I'll call you if it's her."

At the door, the woman opened the door before Pace even knocked. "Oh. It's you."

Knowing his brows were lowered and his mouth was downturned, Pace did not try to sugarcoat his voice. "That's right. I came and talked to you asking about a little dog. And then you called Soft Paws saying one was found in your basement."

She swallowed and coughed a little. "Do you work for Soft Paws?"

He stepped closer. He kept his voice low and spoke slowly. "I run Soft Paws. And Hana Willis is my friend. Do you have her dog?"

Turning halfway, the woman called for her daughter. "Bring the dog here. Now."

As Pace expected, the little girl he had met before—nearly Hana's height with a sandy blonde ponytail—came to the door carrying Lulu. Upon seeing Pace, she struggled in the girl's arms, trying to get down.

Pace took the dog and checked her over. For her part, Lulu wiggled and licked him incessantly. She seemed fine, but Pace wanted a vet to check her over. But first, he needed an explanation.

"How did Lulu come to be in your care?" He clipped the thin leash that he carried around her neck so she couldn't run off, but she made no efforts to get down from his arms.

"I found her in our basement not an hour ago." The mother's exasperated look towards her daughter told Pace his hunch was correct.

"I hate Rocket. Lulu is a perfect dog, Momma." Huge tears slipped down the girl's cheeks. She stepped toward Pace and Lulu, but Pace stepped back. "She's been so good. She never barked once. We've played outside and she gives me kisses."

Biting his tongue, Pace looked to the mother.

"She is not your dog, Violet. Not at all. She has a home. You stole a lady's dog." Looking to Pace, the mother clenched her fists and released them. "I am so sorry. Please take her home. I'll be dealing with this one." She motioned toward her little girl.

Callously, Pace's gaze went from child to parent. "It will be up to Ms. Willis if she decides to press charges. I have a camera on my truck that has recorded this whole exchange, by the way." With that, he strode off, a happy Lulu in his arms.

He made a call to Hana, but it went to voicemail. "Hana, come straight to Soft Paws as soon as you can." What a happy reunion it would be.

※

Calls were pouring in about that little dog. Someone spotted her in Simpsonville, or in Traveler's Rest. One call said the dog was on Clemson's campus, trapped in a classroom. Most were pranks or mistakes and Chas didn't have time to check on each one. He forwarded each viable lead to the police, who said they didn't have time to go on wild chases after a tiny dog either.

But Chas had said he would help, and help he would. He upped the reward to six thousand dollars. After all, Hana's dog had been gone a few days and the odds of her returning were getting slim.

Knowing it was better to think smart, not hard, Chas sat at his computer and started to research dog breeders in the area. If they couldn't find Lulu, he would offer to get Hana a new puppy. He knew to avoid puppy mills, but finding a Cairn Terrier breeder within two hours of Greenville was proving to be difficult. He expanded his search a little further.

It would cost less money to buy a new dog than to pay out several thousand dollars for the missing one.

"Jamie Huntington is on line one for you." Barbara's voice on his intercom made him jump.

The name Jamie Huntington made him jump as well. He cleared his throat and picked up his office phone. "Chas Rossi here."

Her smooth voice nearly purred. "Mr. Rossi, so good to hear your voice. Have you heard back from the owners on Queen Street?"

"Not as yet, Miss Huntington. I expect to hear from them at any time." He pulled up his email to double check. "I will let you know the minute something comes through."

"Of course. And will you help me once I'm ready to open it? I'm going to have a big party and will need caterers and decorators, the whole works."

Furrowing his brow, Chas wasn't sure what to make of her request. "I can certainly help you, but there are event planners who can get all that set up for you. I can get you in touch with the best one in the area. I'll get her number and text it to you."

A sultry laugh came through the phone. "Oh, but Mr. Rossi, I would love a personal helping touch from you."

He would be lying if he said he wasn't affected by her words. His body certainly reacted. But his mind reminded the rest of him that it was Hana he was after. And once he found her dog—or got her a new one—Hana would be eternally grateful and they would be a couple.

Was it supposed to be so hard, though? Chas realized he was going through a lot of effort for someone who wasn't guaranteed to fall into his arms at the end of everything.

"Mr. Rossi?"

Snapped from his thoughts, Chas coughed and brought his attention back to the woman on the phone. "Of course. I'll get you that number and send it to you. And I'll let you know the second I hear from Queen Street."

He hung up and shook his head. He didn't need a flirt who was throwing herself at any available man. Even if she was a verified beauty, a businesswoman, and knew exactly what she wanted. Hana was the woman he had set his heart on.

To prove it, he called Hana. After three rings it went to voicemail.

"Hana, it's Chas. I just wanted to see how you are doing. I upped the reward to six thousand, but listen. I was thinking, I would be more than happy to get you a new puppy if Lulu can't be found. If you want, that is. Think about it."

He hung up, satisfied with both upping the reward and offering to replace the dog. That would show her how much he cares.

❦

"He offered to buy me a new dog. I couldn't believe it. My blood is boiling." Hana paced her living room floor with Jenna on the phone. She had heard his message after getting out of the shower.

Chas's offer of reward money was beyond generous but offering to just replace Lulu was outlandish. You don't just replace members of your family. The very thought made Hana cry.

A sigh came through from Jenna's end. "He's not trying to devalue Lulu's place in your life, Hannie. He's just trying to be helpful. You said before he's not a big animal person. Pets are just pets to him, not family." When Hana didn't respond, she spoke louder. "Hana. He cares for you, he's just trying to help."

"Well, it wasn't helpful. It was hurtful." Hana threw herself on the couch.

"No other leads?"

It was then Hana remembered that she had a missed call from Pace as well. Her voicemail had played Chas's message first and she had completely forgotten about Pace. "Oh, I got to go. Pace also called."

"You've got two princes vying for you, big sister. Call me later."

Two princes indeed Hana thought. Completely different princes. Though Jenna was right, they were both generous and only wanted her to be happy.

Without listening to the message, she dialed Pace's number. "Pace?"

"I called, but you didn't answer." He sounded out of breath.

"I was in the shower, then Chas called. No leads from him. What's going on?" She dared not be hopeful, but something inside her started tingling. He had news.

"You need to come to Soft Paws right now."

Her breath caught in her throat. "Lulu?"

Then he delivered the best news she had ever heard. "I got her. Quent is checking her over right now. Come on." A hearty laugh came through the phone.

The squeal that came from her mouth couldn't be helped. "Oh, Pace! I'm getting in the car right now. She's okay?"

"She looks great. She's been a puddle of wags and kisses." She heard him move a little. "Lulu, I got your mommy on the phone. Say hello."

A noise of squeaks and phone kisses rang in her ears and Hana began sobbing. "Lulu! My sweet girl. I'm on my way!"

She made it to Soft Paws in record time and burst through the door. "Lulu! Pace!"

When Lulu came running around the corner, Hana dropped to the ground. With a mighty leap, Lulu bound into her arms and began licking her all over. The tears couldn't be helped as Hana checked over the dog as if she were a child.

"Quent said she checks out just fine. Perhaps a hair dehydrated, but she's been eating and playing." Pace stood several feet back from them, watching.

The errant collar was replaced on Lulu's neck and double checked. Hana stood and Lulu snuggled in her arms. "Where was she?"

When Pace motioned for her to sit, Hana began to worry. He sat across from her. "That little girl you suspected? Violet? She had Lulu locked in her basement. The mother just discovered her this afternoon and called Soft Paws."

Stunned silent, Hana could only blink. Violet? And they had called Soft Paws? She had been there. She had talked to the mother and given her number. Why could they not have called her directly? Nothing about the situation made sense.

"Hana?"

"Thank you, Pace, for finding her. Please thank Emmie and Quent as well. I want to get her home." She stood and Lulu jumped down to the ground. "Maybe I need to go talk to this girl myself."

Taking a step toward her, Pace shook his head. "Is that a good idea?" But when she glared at him, he nodded. "Only if I come with you."

Together, they got into Hana's car and she made her way to Violet's house. Hana left Lulu in her car with the windows cracked. She didn't want Lulu near that house again. While she meant to knock, her fist instead pounded on the door.

When the door opened to reveal a simpering child on the other side, Hana's fiery temper doused slightly. A man stood behind her. "You're the dog's owner?"

Hana stood to her full height in front of the man. She was glad Pace was behind her. "I am."

The man put his hands on the girl's shoulders. "Violet, what do you need to tell her?"

The girl broke down in sobs, her hair falling in her face. "I'm so sorry, Miss Willis! I just love Lulu and I'm so sorry. I won't touch her again."

Violet's tears softened Hana slightly, but she was still upset. She folded her arms in front of her and scowled.

"Do you mean to press charges? We know you have every right to." Violet's father hung his head as he rubbed his daughter's back.

While she could go to the law and file charges, Hana shook her head. "No. But you need to promise me you won't come near Lulu again." When the girl nodded, Hana turned to the father. Many thoughts went through her mind, but she bit her tongue. "Good day, sir."

They turned and went back to the car, Lulu cuddled up in the sun sleeping. After a bath and a good meal, Hana thought Lulu would be good as new. She would make good on the promise and get both Lulu and Moses a steak. Maybe Pace as well.

"Thank you, Pace." Her voice was barely a whisper.

He reached out and took her hand, squeezing it. Hana returned the gesture and closed her eyes, happy the ordeal was over.

Chapter 23

Hana walked into Rossi Real Estate with her head held high. She felt like a million bucks with Lulu back home and now she needed to make good on the decision she had made before.

Barbara ushered her in and congratulated her on finding Lulu. "I'm so happy for you, Miss Willis. Chas is in his office. He'll be happy to see you."

"Thank you, Barbara." Hana knocked and opened the door when Chas said to enter.

"Hana." Chas sat up straight and put his phone down. "Is everything okay?"

She sat in a chair in front of his desk. Her back stayed straight and she gripped her purse tightly. "It is. I cannot thank you enough for your offer of reward money for Lulu. And the way you jumped into action, it really was amazing. You have a wonderful heart."

He nodded. "As do you. But I sense that's not all you came to say."

A smile spread across her lips but did not reach her eyes, she knew. "You're perceptive as well. I did some soul searching recently and realized I was feeling a little empty and left out because my sister and my friend got married. I felt like life was passing me by. A relationship wasn't in my plans, but then suddenly it was all I could think about." She took a deep breath. "And in doing so, I led you and Pace on. I care for you both, you're both wonderful men. But I don't think I have those romantic feelings for you."

He leaned forward, resting his arms on his desk. "You know what? In the past few days, I think I've also come to that conclusion. You're beautiful inside and out, Hana. And you've become a great friend. But I think I was more feeling pressure from my parents than wanting something myself. At least with you, wonderful as you are."

Hana watched his lips curl upward and a far-off look come over him. "You met someone."

The shock on his face gave way to a deep blush and a look of astonishment. "How?"

"I'm a romance writer, Chas. I know the look." Hana felt an immediate pang, but it was quickly replaced with a desire to see her friend happy. "I hope I can meet her at my book launch. You'll come, won't you?"

He stood and came around his desk. "I would be delighted."

Hana leaned in and hugged him. As she embraced him, she realized there was nothing there. No butterflies, no burning urge to kiss him. Chas was a friend, plain and simple.

She left him and decided she might as well talk to the other party involved.

Not knowing where she might find Pace on any given day, she texted him. He responded that he was at the rescue and Hana bounced in her seat. The rescue had quickly become a favorite place of hers.

When she pulled up, Emmie was outside with a young couple who were fawning all over an adorable little pug. Emmie looked up and winked at Hana. "He's in the office."

Her new friend might not be winking at her when she was done talking to Pace. Emmie was a sweet girl and Hana enjoyed the little bit of time they had spent together, but Emmie might not be so receptive later.

Without knocking, Hana cracked the door open. "Pace?" Since she had texted him, she figured he was expecting her.

"Come on in." Pace sat behind his desk, much the way Chas had been.

Both men were so different. Instead of a meticulous desk with perfectly placed pens and no mess, Pace's desk was cluttered with piles of papers, a few photos, and a pair of soiled gloves.

She stood in front of him, her palms sweaty and her feet unable to be still. Pace leaned back and grinned, propping his feet up on the desk corner. "Lulu happy to be home?"

"She's happy as a clam. She's been sleeping and eating like every day is a holiday. And after a trip to the groomer, she's smelling better, too." Hana laughed. Even though it was only a few days, Lulu smelled horrid and her fur felt like a wire brush.

Nodding, Pace motioned to a chair for her to sit. "I'm glad you're both happy and healthy. And Moses can't wait to play with his friend again."

Hana remained standing and took a steadying breath. "Pace, I need to tell you this. I need to apologize for my behavior over the past few weeks. I like you a lot, but I think with the weddings this summer, I inadvertently created a need for something in my head without having my heart ready. I placed undue pressure on myself, which put you and Chas in an awkward position."

Moving from his chair to the front of the desk, Pace took her hands in his. "Hana, that's okay. Clearly, we both saw something special in you. It's not like you were taking advantage of us. Or, me, at least."

She turned around so he couldn't see her and the tears in her eyes. "But I do feel like I took advantage of your kindness and your trust. You deserve a woman who can love you fully and who isn't so, so wishy-washy."

Moving around to face her, Pace put his hand under her chin. Hana looked up at him. "Hana, I want your happiness. It's all I think about. When you were hurting, I was hurting. Do you not think you can love me?"

His hair was standing on end as usual, and he had a few days of scruff on his cheek. But his eyes were full of something Hana wasn't used to. Something she had only written about. Her heart beat faster and her skin grew warm.

"Oh, I'm sure I could. I can't imagine anyone not falling for you, Pace."

He kissed her solidly, without any hesitation. Hana wrapped her arms around his neck and felt his hands come around her back. Suddenly, he lifted her while deepening the kiss. They tightened their grasp on each other, clinging as if their lives depending on it.

When they broke apart, Pace looked at her and ran his thumb across her lips. "Do you think maybe you could fall for me? Because I'm falling for you, Hana. And I won't take no for an answer."

She giggled and kissed him lightly. "I think that could be arranged."

"I think I'm done here. How about we go get Moses and take him to your place for dinner?" Pace kissed her nose and nipped at her neck.

"I think that could be arranged as well."

They left his truck at Soft Paws and went to get Moses from his apartment. Pace ushered him into the back seat where Moses put his head on the center console between them. But all Moses saw was a view of their arms, because Pace and Hana leaned in towards one another, their hands linked together.

"I thought you weren't going to fight for me." Hana rubbed her thumb over his knuckles.

Pace flashed his teeth and his eyes sparkled. "Ah, princess, that's where you're wrong. I said I wasn't going to fight Chas for you. I said I was going to let you pick me yourself. And you did."

She pulled into her driveway. "No, I didn't. I came by to tell you I wasn't going to string you along anymore. Again."

He leaned in close and brought her face to his. "And you did tell me that. And you're not stringing me along anymore. Because you chose me."

She pulled back and laughed. "How do you know I wasn't going to choose Chas?"

"You went to him first." Pace pulled her in for a kiss.

Hana's reply was full of shock. "What? How did you know I went to him first?"

Pace hadn't known until she confirmed it, but he wasn't about to tell her that. Instead, he winked at her, kissed her cheek, and got out of the car.

Inside, they ordered nachos and wings to be delivered, along with treats for Lulu and Moses. They took turns throwing a ball for the dogs between kisses.

When the food arrived, Pace got the door, making himself at home. Hana brought two cans of Sprite to the coffee table where they set up and turned on the television.

"How about Indiana Jones?"

One of his favorite series, Pace beamed at her. "Oh, which one? As long as it's not that crystal skull one, I'm all about it."

They huddled together on the couch, ignoring the food in front of them. "We can start at the beginning and see how far we get." Hana rested her head on Pace's chest and wrapped her arm around him. "I can hear your heart."

"What does it say?"

She giggled and made of show of listening. "It says we might need to get Moses a dog bed for my house. He won't fit on Lulu's."

Pace nodded. Getting dog beds for each other's places was a good start. He kissed Hana's forehead and they settled in to watch the movie.

This, Pace thought, was the life he never knew he needed. And it was the one Hana had only dreamed of.

Hana greeted her guests as they came into Palmetto Magic for her launch. Her newest book had just been released and was already on the bestseller list. Some of her favorite people were gathered to celebrate with her.

Her parents and brother and sister came in looking awed and a little out of place. Hana made a mental note to watch Nari—she would attract some unneeded male attention if she wasn't careful. Her parents were happy to mingle away from the bar area.

Jenna made an appearance with Will, having come in from Tennessee the night before. Hana hugged her sister and noticed something different. "Jenna! Wait!"

Her sister nodded enthusiastically. "Can you already tell? We were going to tell everyone tonight after this."

Only a trained eye would see the hollow of Jenna's abdomen had become a little fuller. "I'm so excited for you!" As the line of people grew longer, she told Jenna she would talk with her later and kissed her cheek.

Behind her sister was La'Anna with Rob. Always ready to be the center of attention, La'Anna rocked a loud fuchsia dress and had Rob in a matching tie. They kissed cheeks and hugged tight. Hana hadn't seen as much of La'Anna as she would have liked, but she hoped now that she was no longer a third wheel, they could do some double dating.

Emmie and Quent came in a bit later, followed by Pace's parents. Even though there were still a few months left on Emmie's no-proposal agreement, Hana heard they were already planning a wedding. Trey had gone to Atlanta for training to be a counselor, finally with the blessing of his parents.

Near the end of the line was Chas Rossi with a knock-out on his arm. The girl looked like a legit model and Hana realized she was a former Miss America. If she remembered correctly, she now ran a skincare line and promoted body positivity. They were the perfect-looking couple. Both tall, impeccably dressed, with a certain air about them that simply said they had it all together.

Chas kissed Hana on the cheek. "Hana, this is Jamie Huntington. Jamie, this is Hana Willis. " He paused and looked beside Hana. "And this is Pace McCoy."

Hana shook hands with the tall beauty. "It's a pleasure to meet you. Chas told me he had met someone special."

The woman laughed and put her arm around Chas. "I appreciate you letting him go for me."

"Oh, he was never mine to begin with. But you two seem very well suited." Hana looked from Jamie to Chas. They both looked happy.

"She's a dream." Chas's adoration of the woman with him was undeniable. He placed his hand on the small of her back and led her inside.

After everyone had been greeted, Hana turned to Pace. "This is truly unreal. I'm blown away. All these people. And look at the donation box."

A clear box for donations to Soft Paws sat by the bar and it was already stuffed with bills.

"It's all because of you." Pace kissed her temple.

Looking at him, she grinned. "No, it's all because I found prince charming while writing a book. It's like a fairy tale."

"This one is just getting started."

Acknowledgments

Thank YOU, dear readers, for picking this book up. It means the world. If you've read my other books - yes, this is a departure, and I hope you enjoyed it. If you're a new reader, I hope you're look at my other titles. Please leave a review. They are my bread and butter!

I have to thank my brilliant husband, Marshall, first and foremost for being such a rock and sounding board for me throughout every book journey, but especially this one. His encouragement has kept me afloat many times over the years.

A big shout out to my editor Lydia. She is phenomenal and I'm sorry I didn't take all your suggestions. You have been with me for three books now and you're a big part of my journey. All the hugs!

The women of Moms Who Write have also been amazing. This is such a fun group made up of the best cheerleaders a writer mom could want. Big hugs also to the Bookstagram and Booktok communities.

The Bacon Tribe & MMAMMS, y'all are the best! Sallie, I love you!

Stay tuned for more sweet romance books coming soon!

About the Author

Allison Wells is an author, avid reader, and sweet tea addict. She graduated from Clemson University and began writing books as a way to escape the doldrums of newspaper reporting. Allison is married to a wonderful man and they are raising four children in the foothills of the Blue Ridge Mountains. Check out her daily adventures on social media. Her motto is, Life is Short, Eat the Oreos."

Find me online at www.allisonwellswrites.com

Also By

Other books by Allison Wells

Bluebell was sold to a well-known Storyville madam as a child. Now Bell is numbed to her life—until an optimistic preacher named Teddy Sullivan comes to New Orleans, intent on saving the sinful souls of the South. Teddy is instantly drawn to Bell and longs to rescue her. But she decides that saving her friends from selling themselves in the Storyville cribs is more important than saving herself.

Roxie has been married five times and has lost more than most people could bear. But she still wonders what unconditional love is like and how to gain it. A modern retelling of the Woman at the Well in the New Testament, Living Water shows us that no matter our past, it's God's love that truly quenches the thirst of our souls.

Abby Walker has waited faithfully for the return of her fiancé Harvey Nicholas from the war against the Nazis. When he finally returns after an injury, Abby discovers another woman plans to marry him instead. Can Abby keep her faith while finding out what really happened?

When the Free Love movement leaves twins Eve and Juliette Nicholas feeling like they're drowning, they must learn that love always has a cost and to hold fast to the One Who can calm the waves.

Learn more at www.allisonwellswrites.com